The Ex Project

Jennifer Aline

A MERLIN HEIGHTS BOOK

BOOK & BREW CREATIVE LLC
FRESH STORIES & BREWED WORDS

Dedication

To the team of writerly mamas who've been there every step of the way (you know who you are). Without you ladies, this book wouldn't be out in the world.

To the friends and family who supported my creative dreams even when they seemed unrealistic—thank you.

To the elementary school teachers who stapled paper together so I could write during recess—thank you.

And to my brother, Matthew. I will forever dedicate every book I write to you. Thank you for always pushing me to create, imagine, and write from the heart.

Content Warnings

- Alcohol use and discussions involving drugs.

- Religious trauma and the mental abuse associated with it.

- Curse words.

- Very light mentions of BDSM.

- Slight homophobia from occasional side characters.

- Poop jokes. Hey...it's worth mentioning.

- Memories of being "fat shamed."

- Some steamy scenes leaning toward the more explicit side of things.

- Throuples, threesomes, and non-monogamy galore.

- Light jokes involving race, sexuality, religion...and adulthood in general.

- Some sexual coercion from a side character.

- INTENSE SIPPING. Like...a lot of it. You've been warned.

MY CUP ☕' JOE

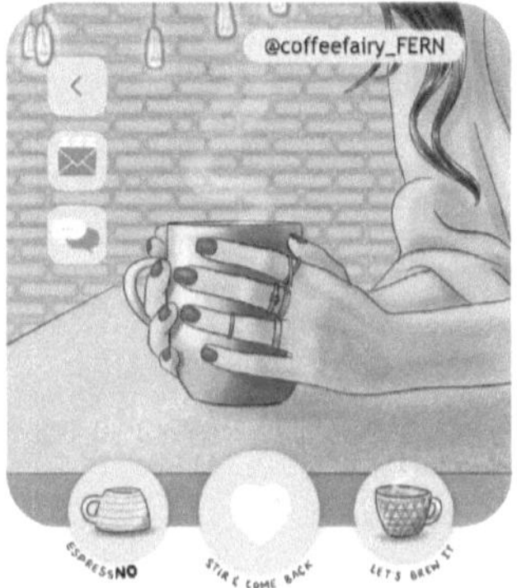

Fern, 27

Graphic Designer
Sips with MEN
Looking for RELATIONSHIP, MARRIAGE

Hot or Cold

I hate making decisions 😩 If I MUST choose...it'll have to be...both. Yup. I'm THAT person. 🔮

Sweetness

All the sugar, please! Cubed, cane, fake (yes I said fake). I want all the sweetness all the time.

With A Side Of

A vegan pastry and my planner! Sure, some crumbs may get on the pages. But that adds personality? Flair? Mystery? ... Right?

Chapter 1

FERN

I couldn't take my eyes off the couple making out by the registration table.

No. They were *on* the registration table.

The second I watched him lift her up onto the table and thrust his tongue down her throat, wine dripped from my lips back into the glass between my palms. I couldn't look away. My eyes locked onto them like the eyes of a teenager to their first porno. It felt wrong, but my eyelids physically wouldn't close. I couldn't even lift my elbow to nudge Emmie, who leaned against the bar beside me, still as a board. All I could do was awkwardly linger above my wine glass, with beads of riesling dripping down my chin, and stare.

The volunteer behind the registration table tumbled halfway out of her chair before tapping the couple's shoulders—a gesture they both blatantly ignored. My gaze narrowed as he plunged in for a deeper kiss, and my eyes shifted to a small, three- or four-year-old girl tugging at the woman's shirt. Once I noticed the child standing cross-legged with her lower lip trembling, my trance broke.

I officially disgusted myself.

Humanity also equally disgusted me.

Looking down into my glass—and at the backwash staring up at me—I tried again at the sip I'd failed to complete seconds before.

"Why is everyone acting like it's their first time drinking?" Emmie jiggled ice cubes around the vodka soda she was holding, her eyes thin above dark frames as she scanned the room. "Are reunions usually like this? I skipped mine—or I was never invited. I'm the biggest reunion virgin here."

"Greg Turner is probably *still* the biggest virgin here." I nodded toward a gnome of a man, slumped at the bar, wearing an ashen tuxedo. He sat smiling into an overflowing glass of sparkling wine, nodding at those who used to stuff him into lockers nearly a decade before.

I truly cared more about how the hell he'd gotten so much wine in his glass than whether he was still a virgin.

I shrugged and watched Greg Turner take a long sip. The thin mustache he probably hadn't shaved since sophomore year hovered above the rim, and disgust whispered down my spine. "I have no idea. I'm surprised this many people brought their babies after *18+* was mentioned in every single email."

And we'd received about seven emails just in the last month.

"I actually thought reunions were where people showed off their ridiculously big families or flaunted the rock on their hand," Emmie said, eyeing the couple across the room leaning against the registration table. Their daughter was now on the verge of tears as her knuckles whitened against the edge of her mother's shirt. "And also show off their improved public make-out skills, apparently."

"Apparently, Mary wanted this to be more like a college party than a daycare. Honestly, I'm not feeling either of those options." Mary—still blonde and wrinkle-free—rolled a cooler to the folding table with a bag of red cups pinched beneath her arm. I expected Bailey and Kayla to still follow her every move, but her devoted ducklings were nowhere in sight.

Perhaps they had grown up and grown away from her malicious high school reign.

Emmie's jaw dropped. "Is she seriously setting up a drinking game?"

"I wouldn't be surprised," I said, finishing my wine and setting it on the bar behind us as Mary did, in fact, start lining up cups into their recognizable form. Almost on cue, Kayla skipped to Mary's side. Her pout looked newly prodded and her hair lightened to an even more unrealistic shade of blonde than what we knew her to have.

My fingers brushed my roots as I realized my burgundy locks were probably more luminescent beneath these bar lights than usual. I was in the ideal position for public scrutiny.

A decade after seeing most of the people in here, I had zero fucks to give. These people could scrutinize all they wanted. They could mock the fairy figurines I'd kept in my locker for those four years or pick fun at the little hop in my step I'd learned to embrace since high school. They could cackle at the time I got a bloody nose in the middle of ceramics class and cried in the bathroom until the end of the day.

I welcomed the scrutiny. My care for most of these people disappeared the day I walked across the stage at graduation.

Well, *tumbled* was a better word. Tripping down the stairs and fracturing my index finger on the way back to my seat was one of my greatest achievements to date.

"Unless Al lets me twist the topic up a bit, I may need to crash someone else's reunion for this blog, Fern. I don't know why he insisted I focus on classic reunions when, obviously, *this* is where the good content is," Emmie said, polishing off her vodka soda and sliding it beside my empty glass. "He wants the cheesy slideshows and photo booths. I don't even see any nauseating door prizes here."

I shrugged, looking around the room. "Where are the high school sweethearts who *didn't* last?"

Emmie twisted on her heel, asking the bartender to pour us each another glass. "High school sweethearts never work out. If they do, they're missing a billion chances with other fish in the sea more likely to break their heart, stomp on it a little, or be a much more perfect match."

"I've seen three couples so far who, apparently, made it work. There are two other couples here, too, who weren't even dating in high school and must have found each other after graduation." I pointed to Cassidy LaFavre, one of the many mediocre varsity cheerleaders in the room. She was snuggling Jared Martin, the asshole who would dangle my history tests in the air before I could snatch them from his clammy hands. "I never would have put those two together, and I heard they only started dating, like, four months ago. Now they're engaged."

"Engaged and acting like middle schoolers at their high school reunion...just like the couple at the registration table," Emmie said, passing me my wine. We both gazed over the rims of our glasses toward the front table where, thankfully, the couple and their poor child were nowhere in sight. I dearly hoped they had taken their daughter to the bathroom. "One thing I've learned is, those who've lasted beyond their honeymoon phase barely cuddle or make out anymore. Hell, they barely have sex without rolling their eyes beforehand."

"Shut up! That's not true," I said, hoping my smile didn't look as forced as it felt.

I knew couples that were still scheduling date nights once a week. I had friends with partners from high school still coming home to an unexpected bouquet of lilies or hydrangeas on their kitchen counter. One of our co-workers came into the office last week, flaunting her lavish diamond after barely dating her fiancé for six months. Though I knew Emmie was partially playing devil's advocate, this was a topic she was ready to sink her teeth into. She was leaving bite marks on every word I spoke and loving every second.

"Ask almost anyone who has been in a long-term relationship or is a new mom." Emmie had practically finished her third vodka soda, her eyes already growing glossy. "I mean, I'm neither of those things, but I've been told it's the truth no one warns you about."

"It's not that they *don't* warn you. I just think it's not as common as people think." I shrugged and ran my finger around the edge of the wineglass, pressing my lips into a tight smile.

"Do we even know who *they* and the *people* are that we're talking about?" Emmie asked.

"Society? Social media?" I raised my eyebrows in her direction, flinging my hand into the air. "Almost everyone in this room?"

"Fern Powers? Look at that *fabulous* hair, girl. Hug me!"

I turned to find Roona Adel forcing me into her embrace. Garnier wafted from her inky hair that now had a hint of silver sneaking through at the roots. Three miniature versions of herself clung to her ankles, and beside them stood a tall, dark, and *very* handsome man staring down at his phone.

"Oh, my hair?" I ran my fingers over the shoulder-length coiffure I took way too much pride in. "Thanks. It changes every month or so."

"You never stop surprising people. I'm glad to see you haven't changed." Roona loosened her grip, stepping back and practically thrusting sharp heels into the smallest of her three clones. "What have you been doing with yourself?"

"Oh, you know...working. Adulting. Doing all the things." My body began swaying side to side to the invisible beat of some 2000s pop song only I could hear. When social anxiety bit me in the ass, all I needed was a little Avril Lavigne or Paramore to dull the pain—even if it was all in my head. Emmie elbowed my ribs, and I straightened my stance, clearing my throat with a grin. "I'm a graphic designer."

"Graphic design. That's very *you*." Roona's eyes shot toward Emmie. "Is this your partner?"

"Holy shit, no," Emmie said, practically spitting out the rest of her drink before sliding the empty glass behind her. "I'm attracted to everyone, don't get me wrong. I'm just Fern's good friend. We work together."

"Yeah, I'm *still* just into guys." The word vomit floated through the air in front of us, and I watched Emmie's chin fall to her chest, curls shaking over her eyes.

"Oh. That's nice." Roona cleared her throat, stepping back and—again—almost pummeling her children as they scattered like flies at her feet. She linked arms with the man still staring down at his phone until Roona's touch woke him, his head thrusting up. "This is Archer. Archer Callum? The guy I wouldn't shut up about during study hall the last semester of senior year?"

I only remembered her throwing her flip phone at the chalkboard on a weekly basis or randomly running out of the room in tears. Occasionally, she would turn to me and vent about some guy not answering her calls or her mother's latest trip that left her house empty and open for all kinds of extra-curricular activities, but that was it.

I always wondered about those extra-curriculars she never invited me to.

"Archer. Study hall. Of course! That guy you always talked about." I nodded, gazing down at her three children. "Looks like you didn't waste any time."

"Would you expect anything less? We're trying for number four soon." Her eyes darted to Archer, who obviously couldn't care less about the conversation going on. "Maybe four *and* five since twins run in *both* of our families."

My lips mimicked a Cheerio as my eyebrows lifted, nodding as the very necessary wine cooled my tongue.

"Sign-ups for the tournament are up!" Mary shouted from the other side of the room. Roona hopped in her heels, elbowing an unfazed Archer.

"I'm absolutely going to play. I'm *sure* we'll catch up later, Fern." Roona leaned in and kissed my cheek before dashing to the opposite side of the room, leaving her family to slowly follow her.

"I may have better content for this blog than expected," Emmie whispered.

"I can't believe they ended up together." My eyes followed Roona's line of kin toward the opposite side of the room as Archer remained angled down to his screen.

"*That's* what you can't believe?" Emmie threw her arms into the air, practically knocking my wine glass into the person behind me—who I think I once made monkey bread alongside in my middle school Home Economics class.

Did they even offer that class anymore?

If they didn't, they needed to. It was a life necessity to learn how to make top-notch monkey bread.

"I wonder if they've been together all these years or if they broke up...or if they tried it out again." My glass bounced from one hand to the other, the dew dampening my palms.

"She either drugged that guy or he's scared shitless of her. I think *that's* how they make it work," Emmie said.

"Oh, stop. I'm serious!" I leaned against the bar and crossed my arms, watching people hand phones to their children to distract them from the binge drinking about to happen. A few people poured out crayons and paper from their purses so they could drink with less guilt. "I just wonder if I'd tried harder or cared a little more, if one of those relationships would have worked for me too."

A throaty laugh echoed through the room, followed by a recognizable snort. My gaze shot toward the registration table where three men walked in, hugging and throwing themselves at the alumni surrounding them. The group's inebriation was obvious—probably because they didn't want to cave to the insane prices at the bar.

The sound of that rugged snort lingered in my ears.

Then I saw his face.

"Tim Bing. I know that laugh," I whispered.

Emmie slowly turned to face me. "Someone's name is Tim Bing?"

"Well, Timothy Bing. He was a new student my senior year, and his British accent made everyone obsessed." I watched as he shook hands with two former lacrosse teammates, ruffling their hair—or lack thereof.

"Okay, and...did you guys hook up? Or did you just listen to him talk?" Emmie wondered, watching the scene unfold as one of Roona's three children threw a tantrum in the opposite corner of the room.

"Well, I guess we hooked up. We played around a few times throughout the year." I finished my wine, wiping my lips on the back of my hand where the last traces of mauve lipstick now showed. "I don't know if I'd call it dating, but we definitely enjoyed each other."

That was an understatement.

"It looks like everyone's *still* enjoying him." Emmie gestured toward the door where Tim continued greeting classmates with the same toothy grin and accent that pulled me in all those years ago. "Why'd you guys stop hooking up?"

"He moved to New York City and then to LA and still lives there—apparently with a model fiancée. Plus, that was all it really was—hooking up. A dinner here, a make-out session there; a graduation party here, a car blowie there."

"Please never say *blowie* again." Emmie nodded at my empty glass. "You told me to let you know when you started acting weird. You're acting weird."

"If I stop acting like myself, people will really start wondering what's wrong with me." I circled the rim of the empty glass with my fingertip, then looked up and immediately met eyes with Tim Bing, who was walking toward the bar with his arms open wide. Twitching out some sort of smile, I shoved the empty glass at Emmie, who quickly flagged down the bartender.

"Fernie girl! How long has it been?"

His accent was just as comforting as the embrace I now sunk into. He'd put on muscle since graduation, adding warmth to his naturally slim frame. The occasional patches of acne that his accent once distracted us from were now nowhere in sight. Then there were his teeth. His stupid, perfect teeth. When he told people he was genetically blessed with those flawless fangs of his, I had never believed him. His accent and smirk helped divert the truth if what he told us wasn't all of it.

"Since your graduation party, I believe." The wine glass found my fingers just in time, and I took a long swig, eyeing Emmie who stood with another cocktail cooling her palms. Was she really onto her fourth drink of the night? Or was it five? "You flew all the way to Merlin for *this*?"

"I sure did." Tim nodded at a couple walking to the opposite side of the bar and waved down the bartender. "Aleena had to stay back. She has a show tomorrow night. But I couldn't let the biggest party of the year go on without me."

It was clear he was making a noticeable effort to enunciate the words *show* and *me*. I often gave people the benefit of the doubt, but it seemed like Tim let the upscale life get to that perfect little brain of his. He ordered some kind of cocktail with an orange and lime peel wrapped around the straw and a cherry situated perfectly atop crushed ice. Sliding several dollars toward the bartender, he clinked his glass against mine, and a suave smile dimpled his cheek.

"You look like you're doing well, Fernie girl." He started walking backward, taking another sip and licking his lips. "The hair. I like it."

Emmie snickered the moment he turned on his heel toward the folding table in the corner, Roona's husband failing to keep their children occupied as cheers bounced off the walls.

"What a dick," Emmie scoffed. "The accent? Okay, it's nice. The personality? No thanks. He thinks he's hot shit."

"He is. Well, he *was* ten years ago. He was definitely more attractive before California happened." I heaved myself onto the stool beside Emmie, watching twenty-somethings attempt to relive their past or brag obnoxiously about their present. "Maybe he wouldn't be some Hollywood wannabe if we'd kept hanging out."

"Fate. We all end up where we're meant to go." Emmie brought the straw to her lips and nodded toward Tim Bing. "That guy, right there. He was meant to swoon models with his British accent and spread his cockiness—and cock—all over Cali. You're too good for him."

"But what if he was single right now and not across the country? We're different people in different places. It could work." I could tell my naivete was showing.

"You're walking on hot lava with this, Fern," Emmie said monotonously. "Second chances with exes never turn out well."

"I don't believe that. There are *so* many couples here who either knew each other in high school and ended up together or were high school sweethearts. Some people dated, took a break, and then made it work out. I could join this club of reunited lovers."

"You'd seriously date your exes?"

My nod radiated confidence. "Yes."

"Just to see if you can handle disappointment better in your twenties?" Emmie asked.

"Just to see if we've changed enough to finally click the way we'd hoped we would before. There was a reason we were attracted to each other."

A roar of cheers burst from the corner of the room where glasses clinked and red cups went flying. Toddlers cried, clinging to whoever was closest to them—some adults unsure who the child was clawing at their calves. Roona swerved toward Archer, grabbing his face and pulling him in for a kiss similar to what we experienced an hour before on the registration table. Tim Bing threw his hands into the air, high-fiving everyone around him before wrapping his arms around some girl I remember failing out of our ceramics class.

I wondered if wine was muddling my thoughts, or if they were as clear and truthful as I believed them to be. I believed anything until proven I shouldn't. Giving people more chances than they deserved was my biggest flaw. In a world painted in hatred, I believed people were naturally good. My parents taught me to see one evil act as a reason to be wary and the second evil act as a reason for caution. Whenever I asked about the third evil act, a different response fell from my parents' lips each time. Some days, the third act was reason to run, while other days it was reason to forgive.

Growing older with this mindset wasn't easy. It also wasn't realistic, as I experienced a world riddled with drunken liars, cheating roommates, and apparently, cocky Brits.

"You wouldn't catch me dating an ex. Hell no." Emmie shook her head and leaned against the bar. "Most of them cheated on me. Actually, I think *all* of them cheated on me."

"That can't be true. Why would they cheat on *you*?"

"Some people are just genetically born as cheaters. Those people saw me as some smart, fat chick to help them with homework who wouldn't decline a hook-up when they weren't getting it from anyone else." Emmie brought the drink to her lips and snickered above the rim. "If only they could see me now. One hundred pounds healthier with hair I know how to manage and a few words I'd love to stick up their ass."

"Well, why don't you?" I snatched the phone from my back pocket, scrolling until I found the My Cup O' Joe app. "Give me someone's name. Sticking words up people's asses is my favorite."

"Don't waste your time." Emmie also reached for her phone that laid buzzing on the bar. Scrolling her thumb over the screen, she shook her head. "And there it is. Al just emailed me, saying that my blog is due Monday morning, and he moved our staff meeting to Monday afternoon."

"He emailed you on a Saturday night?" I clicked off the app and slid the phone back into my pocket, doing my best not to focus on work even as Emmie discussed her supervisor's antics.

Though our jobs often meshed into our personal time, we tried to push aside anything work-related outside the office. Working for a dating app exploding in popularity meant constant notifications and accidental app clicks even when we didn't want to look at that damn coffee cup logo for another second.

"The content team must be in serious shit. That or he's bored and alone and felt like shaking things up," Emmie said with an apprehensive sigh.

"I thought they were just downsizing. Aren't you safe because your page is still ranking?" My eyes shot to the registration table that two of Roona's three children were now dancing on top of. The third child lay hidden beneath the table as papers and pamphlets rained onto the tiled floor.

"I think I'm still safe, but I think he wants an enormous change to happen. So, we're being forced to follow current trends," Emmie said.

The content team at My Cup O' Joe was the most envied team in the company. This was mostly because of the lackadaisical energy floating from their office corner, their weekly cupcake deliveries, and their ability to work from home three days a week. Though I sometimes grew jealous of their nonstop laughter, I knew how uncomfortable I'd be writing about anything related to relationships.

Or lack thereof.

"Well, then change it up." I shrugged, lifting the wine glass into the air. "If there's anyone who can change shit up, it's a gorgeous girl ready to chase down all the cheaters who screwed her over in the past."

Emmie laughed before raising her eyebrows purposefully, a spark of consideration hiding behind her glasses.

"I still don't think I'm actually as serious as you are about checking back in with my exes." Emmie slid her empty glass across the bar. "But going after cheaters? That could be something."

"What kind of something?" I mimicked Emmie and finished my last glass of rosé, sliding it onto the bar.

"It's the kind of something Al would be into. A catchy name for a blog with a catchy game to go with it. A messed-up game, but catchy nonetheless." Emmie pulled her phone back out and swiped her thumb across the screen with unexpected enthusiasm. "Monday's meeting may be more hopeful than expected, and I have your weird-ass reunion to thank."

MY CUP 🫘' JOE

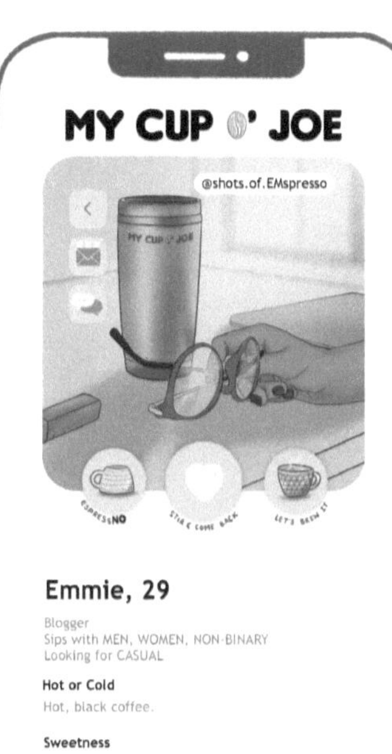

Emmie, 29

Blogger
Sips with MEN, WOMEN, NON-BINARY
Looking for CASUAL

Hot or Cold

Hot, black coffee.

Sweetness

The more bitter, the better.

With A Side Of

Whiskey? Beer? If alcohol doesn't count, throw a pillow my way. Yes, I can nap no matter how much caffeine I consume.

Chapter 2

Emmie

"We are putting a temporary pause on *Bean Banter* and *TEAse Me*." Al's voice was as solid as cement. This either meant the management meeting had been a disaster or he'd gotten laid over the weekend. The mere thought of Al having any kind of sexual interaction made me want to vomit on the spot. Whatever the reason was behind Al's tone, I wasn't in the mood for it. I wasn't in the mood for his lackluster attitude, and I wasn't in the mood for this news. "Izzy and Kyle, you guys will join the editorial team for the next several weeks until we see ratings change."

"Kyle? Why? He's probably the most creative one here," I said, eyebrows slamming into my hairline.

"And Izzy's blog always gets a ton of engagement," Melanie said from across the room, her arms crossed. "Why not keep her blog active and, well...pause something with less reach?"

"When My Cup started beta testing three years ago, our goal was to bring people together through coffee. We're realizing, one year after going live, that content unrelated to coffee doesn't have consistent engagement. That's just that."

"Izzy compares sex to tea. It's genius. *TEAse Me* should stay," I said, gesturing toward my right where Howie was staring down into his phone. "Pause *Howie's How-To* column. People can Google recipes or use AI when they need to make drinks."

"Fine by me." Howie's eyes remained locked on his phone, stale sweat drifting in my direction. I adjusted my stance, forcing the vomit back down my throat.

"It's all about keeping the company goal in mind while gaining engagement. I'll review Izzy's stats again, and if Howie wants to help editorial for a bit, that's fine." Al leaned back to grab his glass of water, taking long gulps as if this discussion was a strenuous workout. We all knew he could use one of those. "The truth is, blogs just aren't as trendy as they used to be. If we want to keep them afloat, something must change before we strictly switch to podcasts."

A stir hummed across the room.

"I will *not* make people listen to my voice," Colleen whispered from beside me, nudging my elbow. "You'd probably still rank at the top as a podcaster, though."

My eyes practically rolled into the back of my brain. "I'd rather write than talk, believe it or not."

"That *is* a surprise," Colleen said. "You're the best talker I know." She turned back to face Al, whose lips held an uncertain grimace. My stomach churned against my palm, and I crunched forward slightly, hoping to calm the discomfort. Everything around me was causing my stomach to flutter in the worst of ways. I hated caring so much about this damn job.

I also hated how much my digestive tract despised me.

I seriously wanted to rip my intestines out on a daily basis.

"I need to meet with Colleen, Ahmed, and Emmie. One at a time. Thanks, guys." Al pushed away from the wall, opening the door and nodding at the five other staff members trudging back to our content marketing corner.

The other employees were probably confused by the silence sweeping our side of the office—a corner typically bursting with bad, alternative 90s music and burned popcorn. I was lucky to be part of a team who worked together flawlessly and supported the content their co-workers created. That kind of cohabitation was nearly extinct in most workplaces. I indulged myself with donated cupcakes from Greyport and free Spellbound Beans coffee on a weekly basis. Though I felt our team deserved the praise we received, I quietly wished other departments received the same.

Fern worked her ass off and, though recently promoted, only received a company-wide email as congratulations.

Luckily, I had vegan crullers, confetti balloons, and a latte ready at her desk the day that pathetic email landed in her inbox.

The three of us knew we weren't in trouble, even though other co-workers would jump into panic mode if they walked by the door. Colleen, Ahmed, and I had been the top bloggers at My Cup O' Joe since the dating app went live several months ago. The public immediately connected with our brand, and to our surprise, the ballsy blogs we took a whack at each week didn't hurt the rankings.

The caffeinated singletons of the world liked gutsy content.

I was damn proud to be one of those gutsy, caffeinated singletons.

I hated being as cocky as Tim Bing about my work, but I deserved it. I was nicknamed the Mixed M&M in middle school not just because of my name and ethnicity, but also because of my weight. That name followed me through high school, where I'd just scribble across papers when forced to check off my ethnicity, never knowing what to pick. I'd find Post-its stuck to my locker saying, *Wanted: More Lasagna*, because people thought it was hilarious that my weight and last name, Garfield, coincided so wonderfully.

I had every right to be proud of how far I'd come.

Though I tried holding onto every ounce of confidence within me as I sunk into the chair in front of Al's desk, I felt it slipping. I'd worked too hard injecting that confidence into my bloodstream for it to retreat this quickly.

"Emmie, Emmie." His voice had a sing-song ring to it as he leaned back and swiveled himself side-to-side. "I got your blog this morning, and *Emmie's Expresso* is still ranking high, per usual. There's not really much to discuss."

"Not *much*?" I laughed, adjusting my glasses with raised eyebrows. "That still means there's something to discuss, Al. Spill the beans."

"Clever pun," Al said with a chuckle.

I pressed my lips together and leaned forward. "Tell me what's going on."

"Okay, well..." Al placed his elbows on the desk and leaned over his arms, the silver goatee circling his mouth less groomed than usual. "Honestly, corporate is on a trend-chasing rampage. They fear blogs will continue to plummet, and podcasts and vlogs will take over sooner rather than later. Most dating apps are already there...so I'm sure we will follow suit. They want the content team completely switched over to podcasting by spring—by the My Cup Anniversary Gala in March."

I immediately wished I had vodka in my latte.

"I've been fighting for you guys, though," Al said, adjusting himself in his seat. "You bring in a ridiculous amount of interest, and paid subscriptions increase whenever your blogs go live. Even the funky twist you put on that reunion blog will be a hit, I'm sure! Corporate just has other plans."

"What do I have to do?" My legs and arms crossed in unison as I leaned forward. "My voice is atrocious, and if I'm forced to turn to podcasts, all I'd create is a shitshow—not beneficial content. I'd suck in front of the camera too, and joining editorial full-time isn't a good route for my talents either."

Pretty much, I needed to save my job or find a new one.

And the latter made me sick to my stomach.

My finicky stomach couldn't take anymore of this.

"My goal is to keep Colleen, Ahmed, and your blogs active if stats don't fall. Izzy's is a possibility too. The thing is, we need to up the engagement. Like...double or triple it within the next six months."

"That's fucking impossible, Al!" I practically peed myself at the thought of creating content that would drag in triple the amount of reach than usual. Being that My Cup O' Joe was, foremost, a dating app, entertaining content was for additional revenue and subscription growth. We created the fluff that produced dating profiles—and lasting relationships.

Or so corporate thought.

"Well, it's not impossible, Emmie," Al said. "If anyone can do it, you can."

The déjà vu made a drunken memory crawl from my brain.

"What if I hunt down all the exes who cheated on me?" Al's eyes widened as my words quickly spewed out.

"What?" he asked, eyes pinned to mine.

"Fer—my friend…wants to go back and date all of her ex-boyfriends to see if one will *magically* propose to her within the next several months." I couldn't get Fern caught up in the middle of my experiments. Her becoming the butt of new office jokes if people found out was not something she deserved. She would stay true to her side of the experiment if I jumped on board with this insane project, but I feared her emotions would get the best of her. I loved that girl like a sister—as cliché as it sounded. But damn, the way her emotions took control of her every move and decision kept me on edge. "There's no way I'd do what she's doing, but I could chase down some of the local, cheating scumbags and give them a taste of their own medicine if it would help secure my job."

Al pressed his chapped lips together and sat back in his chair, his forehead wrinkling into cavernous trenches even Botox couldn't save. "And what would you do?"

I narrowed my gaze and repeated myself. "I'll chase down my cheaters."

The phrase was so damn pleasing to say.

"I get that," Al said. "What will you *do* once you meet up with them? How would you make this venture interesting and relatable? How will you get more people to make profiles and believe they'll find love after being cheated on? Believe me, I see the comic relief in this, and I'm sure others would too. I just want it to be as engaging as it is funny."

If I had a quarter for every time the word *engagement* was discussed during content meetings, I wouldn't need to fight for my job—I could quit. "That part I still need to think about. I'll have to do more than just show up looking fine as hell."

I wanted to strut right up to one of those assholes in my size-ten skinny jeans with a plaid shirt knotted at my navel. A frilly bralette would peek out just enough to showcase a curious amount of cleavage before my hand lifted to smack them across the face. Just thinking about the sound of my palm against their skin made my adrenaline bolt. Watching them grab their shocked, swollen face, wondering how I'd gone from Mixed M&M to Mixed and Magnificent sent me on a high no drug could compare to.

But I knew this wasn't the point. The blog couldn't solely focus on stalking my exes just to get a rise out of them. I needed to connect this daring venture to the big, wicked world of virtual dating. I wasn't exactly sure how I was going to do that, but I had no choice—I had to figure it out.

Soon.

"It will relate." I lifted my chin, smiling inquisitively. "It will connect and maintain engagement."

That damn word haunted my every move.

"Not just maintain, Emmie," Al said sternly with a bushy brow lifted. "Improve and increase."

"Yeah, yeah. It'll do all that. I promise. Give me a week to research some exes and write up a series outline for you. Does that timeframe work?"

"One week. Next Monday." The corners of Al's lips hinted at a smile before he quickly shoved the emotion down. "You think you can nail down enough local exes before the gala?"

I couldn't help but snicker at his question—both because I'd never *nail* any of those jerks again and because I would probably have to use our app's database to find some of their current whereabouts.

"I'll find them." My voice sounded just as solid as Al's had at the start of our meeting. Even though I was masking some uncertainty, the thrill of this assignment overpowered any insecurity I felt—well, at least for now. I knew when reality came careening down on me in a few hours, I'd panic. Until then, my confidence could take center stage. "We work for a dating site, after all. I'm sure some of them are on there—maybe with multiple fake profiles. I'm sure I will find them. Most of my exes were *that* kind of shady."

And I was about to walk right back into that shade.

Chapter 3

FERN

My middle finger pressed right through the clay when the knock on my door sounded, a continuous dent spiraling as the wheel spun to a halt. I turned off the bat and watched the clay slow to a standstill, rinsing my hands in the bucket near my feet before poorly attempting to dry them on my jeans. Porridge rubbed up against my naked ankle, clawing at threads dangling off the cutoff denim and purring ferociously.

Emmie's knocks typically sang a slow, monotone tune, but this time, the sound was abrupt. This sound was angry...or worried.

Or both.

Curiosity clung to my fingertips as I opened the door. "Well, that was different."

Emmie shoved her way into my apartment with a tablet pinched beneath her arm and a shoebox pressed against her chest, college-ruled paper and photographs bursting out of the cardboard. I kicked the door shut and followed her to the kitchen counter where she set down the tablet, immediately throwing the shoebox cover onto the ground for Porridge to climb into. Emmie usually stopped by my apartment before dropping off her recyclables every Thursday, knowing Porridge appreciated an empty case of beer—or two. Getting gifted a cardboard castle early made Porridge's purrs vibrate against the walls, becoming our own miniature white noise machine.

Or was it technically a pink noise machine? I never quite understood the difference between all those sounds.

Emmie leaned over the counter, saying, "I need your help."

"Those words make my heart sing!" I galloped to the other side of the counter, placing my elbows on the turquoise plastic and setting my chin into cupped palms. "I'm guessing that delightful meeting was just as delightful as expected?"

"Sarcasm and delight don't mix, Fern." Emmie took out a few pieces of lined paper, purple gel pen scribbled on them from top to bottom. Nostalgia hit the pit of my stomach. "I used your idea. You know, the whole *tracking-down-my-cheaters* thing? I have one week to prep a blog series. This means I need to chase down some of the local assholes—and assholettes—I used to date."

"I like your take on female assholes." Our eyes remained hitched, our faces expressionless, before I let a high-pitched giggle escape. Shaking her head, Emmie turned on her tablet and placed it beside the shoebox, immediately pressing the My Cup O' Joe app. "They're going to go completely insane when you walk right up to them and smack them across the face—well, with your words, of course...or your hand. Either or."

Emmie snickered, her thumb scrolling over the tablet screen. "You don't get to just watch and laugh, you know. You're in this too."

I dramatically placed my hand over my chest. "Me? Why do you expect me to jump on board so enthusiastically?"

"Because you're the one who was swooning over all of your exes last weekend." Emmie continued scrolling, taking a second to look above the dark edge of her glasses. "And this was *your* idea to begin with. So, you're in this no matter what."

"I think I can play this little game of love." My other hand met the one already covering my chest, and I watched Emmie silently—and dramatically—gag. I always found it strange that she passionately worked for a dating app and just as passionately hated anything to do with love and relationships and dating. "The Romantic and The Cynic are going into combat together. The Romantic, to find love. The Cynic, to find herself."

"And to save her fucking job." Emmie nodded toward the fridge. "We need wine if you're going to pull these poetic lines on me."

"Wine *and* I need my journal. I'll do some research too." I twisted on my heel with cupped hands and hopped around the potter's wheel toward the small secretary desk sitting in the corner of the living room. Wiping hands crusted with dry clay on my tunic, I pulled out the leather-bound bullet journal I lived by.

Practically every movement of every day was delicately written in this book. There was never a drop of white-out smudging my cursive script or a misplaced sticker to ruin the theme. It was more than a planner—it was a lifeline. It was my adulthood diary, per se. I needed the organization just as much as I needed the charming decals and stickers to brighten the pages. Emmie laughed every time she found me sitting cross-legged on my apartment floor, smiling to myself as I opened my monthly sticker subscription box.

She'd witnessed this scene more than once.

"What research do you have to do? You just get to pick a few exes and meet them for free drinks. Maybe have some sex and hope somebody turns out to be *The One*." Emmie sighed and sunk onto the stool with shoulders slumped. "I have to become a stalker and figure out what the heck I'm going to do once I find them. This blog series needs to kick major ass before the My Cup Gala in March, or else I'll be forced to do podcasts."

"I'm hoping for more than just one-night stands, Em. Plus, you're halfway through your research already, it seems. You just need the who, what, and where parts." I slid my fingers over the leather and stuck my pinky into the paper-clipped week of the planner. I'd decorated the week in yellow and periwinkle, lining the edges with sepia-toned foliage and peonies.

The late-summer subscription decals were my favorite: intricately sketched florals with color suggestions for all those planner-hungry lunatics out there.

I was proud to be one of those lunatics.

"I can find enough old flings to track down, but I can't throw a drink in their face, spit at their feet, and just walk away. That wouldn't be My Cup appropriate or point people toward the profile builder." Emmie's eyes scanned the tablet in front of her, chipped nails sliding across the screen. Her words were not smothered in sarcasm for once. She was serious about all of this. "What's *your* plan since I'm sure you already have one stirring in that sparkly little brain of yours?"

Emmie's fingers skimmed the surface of her tablet again, profile pictures of steaming lattes and cold brews passing through our vision. Usernames were connected to these photographs along with caffeinated details many people overlooked. Real names wouldn't appear until someone matched, and only then would answers to typical dating questions be visible: *What's a quote you live by? What does an ideal date night look like? Are you an extrovert or introvert?*

However, the coffee-focused elements made My Cup the top dating app it was—even if most users put little time into genuinely answering those questions.

Most people didn't even know what a cortado or flat white was, let alone if they preferred sugar cubes or artificial sweetener. Not everyone wrote down their favorite coffee style, signature syrups, or the coffee shops they frequented in their profile. That last part seemed a bit stalker'ish, but I never questioned corporate's motives. Typical profiles consisted of ceramic mugs of coffee or pictures of latte art no coffee aficionado could pass by. Users often included trimmed nails or a stained napkin alongside their drink to give viewers a glimpse of their personality. Some lifted the drink to cover their face so a trace of hair color or the upturned corner of their lips was visible.

My Cup O' Joe allowed tiny facial features to appear on that initial page, but nothing further. If more than a quarter of face showed before someone clicked the *Let's Brew It* button, the profile was immediately deleted. Though the interns were the main *face detectors* of the company, we all had the power to delete. It made working for My Cup *that* much more exhilarating.

The first face I deleted was my cousin's ex-boyfriend. He had ghosted my cousin the night he was supposed to meet most of our family for the first time at a Two Mighty Pillars retreat, where we would all be stranded in the woods, hoping to connect with God...or something like that. My cousin waited on the cabin porch, shivering into a fleece blanket for hours, before his boyfriend texted him to let him know he *'just couldn't do it.'*

He also added that he needed someone with a less abrasive, more inclusive family.

It felt damn good clicking DELETE when I saw half of his face on the initial profile.

"Well..." I said, opening the planner and pointing to the first bullet point. I felt guilty jumping right into a plan I barely had before helping Emmie untangle the knots in hers. She just seemed so desperate for motivation or inspiration. If a motivational push was what she thought I could hand her, I'd do just that. Grabbing a pencil from the side of the journal, I began writing. "I can think of about five local exes from the past decade who may be single. They *all* weren't total jackasses when we dated, so they should work."

Emmie lifted an eyebrow. "Why would you even consider meeting up with those who were minor jackasses?"

"People change. Isn't that the point of this? At least for me?" I nodded toward the bottle of zinfandel on top of the fridge, forgetting about the wine we'd mentioned ten minutes before. "Plus, I've always wanted to give Isaac another chance. He deserves it."

"How many times have you said that about him?"

I pressed onto my tiptoes, grabbing the bottle from atop the fridge and placing it on the counter beside the shoebox. My close-lipped grin against the cold side of the wine bottle told her I'd already dismissed her last statement. "Have you met Zin?"

Redirection complete.

"Fill her up good, Fern," Emmie said, taking a deep breath and walking her fingers into the shoebox. I'd never seen her wear this mask of panic before, and honestly, it was a little concerning.

I poured us each a glass, filling Emmie's up a bit more than my own, and watched as she unwrinkled lined sheets of ripped paper. She lifted faded photographs from the box as well but would only huff at the pictures and toss them aside. She did this with every single photo before placing them into a pile and sipping her wine.

I knew better than to question her organizational skills.

Instead, I walked toward the wheel where I had placed the half-destroyed, half-abstract pot I'd been working on into the cooler, hoping to return to it sooner than later. I packed up the clay and pushed aside the stool, emptying the dirty water into the bathroom sink. Leaning against the sink to give Emmie some necessary space, I sent a few text messages before heading back into a less cluttered living room. I folded myself back over the planner sitting on the counter, Emmie continuing to grumble and sort through the box.

"Any luck?"

"Belinda was kind of a bitch when we hooked up in high school, but she moved to Greyport after graduation...and I'm not trekking across the state for this project, even if she's only a few towns over. Marc is deployed, so he's out. Savannah is married with two children and living—I don't know—in Hawaii or something. I did find this, though." Emmie reached for a wrinkled Post-it note, blue writing scratched across the top. "It's a note from Jake. We sort of dated senior year. He never talked to me publicly, and we kind of hooked up in secret—which should have been my first red flag. Does the name Jacob Merchant ring a bell?"

"You dated the *Real Estate Ringleader*, Jacob Merchant?" My jaw almost hit the planner between my hands. "His face is literally on every single lawn between Merlin Heights and Greyport. I also think he went to St. Merlin Academy for a few years. He's always looked so familiar. How've you never told me you guys dated?"

"The thought of him being forced into a uniform and going to your fancy Christian school is ridiculous." Emmie snorted. "I've also kept the past in the past until you forced me to puke it up."

"Swallow it down, sister, and make him the first cheater you chase." My index finger tapped her tablet as I practically lay stomach-down across the counter. "Make a spreadsheet or email a list to your My Cup portal. You don't want to forget anyone!"

And there was my attempt at keeping her planner-less ass organized.

"Well, you *apparently* have a solid list already. Give me the names." Emmie leaned back and slid the tablet away from her, rustling fingers through her dark, short locks.

I sat back and crossed my legs, taking a sip of the zinfandel before lifting the planner. "I'm starting with John Lionne. We dated for a few years from middle school until ninth grade. I can text my cousin who used to be best friends with him and see if he is single. Or I'll just see if he's on My Cup."

Emmie's lids lowered over her eyes, and she bit the inside of her cheek. "You already texted your cousin, didn't you?"

I swallowed and pushed out a square grin. Well, shit. I needed to work on making my little white lies more believable, which was something St. Merlin Academy did not include in their curriculum. "He's single, living in town, and is a freelance illustrator making logos and creating brand strategies for legal companies."

"What the fuck, Fern!" Emmie threw her hands into the air, barely missing her wine glass. "You cleaned up your shit, walked around for barely ten minutes, and you come back with all of *this?* I guess you are serious if you've already planned your wedding to this guy."

Emmie's dramatic enthusiasm was one of the many reasons we clicked so well. We both were intensely dramatic. We just sat on opposite sides of the drama spectrum.

"When I told you I was serious about this at the reunion, I wasn't lying." I cleared my throat before taking a sip of wine and sitting up a little straighter. "If John doesn't work out, there are back-ups: Davis, Isaac, DJ, and Christof. They're all local, and I'm doing this in chronological order from when we dated. Davis, John, and Christof went to St. Merlin, and Isaac and DJ went to your beloved Claus Public School."

Impressed with my detailed memory, I confidently finished my glass of wine.

"Why don't you just get all these dates done at once? Schedule a date each night of the week, and see who you click with."

My jaw practically smacked the countertop. "Emmie, no. I can't date multiple people at once!"

"Maybe someone on your list is non-monogamous." Emmie sat back with a grin. "I mean, you didn't know I was poly until you caught me with Rae and Kyle. Not that you weren't freaked out by that or anything."

"Did you expect me *not* to be shocked by that, though? Rae was ass-naked in your hallway, and then I saw Kyle sitting on your bed...all of this happening within seconds." My voice was hushed, as if one of them could walk into my apartment at any moment. "I mean, she has really nice tits, and a good set of knockers is to be appreciated. I just didn't expect to walk into that kind of show when dropping off your wine from the auction."

"Good tits, good wine, and I can't complain about what Kyle's packin' down there. What can I say? It was a very *good* night. It always is with them, though." Emmie's eyes went wide behind her frames with her fingers parted atop the tablet. "I also don't know whether to laugh because you dated guys named Davis and Christof or be jealous that you're so prepared for all this."

"Are you surprised, though...by either of those things?"

"Not at all." Emmie finished her wine, sliding her glass toward the bottle with lifted eyebrows. "So, did the illustrator guy text you back?"

"He hasn't yet. No. My cousin said he rents an office close to the My Cup office. Maybe I could casually stop by?" I pictured myself knocking on the door of his little office, tripping over my words as I tried explaining why I was there. I couldn't just show up. I didn't have the courage—or social skills—for something so spontaneous.

I also didn't want to come across as creepy.

"Yeah, no. Don't do that," Emmie said, shaking her head.

I pursed my lips together, reaching for the wine without breaking eye contact. "I'll figure my shit out later. You, on the other hand, need to step it up. You have the public depending on you and your little experiment. I get to do this to, hopefully, find true love."

Emmie's laugh made her almost knock over the shoebox by her elbow, causing Porridge to jolt from her spot in the cardboard boxes onto the living room sofa. "You really think you'll find true love by dating your exes for a second time?"

"I don't do things I'm not sure of." I lifted my chin into the air ever so slightly, unexpected confidence clinging to my words.

"What about that My Cup logo edit you did in January?"

"Okay, *that* I wasn't sure of," I said as my chin lowered. "But I think this could be a smart decision on my part. I'm rediscovering the past first-hand through present eyes. Maybe I'll even get proposed to by the anniversary gala in March. Then I'd have a date *and* a diamond to show off."

"And your parents would get off your ass," Emmie added.

The truth burned my cheek as it smacked me across the face, and I reached for the bottle of zin. Emmie nudged her wine glass closer to my hand, and she nodded at it again. After her last comment, the bottle felt heavier than it had twenty minutes before—which was impossible because we'd almost emptied the damn thing already. I pushed aside the weight of my anxiety and began pouring. "Is the anniversary gala a deadline to add to our lovely list of deadlines?"

Good job, Fern. Confidence. Keep sounding confident.

"Well, are you *really* going to find love by the time my blog is either canceled or continued?" Emmie leaned forward and peered over her glasses. "I'm doubtful of an engagement, Fern, but maybe a serious relationship by March? Maybe, at least, a date to the gala?"

"You might be doubtful of a diamond, but I think it's possible. I've seen so many couples get engaged after only a few months of dating. Plus, if we add these months of dating to our past timeline, it becomes a much longer timeframe altogether." I slid Emmie's glass into her hand and tipped the rim of mine in her direction.

When her glass kissed mine, the *clink* was majestic.

"Sure, Fern. By the My Cup Gala—"

"*And* the weekend of my twenty-ninth birthday!" The realization made me throw my hands into the air, wine spilling over my fingers. My lips immediately began slurping up the sweet liquid coating my hand.

Wasting a drop of wine was forbidden.

"Okay, yes," Emmie said. "On your birthday and the gala weekend, I will save my blog, and you will find The One."

"I may ask my cousin about John again, just so he knows I'm serious." After dabbing my hand with a napkin, I straightened my spine a little more. "Maybe I'll even let my parents know I'm honestly dating and looking for commitment. If they hear that, they'll at least give me room to breathe."

"Or they'll climb back up your ass with even more questions." Emmie grabbed the bottle, pouring the last of the wine into her already filled glass. My bartending skills never satisfied her. "You get ahead of the game, but don't be needy. You don't want to come across as desperate and clingy. Besides, you'll be miles ahead of me when I figure out how to screw over Jake."

"I thought the point wasn't to entirely screw them over?" I asked.

"At this point, it may be the only option I've got." Emmie took a long chug from her glass, wiping chapped lips on the back of her hand. "If anything, it'll be a personal confidence booster, and My Cup loves anything that gives people positivity and confidence."

"Positivity and confidence with a hint of revenge," I said, lifting my glass to meet hers, the wine safely remaining inside.

"I love when Feisty Fern comes out to play." Emmie's eyes brightened the tiniest bit as I threw her a casual—and inept—wink.

"I learned from the best."

Chapter 4

Emmie

All I'd done this week was sit in my little cubicle and rummage through the past. I'd clawed through Post-its painted in chicken scratch and squinted at worn photographs at a face I barely recognized. By Friday, I thought leaving the shoebox in my bottom desk drawer would make memories less likely to haunt me throughout the day.

I was wrong. The shoebox haunted me from that damn desk drawer all the way to Spellbound Beans Coffee where I worked from on Fridays.

I swear I saw it magically appear at the table I always sat at.

Waiting.

"What's with your face?" Oliver grunted, slowly sliding black coffee across the counter. "Your forehead will stay like that if you keep it all wrinkled. It's not a good look."

"Just give me the drink." I stepped away, wrinkling my forehead even more aggressively, and walked toward the table against the brick wall. Thankfully, there was no haunted shoebox sitting in my usual spot. "This new assignment is kicking my ass, and I purposely forgot all of my research at the office."

He brought fisted hands to his eyes and pouted his lip, dramatically letting out irritating sniffles. I wanted to comment about all the stupid forehead wrinkles I saw curling into his skin as he mocked me, but I held my tongue.

"I'm sure this blog is no different from the others. Suck it up." He flicked his hand in the air a few times, as if I were a fly getting in his way.

Ignoring the petty remarks I'd grown used to, I adjusted my glasses and hunched over my laptop. The cursor clicked the six tabs left open from a week of searching—more like stalking—people I never expected I'd think about again, let alone see or talk to. I sighed into my coffee, knowing I'd need another one in ten minutes once I chugged the torrid liquid.

My throat was numb to the inferno sliding down it.

Oliver shifted behind the counter, taking orders and fluttering dark lashes at twenty-somethings naively laughing at his bogus quip. He didn't hurry the orders, even when an older woman impatiently appeared behind some giggling brunettes. Benji flew through the kitchen doors, popping behind the extra cash register to care for the woman waiting. His calm voice never once hinted at the irritation flushing his cheeks as he took her order.

Benji swiped her card, poured a large coffee, and thanked her all before Oliver finished running a single espresso.

I clicked and scrolled, casually listening to Oliver's obvious flirting as he finally began mixing the lattes. He was now interacting more professionally with the cluster of brunettes and moving swiftly behind the counter, which was his way of silently trying to push Benji back into his office. Oliver liked to run the show at Spellbound Beans even though Benji had graciously made his cousin lead barista out of pity. Oliver had a personality that employers did not find attractive or worth their time. Not only was he abrasive and lazy, but it was also obvious he only took the job to flirt with the naïve Merlin Community freshmen who wandered in each morning.

However, Benji was a lot like Fern: too kind and too willing to give second chances.

Too bad Benji was married and *very* monogamous.

I peered at the clock above the doorframe, awaiting Fern's timely arrival. I'd shown up a few minutes early, hoping to get ahead, and only managed to re-open a few tabs while rolling my eyes at Oliver from across the room.

Little did he know his name was on one of my open tabs.

"I'm here! I'm here!" Fern appeared at the table, scratching the chair across the cement floor. She tossed her leather bag around the back of the chair and reached for her tablet, looking over her shoulder to see if there was a line at the counter. "I need a latte. Did you knock before leaving the building? I must have been in the shower. Dammit, I'm sorry I'm late!"

"You're not late. I'm early. Get your latte." I nodded toward Oliver who was now leaning against the sink, sliding his thumb over his phone screen. His growing grin meant he was either texting some customer he'd met the day before or scrolling through his My Cup inbox.

His My Cup profile name was *oliVERYcaffeinated*.

Annoyingly clever for the not-so-clever human he was.

Fern hopped to her feet, and when Oliver caught her gaze, he immediately set down his phone and twisted toward the espresso machine. Oliver never messed with Fern. Maybe her vibrant energy made him uncomfortable, or her heavy social anxiety turned him to stone around her. Whatever it was, I used her as my shield whenever I was about to go off on him.

And I often wanted to.

Fern was probably going to work on some new advertisement campaign or start prepping the website's design update two months in advance. She didn't have to sit and stalk all her ex-partners because, well, she already had—and done so willingly.

At least I was getting paid to scan through pathetic photographs of the scratched-up coffee mugs my exes used in their My Cup O' Joe profiles. I was even more thankful to have the power to slide right into the backend of their profiles without clicking *Let's Brew It*. Seeing the actual faces I was planning to confront in the coming months made my stomach sink into my Converse sneakers.

"Okay, okay. I need to email Najma about this new template before I just dive right in. They want it to be modern and all straight lines, but I have no idea what else they want. Color palette? Symbols? Messaging? They could have at *least* sent me a spreadsheet." Fern looked up to meet my pointed stare, my face angled at my laptop with knuckles white over the keys. "I'm sure you care deeply about the rebrand."

"The care I feel is tremendous." My emotionless eyes shifted back to the laptop screen.

Fern laughed into her mug, steam brushing her pale face as she lifted the drink with both hands. "Well, then, how's your outline for Monday coming along?"

"It's not."

"Stop it. You've had all week to prepare." Fern sat back in her chair, hugging the warm mug close to her body as she pushed out a lackluster yet confident smile. "I'm sure you're fine."

"Do you realize how fucked up this is?" I cocked my head to the side, the sweat bubbling at my hairline causing frizz to crack the hairspray. Dammit, I never should have tried that new product the ad algorithms sold me on after a night of insomnia-fueled social media scrolling. "We are using our job to legitimately stalk ex-partners. I mean, at least your reasons are good. Mine? I still don't know what mine are."

"Give me someone on your list." Fern leaned closer to the table, and I eyed the coffee bar behind her. Oliver's eyes caught mine, and he lifted his eyebrows, silently asking why I was staring. I swear that guy had a sixth sense and could tell when people were looking at him.

"Oliver."

Fern immediately looked over her shoulder to awkwardly join our staring contest before leaning closer to the table. "You guys hooked up, like, twice. Right? Does that even make him boyfriend material?"

"He's a jackass. It counts."

"He *is* a jackass," Fern whispered, thinning her eyes. "I still can't believe you caught him in *that* bathroom right before you—"

"Shut it, Fern," I said, pursing my lips and glancing toward the single door in the space's corner. I immediately felt the IBS monster clawing at my intestines. Why did I always have to be the one thrown life's embarrassing curveballs? "We can talk all we want about my shitty exes, but let's leave my viral shit out of this. Literally."

"Noted," Fern said, gesturing over her closed mouth and flicking her hand to mimic throwing away a key. "Who else is on there?"

I turned back to my laptop, glancing at the first name on my list. At least I had a list—even a spreadsheet with multiple tabs I knew would make Fern proud. That was a start. "*The Real Estate Ringleader.* Jake."

"Okay. Good! I'm glad you made him your first mission." Fern's tiny plum lips twisted into her cheek. "Maybe use his job as a starting point. Use his job and—since they all cheated—use their reason for cheating. Maybe? I'm just brainstorming for you before I design this logo and am useless to you for the next few hours."

"He cheated because people were spreading lame-ass rumors about us, and he didn't want a bad reputation." I breathed heavily into the black coffee, now lukewarm and way too easy to sip. "I guess the reputation of dating some frizzy-haired, fat chick is worse than the reputation of being a cheater."

That truth still stung.

"You're making me want to take on this assignment for you." Fern's ringed fingers balled into fists, her typically saucer-shaped eyes shifting into thin lines. "Why not show up to one of his open houses looking like a fucking goddess? Replace all the pamphlets with fake ones that say, like, *Living with STDs* or something."

"Or I just walk around the house talking about how he cheats people out of what they deserve? People would think I'm just talking about the housing market all while I give him a spoonful of his own medicine." For the first time since taking on this foolish project, I felt my heart pump with a weird wave of electricity. Maybe this project wouldn't just help secure my job but also improve my confidence—in a ridiculous, messed-up way. Though I now had sky-high self-esteem after suffering years without an ounce of it, I knew I could benefit from a good kick in the ass. "He probably wouldn't even recognize me if I showed up with big sunglasses on."

"Emmie, I like it." Fern's little frame slowly straightened as her eyes widened and her hands flattened on the tabletop. "Actually, I *love* it."

"Then there's Manny." I scrolled down to the second name on the list, my fingers flashing over the keys. "He cheated on me with two sorority sisters—at once."

"Ewww." Fern crinkled her nose before adjusting the delicate, circular septum ring peeking out. Yesterday, she'd worn a simple silver barbell, and today, she donned an intricate ring with tiny sapphire gems lining the silver.

I swear she had a different piece of jewelry for every day of the week.

"He's the campus life director at Merlin Community College. Maybe I can look at the calendar and walk into an event he will be at." I clicked the third tab, and a bright-red and purple activities calendar shocked my eyes into a squint. "I'll look damn fine and flirt a little. He won't be able to resist some stranger giving him sex eyes from across the cafeteria—or wherever we end up. I'm sure he hasn't changed so much that he would ignore an opportunity to hookup."

"And you said ten minutes ago you didn't have a plan," Fern said slyly, crossing her legs beneath her on the chair. She was the queen of *criss-cross applesauce.* Whether in the office, at Spellbound Beans, or at a fancy restaurant with a maxi dress that should never be shoved into this seated position, she always found a way to sit like a kindergartener. "You're more ready to go than I am."

"That's a lie," I scoffed. "When's your first date?"

"Monday. John and I are getting drinks at Thirsty Theodore's after I meet my mom and Marian for coffee."

"Coffee then cocktails? You're going to get hopped up on caffeine before downing some drinks with a guy you haven't seen in well over a decade? I'm terrified and a little impressed." I slapped my hands down on either side of my laptop as a laugh bubbled in my chest. "Oh, I will definitely need to hear about this."

Fern sat up a little straighter in her chair, as if she had to physically remind herself of the tasks ahead of her and her ability to conquer each one of them. They weren't just tasks for Fern, though. They were second chances at a lifelong relationship.

This wasn't just a game to her.

"I texted him last night and he actually answered," Fern said with her signature, overly confident shoulder-shimmy. "I'm guessing my cousin gave him a heads up."

"Are you going to add a little rum to your coffee? Maybe dabble with the CBD oil in your medicine cabinet?" I didn't want Fern's perfectionist anxiety to consume her between coffee with the Devil—and her knockout little sister—and her unofficial first re-date.

"He dated me back when awkwardness was just a personality trait of mine. It may have been a trait other people laughed at, but John never cared. He thought it was quirky—cute, even." Fern cupped her coffee close, her spine still strong and her chin still raised. "Plus, John was always a little...odd. If I show up acting all smooth and sexy, he'd probably walk out."

"Could you pull off smooth and sexy?"

"Nope."

I finished the last drop of coffee and set the cup down, smearing the damp circle away on the tabletop beside my laptop. The spreadsheet stared at me, burning through my skin to a heart not fully prepared to face such a grim past.

However, I had no choice. I had to save my job. Not because of all the bills I had to pay, but because I actually liked it. It was rare these days to absolutely *love* the work you did.

And dammit, I loved it.

"I'll find out when Jake's next open house is. There must be one next week sometime." I looked over Fern's shoulder, deciding what latte to attack before submitting the finished outline to Al. Though black coffee was my go-to, I felt oddly inspired to add a little flair to my morning. Maybe I'd reward myself with a drop or two of creamer. "By Monday, I'll be ready."

MY CUP O' JOE
@OliVERYcaffeinated
ESPRESSO NO
STIR E COME BACK
LET'S BREW IT
Oliver, 33
Barista
Sips with WOMEN
Looking for CASUAL
Hot or Cold
Hot. Very hot.
Sweetness
A little sweetness is okay, but I prefer bold coffee.
With A Side Of
Dirty talk, hair-pulling, spanking...I'm open to every side and snack.

Chapter 5

FERN

My palm swiped the switch beside the door, and the office lit up, some lights flickering to life hesitantly in the back corner above Emmie's and Ahmed's desks. Now knowing the tension building in the content department, the skeptical lights seemed ironic—even though Emmie and Ahmed were probably safe from the feared podcast transition.

Probably being the key word.

I hung my bag on the hook and sunk down into the swivel chair, adjusting my posture and taking a sip of lukewarm coffee from my travel mug. I only allowed myself five purchases from Spellbound Beans a week, and even though it was Monday, I knew I'd desperately need a latte by lunchtime.

I absolutely had a problem.

The closer the clock ticked toward my date with John—and the late-afternoon coffee date with my mom and sister—the more I needed those extra shots of espresso.

"Did you look behind Spike?" The baritone voice broke my trance, and coffee dripped over my bottom lip, my tongue struggling to catch it. Hopping to my feet, I looked up to find Chase grinning over the cubicle's ledge, his eyes darting to one of the many miniature plants balancing on the separator between our cubicles. His chest and shoulders hovered far above the line of plants while I had to practically climb on my desk to reach behind the barrel cactus we kept in the corner.

Behind the ceramic planter sat a blue Warhead, immediately throwing me back onto a patched-up, leather school bus seat on my way to third grade.

"No way!" I snagged the candy and tossed it into the air, fumbling to catch it as I sat down to unwrap the package. With a snicker, Chase showcased the blue Warhead between his index finger and thumb and began opening it as well. "My Monday has been made. Were you one of those kids who sat in the back of the bus and tried not to make faces when you had these?"

"Who *didn't* play that game?" Chase had already removed the packaging while I continued to pick the plastic with cracked nails. "I was trading my Charmanders and Bulbasaurs for Mewtwos and Dragonites while trying not to pass out from having two of these in my mouth at once."

"Two of the *blue* Warheads at once? Blue is the sourest one! There's no way you made it without cringing." My mouth immediately began to water.

"Is this a challenge, Ms. Powers?" Chase rolled the Warhead between long, dark fingers, his even darker eyes darting from mine to the candy and back. "Do you not remember our Sour Punch straw morning last March?"

"You don't forget seeing someone swallow an entire package and continue on with their day like their throat hadn't been clawed by a cat."

"Sour is sweet to me," Chase said. "My taste buds are backward."

"*Just* your taste buds are backward? Try brain cells."

"Be kind. You're speaking to the winner of the Warhead challenge happening in sixty seconds." Chase lifted a thick eyebrow, stepping around the cubicle separator and leaning his elbow onto it casually.

I sprang to my feet because I couldn't take on one of our usual challenges slumped over in my chair. I was in my competitive stance—a stance I rarely visited. Standing only a few feet apart, I looked up to meet Chase's eyes and broke my serious façade with a grunt of a laugh.

Chase lifted an eyebrow again. His ability to turn his eyebrows into wiggling caterpillars was a talent. "What?"

"Flamingos. Flamingos in sunglasses," I said, taking a step back to consume Chase's ensemble. He pulled at the bottom of his button-up, snickering before shaking his head.

"They're wearing little sandals too. Some are even wearing socks *and* sandals." He pointed to a few odd flamingos scattered across his chest before leaning back against the cubicle. "You're deflecting, Ms. Powers. Thirty seconds."

"I am just excited to see what your fall wardrobe entails. Black cats strangled in scarves? Pumpkins puking up their own seeds?"

"Watch it, sicko. Don't rush summer." Chase looked over his shoulder as Al walked into the office, whispering something to Ahmed who trailed behind him. "I have one with turkeys eating giant turkey legs, though."

"That's cannibalism. I'm definitely not the sicko here." I lifted my blue Warhead so it was inches from the one between his fingers. He gently bumped his candy against mine and nodded in my direction with playful competition glinting in his eyes.

"No laughing. No smiling. Nothing until the candy is gone," Chase demanded, repeating the usual spiel he gave before each challenge.

"Three, two, one. Gobble time."

"Clever." Chase tossed the Warhead into the air and caught it flawlessly in his mouth.

My attempt at mimicking him turned into my knees hitting the floor to crawl after the candy as it rolled over the office rug. Practically pouncing across the space between cubicles, I snagged the candy before it rolled beneath Maura's desk, who now stood, staring, at the end of the aisle. Rubbing the candy on my dark blouse and skittering back to face Chase, I hoped the janitor hadn't skipped our section during the weekend cleaning.

I caught Chase's stern gaze. No muscle shifted on his ebony face, his thick lips contently curved into his right cheek. I looked down at the Warhead in my hand, back up to meet his stare, and then tossed the candy into the air again.

The second it fell to the floor again, Chase's laugh echoed through the office.

I magically ignored my need for a midday latte and survived the afternoon on the office's mediocre brew. By five minutes after five o'clock, I was already sitting at the table Emmie and I frequented at Spellbound with a hot mug between my palms. My feet quickly tapped the cement beneath the table as my eyes stared at the door, occasionally lifting the mug to my lips.

It felt like swarms of customers entered and left through that damn door before my mom and Marian slid inside. My little sister's face brightened my own as I got to my feet and felt her warm arms squeeze me close. I didn't want to let her go. I even curled myself into the sweet lavender scent of her jacket before opening my eyes to see the woman standing behind her. When our identically shaped eyes clicked, I shifted away from Marian and embraced my mother robotically. I pushed out the same mechanical grin I always managed before sitting down at the table.

"I'll grab our drinks, Mom," Marian said, backing up toward the counter where Benji stood, patiently waiting. "Do you need another, Fern?"

"I'm okay. If I drink back-to-back lattes, I'll pee every five minutes at my next stop."

"It's Monday Mojitos, right?" Marian asked, her voice echoing slightly before she turned to give Benji the orders. "At Thirsty Theodore's? Do you all still do that?"

My sister was somehow on top of my social schedule better than I was—and she didn't even need seventeen different planners.

I immediately grabbed my phone to send a message to our My Cup co-worker group text, remembering that the usual crew would likely be at Thirsty Theodore's around the same time as my date. After casually suggesting they switch the bar of choice to the Claus Cave—just this time—I slid the phone into my bag. I knew Emmie would immediately pick up on my anxious, textual tone and organize a new plan of action. "Not tonight. I'm meeting a friend."

Life finally colored my mom's cheeks. "A date?"

Taking a deep breath, I straightened my spine and laced my fingers together on my lap. "Yes. I have a date."

I didn't think it was possible for my mom's smile to grow larger, but it did. It was like staring at a silver-haired mannequin wearing a perfectly tailored tweed jacket with an oversized plastic smile stitched across her face.

Just this time, it wasn't so plastic. Her smile was the most genuine I'd seen it in months.

"Did I hear this right? A *date*?" Marian handed the coffee over to my mom and slid into the seat next to me, leaning in. "With a guy?"

"Yes, with a guy," I laughed, rolling my eyes and trying to hide behind my mug.

Marian casually shrugged before lifting the drink toward her perfectly shaded lips. "You never know. Just asking."

"Of course it's a *guy*, Marian. Please." My mom leaned forward, wagging her hand at my sister. "Fern isn't like Emmie. Our girl doesn't just sleep around with every make and model to avoid relationships."

There it was—her first attack at Emmie of the evening. I looked at the clock as I sipped my hot drink, letting the burn contently tickle my throat for an extra few seconds.

The silence was more painful than the heat.

I wanted to get the fuck out of here.

"Well, tell us about the date." Marian obviously felt pained by the silence as well.

"It's John." I adjusted myself again so I was sitting straighter in the chair, my chin lifted. I'd learned that presenting myself with a confident edge made my mother believe I felt that way. The charade was one I'd perfected since childhood and had conditioned my body to understand. At least I looked the part, even if I didn't always feel it. "John, who I dated in middle and high school. We're just going to catch up over some drinks."

"John Lionne? The little artist who used to draw you all those fairy pictures?" My mom took the cover of her coffee cup off, blowing spirals of steam in our direction.

A dramatic nod followed my eye roll. "Yup. That's the one."

"What brought you guys back together?" Marian asked. "I definitely didn't see this coming."

Neither had I. I also should have better prepared myself for my responses to these questions. "We, um…well, do you remember how Riley knows him? Our cousin, Riley?"

"Well, yeah. Riley was the one who broke up with him for you in ninth grade," Marian said, flipping her dark hair so it fell perfectly over one shoulder.

Everything she did looked utterly flawless.

I loved—and hated—her for it, as any sister would.

"Something you should have done yourself," my mom interjected, steam still floating toward the top of my mug. I stared at the steam as it spiraled in front of me until I forced eye contact with my mom. "You were young. You didn't know better. *'Be strong, fear not. Behold your God will come with vengeance.'*"

And there was the always-predictable Bible verse my mom expected me to finish for her.

Instead, my sister jumped in as my saving grace. *"Isaiah 35:4."* Marian quickly sipped her coffee before turning to face my direction. "How's the rebrand at work going? Wasn't there something like that going on?"

Thank you, Marian, for always sensing my anxiety and redirecting with such poise. "Yeah! The logo situation wasn't, well…great over the winter, but the website and font rebrand is looking positive. I'm still not sure why we need to do such an overhaul when the app has been live for less than a year, but that's not for me to stress over. We're also adding some new features to the app to incorporate more pronoun choices and different kinds of relationships."

"That's great! I'm sure you'll win an award at the gala. You've done so much over the last couple of years."

Mentioning the gala made my stomach tremble with thoughts of the evening ahead, my eyes darting to the clock.

"Adding new *kinds* of relationships?" My mom's voice shook me back to the uncomfortable conversation I was trying to avoid. "How can there be anything other than what God so kindly handed us?"

I sensed Marian's grip around her coffee mug tighten, her shoulders tensing before she took a deep, renewing breath. "God was kind to create the human form. However, some people appreciate that human form in different ways. I think My Cup is finding ways to make all humans feel comfortable when finding a partner—or partners."

"Partners?" My mom shook her head and looked toward me, her eyes digging a hole straight into my soul. "Please tell me you are *not* jumping on the train Emmie is riding. That train leads straight to the Devil himself."

And that was my cue to leave.

Chapter 6

Emmie

I would have gone to Thirsty Theodore's for mojitos to casually spy on Fern's date, but there would have been nothing casual about sitting opposite their table alongside ogling co-workers. Instead, we changed our weekly mojito night to the Claus Cave, but not without every single person wondering why the change happened and why Fern wouldn't be joining us.

The answer to their questions seemed pretty obvious to me.

I was better at telling little white lies than Fern, but this was one I couldn't fib about. The truth ultimately would push everyone to a different bar, so the truth was told. I began word-vomiting about The Cheater Chase the second I ordered my drink, hoping to deflect everyone away from Fern's situation because, honestly, I was already sick of being the middle man.

I didn't expect the deflection to be so unsuccessful.

My lying skills were obviously rusty as fuck.

"When did Fern date this guy?" Ahmed asked, stirring his straw around the edge of his glass. I reached for my blueberry mojito, which was filled to the brim—per my weekly request. "I don't think she's ever had a boyfriend since working at My Cup."

Izzy looked up from her drink. "Yeah. I feel like if she had a hookup—or several—we'd all know about it after a few mojitos."

"She hasn't, but you *can't* mention this to her—or anybody." I quickly brought the mojito to my lips, the burn of white rum resting on the back of my tongue contently. My eyes scanned the group of us, silently warning each of them to chill the fuck out with the Fern discussion. *Gossip* was a better word for it. "She really is trying to keep it on the down-low. I, on the other hand, can't really keep my upcoming shenanigans too hush-hush since the My Cup world will be up my ass."

"Is Fern not proud of what she's doing?" Izzy asked, her fingers repetitively combing through her flat blonde hair. "Like, is she embarrassed?"

I took a long gulp, wondering why the hell my deflections weren't working.

Fuck it. I hated talking about myself, but I hated people calling Fern out more.

I needed to dive further into the center of attention.

"I mean, *I'm* a little embarrassed I'm going after the assholes who screwed me over. I think feeling weird about it just comes with the territory until something positive happens." The straw practically floated up to my lips, begging for the burn.

"I dated the same person off-and-on for, like, a decade." Kyle pulled a stool over from another table and dragged it so we sat shoulder-to-shoulder. His thin, warm eyes brought forth a familiar comfort the drink in my hand couldn't. "We still hook up occasionally. I don't see what's wrong with staying connected to the past if it was good."

"We all know what your connections entail, Kyle, and it's not what Fern is looking for." Ahmed looked judgingly above his glasses. "Hookups and nothing permanent."

"There's nothing wrong with that if everyone involved is on the same page." Kyle's eyes twitched toward mine, a subtle grin lingering before settling back on Izzy and Ahmed. "Again, if the past was good, there shouldn't be an issue bringing it into your present."

"But Emmie's past wasn't good, and they *still* approved her blog series." Izzy turned to face me, finally letting go of her hair to firmly grab the sweating glass in front of her. "I wouldn't want this to mess with your head or for Fern to get hurt. Fern is so—I don't know—fragile."

I snorted into my glass and felt mint leaves tickle the tip of my nose. "Fern is *not* fragile. The only thing fragile about her is her body size. I could try to snap her in half, but her spine would barely bend. She may be naïve, but she's not some delicate flower. I'm honestly freaking out about all of this more than she is."

Kyle's hand cupped my shoulder, his fingers pressing down playfully through the oversized sweatshirt, sending a soothing, familiar spark beneath my skin. "I know Emmie won't let shit like this blog get to her head. She's too stubborn to let anything like this in."

"He isn't wrong," I said, lifting my mojito in his direction. He clinked my glass with his beer approvingly and shifted his knee against mine.

"I love hearing that." Kyle's wink and casual demeanor were all I needed to finally take off my brave face and take a needed breath.

It also hinted that we had a good night ahead of us.

And dammit, I desperately needed a good night.

Kyle's knuckles tapped Rae's apartment door three times as his other hand reached to fit the key into his own. Twisting the neighboring door open, Rae's petite frame leaned against her doorway clad in striped pajama shorts and a cropped white tee. The inked cicada reaching down and around her breasts peeked out from below her top, and I couldn't force my eyes away.

Honestly, my eyes always clung to her for a few extra, unapologetic seconds.

She stepped out into the hallway, crossing her arms and closing the door behind her. "Neither of you are subtle at all." She followed us into Kyle's apartment, where I immediately sunk down onto his leather couch, Rae plopping down beside me to the right and setting her bare legs atop my thighs. My hands immediately met the soft, pale skin just below the hem of her pajama shorts, a rousing spark of heat jolting between my legs.

I immediately got wet every fucking time I saw her. Whether we saw each other in passing at a bar or our limbs were intertwined on the couch, I had to do everything in my power not to come on the spot. She knew the power her presence had over both Kyle and me, and she loved every damn second of it.

Her petite frame. Her small, perfect tits. Her stupidly adorable dimples.

She was the walking definition of *cute*.

"I mean, if you had the rest of your shirt on, we probably wouldn't be gawking. Maybe." Kyle opened the fridge to grab three IPAs he then set on the coffee table in front of the couch. A joint sleepover was a weekly staple after Monday night mojitos. It was unspoken between the three of us, really. Kyle and I would finish mojitos with our co-workers, drive to his apartment complex, drink some more, and play video games until we couldn't keep our hands to ourselves.

Kyle reached for a game controller before leaning back into the corner of the couch on my left side with his knees wide apart—a silent plea for me to squeeze between them. I scooted closer so he was straddling me from behind but kept close enough to Rae so her legs were still touching mine.

Her subtle touch and Kyle's earthy scent were home to me.

And like clockwork, I was horny as fuck.

"Nothing we haven't seen—and liked—before," I said, reaching for a beer with one hand while keeping the other around Rae's ankle, my eyes bouncing from her legs to her chest to her lips. I ran my hand gently up her shin before taking a hoppy guzzle, the beer halting in my throat as Kyle's body weight pressed closer to mine from behind. Twisting to look over my shoulder at him, I could already feel him growing hard against my lower back. "Didn't you beat this game last week?"

"And can you get that second controller fixed already?" Rae begged, her head falling back so short, blonde wisps of hair playfully covered her eyes.

Kyle shrugged with a faint grin, his gaze focused on the screen ahead. "I mean, *you* could buy yourself a controller...and let me borrow it once in a while."

"What a rude host." I pressed my cold beer bottle down against the top of his denim-covered thigh, and a subtle tremble filled his body. He paused the game, and his chest hit my back as he leaned forward, wrapping a firm hand around my wrist.

"Do you really want to see rude, Em?" Kyle whispered, his breath wrapping a ribbon of heat around my ear, making me shudder. There was something about his quiet intensity that always got to me. He could snap from sweet to dominant in a matter of seconds, and it always sent an avalanche of chills directly down my spine.

I lived for that chill.

"I've seen it all." My voice was hoarse and hushed as his grip on my wrist loosened, and I silently begged for his hands to grab me again. He was extremely observant, always knowing when I thirsted for intimacy and when I just desired that familiar warmth of his body. As a self-proclaimed control freak, I loved giving Kyle permission to take that control away from me. Completely letting go and softening every rough, guarded edge of me was satisfying as fuck. "Nothing surprises me."

Kyle leaned forward and curled into the curve of my neck, his breath heating the sensitive skin behind my earlobe with both hands pressed atop my shoulders. Goosebumps freckled my skin the second his hands hit the small space above the hem of my T-shirt where my bare skin begged for touch. It was as if his fingertips possessed some kind of dark magic, and my eyes followed those magical fingers of his as they walked downward over my chest. I felt his soft, determined lips careen my neck, his tongue teasing just enough to peak my nipples now rolling between his fingers.

From the corner of my eye, I watched his free hand wander up one of Rae's bare legs, his fingers sliding between the thin cotton of her pajama shorts before sneaking beneath the edge of her lace underwear. He pressed himself harder against the small of my back, and I rolled my hips back against him, watching his fingers dive inside of Rae as she shifted closer to us.

Her giggle was electric.

My pussy was trembling.

I finally leaned forward to set my beer on the coffee table, returning to my spot between Kyle's legs as his fingers pushed deeper inside of Rae's damp heat, her back arching and her eyes shutting tight. She set her legs on either side of my hips, and I felt beautifully trapped between the two of them, with Kyle straddling me from behind and Rae straddling my front. I pulled her in closer so Kyle didn't have as far to reach while his fingers thrusted inside of her with more speed.

We all multitasked flawlessly together.

And I couldn't complain about this view.

I brought her palm to my lips, gently sucking each of her fingers while reaching back to pull at one of Kyle's belt loops with my free hand. The more I yanked at his jeans, the harder he pressed into me, and I fell into that familiar combination of comfort and ecstasy I lived for.

He released the hand hugging my breast so he could loosen his belt, the sweetest moan floating off Rae's lips as his other hand continued to pleasure her, forcing more high-pitched moans from her quivering body. Once his cock was free from the restraints of his jeans and pressing against me again from behind, I felt his fingers gently—yet with delicious pressure—wrap their way around the base of my neck.

Kyle's lips brushed the back of my ear, teeth nipping at my earlobe. His breath was hot and demanding, his fingers tightening on each side of my throat. "Still not surprised?"

Rae's moans grew louder, hungrier.

A greedy smile formed across my face as I met Kyle's eyes.

"Nope," I whispered, melting into his grip. "Not at all."

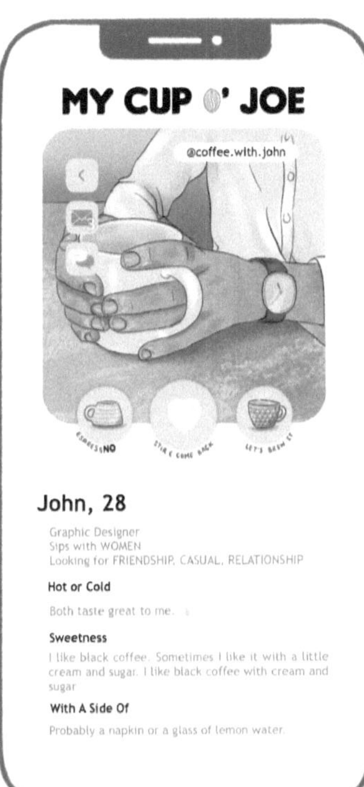

MY CUP O' JOE
@coffee.with.john
ESPRESSNO
STIR & COME BACK
LET'S BREW IT
John, 28
Graphic Designer
Sips with WOMEN
Looking for FRIENDSHIP, CASUAL, RELATIONSHIP
Hot or Cold
Both taste great to me.
Sweetness
I like black coffee. Sometimes I like it with a little cream and sugar. I like black coffee with cream and sugar
With A Side Of
Probably a napkin or a glass of lemon water.

Chapter 7

Fern

There were always too many flickering LED lightbulbs at Thirsty Theodore's. At almost every booth, a rusty mirror hung against the whitewashed wall with bulbs beaming behind recycled glass. I appreciated their attempt at merging vintage with modern, but the lighting made it too easy to see the dark roots anxiously pressing through my burgundy hair. If I were surrounded by buzzed co-workers complaining about being added to another group email—like a typical Monday—I would have cared less about how my dumb hair looked.

I hated that my *caring meter* was now in the red.

My chest slowly lifted, and I released a deep breath, bringing my hands together atop the wood plank table. I immediately stopped tapping my fingers when I noticed three of my nails were chipped, the cracked polish giving me as much of a headache as the damn lights directly above my roots were.

"Francis?"

Holy shit. *Really?*

"John. Hi." I quickly got to my feet, leaning in for a hug before he even set foot beside the booth. "It's still Fern. I haven't switched it back since before, like, eighth grade." I'd also called myself Fern in all our texts. I hadn't written, or called myself, *Francis* Powers in well over a decade.

"Fern, Fran—I never got it straight, did I?" John said, his familiar nasal voice cutting through the awkward fog he'd created the second he announced my birth name. I was thankful *he'd* been the one to build this awkward barrier instead of me.

I was a professional at building graceless blockades.

His arms finally wrapped around me, and my face fell into his chest as the scent of cedar and Pine-Sol tickled my nostrils. I'd forgotten how tall he'd grown once ninth grade hit. During our summers together, I traveled a lot with my family on church retreats. This forced our relationship to survive off calls on my mom's car phone, where reception was less than ideal. Upon each return home, I swear he was another inch taller.

"But you were Francis before your fairy obsession," he continued. It was less of a response and more of a statement. "Is that timeframe, at least, correct?"

Fern Gully was *more* than a 90s fairy obsession for me.

It was a lifestyle.

"Yes, that timeframe seems right," I said, planning my deflection. "How are you, though? It's been, what, fourteen or fifteen years?" Pushing aside the sour starter topic, I nodded toward the booth where he slid in across from me while reaching for two menus, sliding one my way.

With how the night was already going, I thought he may slip into the same side of the booth as me and be one of those awkward shoulder-to-shoulder dates.

"It's definitely been a while." He opened the menu and itched the back of his head. Though his dark hair seemed thinner, it hadn't lost the shocking blue-black shade. It no longer fell jagged above his dark eyes but was clipped short and parted neatly to the side. "Did you go to the reunion last weekend?"

"Indeed, I did." I looked toward the cocktail list above my right pinky finger. Theodore's Kettle—an oversized cauldron of neon-colored liquor with way too much sugar—was calling my name. I didn't need the extra euphoria, but I couldn't resist a pretty drink. "The reunion was...odd."

"Did Mary turn it into a college rager?"

My jaw dropped, and I set the menu down. "How'd you know?"

"How didn't you?" He smiled, revealing white, flawlessly straight teeth. They always hid behind blocks of metal while we were dating.

If anything came from this, at least it wouldn't be a metallic make-out session.

"Did you get any of the emails? I swear all the invites said *18+*, and the place was riddled with toddlers. I mean, I'm not against children, by any means. It just seemed—I don't know—uncomfortable." A slender woman, not much older than us, stepped up to the booth and leaned into one hip. Without hesitation, I lifted the menu in her direction as if she didn't already know what I was pointing at. "I'll have Theodore's Kettle, please."

"Whatever lager is on tap is fine for me. Thanks." John grinned at the waitress as she walked away, and once she was behind the bar, his eyes connected back with mine.

Those dark, russet eyes. They had never looked so bold before.

Maybe it was the irksome lighting giving them a glow I'd never experienced until now.

"Your glasses. Your glasses are gone." I spit the realization out the second it hit me. "Did you get contacts?"

"I got LASIK a few summers back. Right before my senior year at Parsons."

"Well, damn. I shouldn't be surprised you ended up in the big, bad city doing all the artsy things we always dreamed about." A cocktail tub slid in front of me, and almost immediately, the straw found my lips. When the shocking liquid crawled down my throat, I decided it was time to really play this damn game. "So, tell me more about what you do."

I knew exactly what @coffee.with.john did.

"Freelance design. I prepare templates and logos for law firms mostly in Merlin Heights Greyport, and Rockberry Park. Occasionally I'll outsource to Parsons." His voice was so crisp—every word without question or hesitation. He'd always been a straightforward person but never with this type of certainty and confidence. "I hear you work for the app?"

He said '*the app*' as if it were the pimp of dating sites.

I mean, it kind of was.

"Yeah, yes. I'm a graphic designer at My Cup O' Joe." Another sip of the cocktail. "I guess our artistic backgrounds brought us to similar places in life, huh?"

"Seems like it. Dating sites aren't really my thing."

I pushed back the word-vomit climbing up my throat coated in colorful sugar and overpowering, cheap vodka. I couldn't tell him I knew he had a profile—even if he hadn't been active in months.

Hopefully, my stunned eyes and extra seconds of silence didn't say what I was trying to keep quiet.

"You're more into meeting up with ex-girlfriends for cocktails?" I leaned toward the table, raising my eyebrows while stirring the straw around the outside of my oversized glass.

Deflection achieved.

"Well, I'm drinking a beer…and this is the first time I've ever agreed to meet up with an ex," he admitted softly.

I was about to slouch back into the booth when hearing another precocious retort, but the last part of the sentence caught my interest.

A second chance at a second chance was fine, right?

"Really? You've never been interested in catching up with anyone from your past?"

"Not really," he stated, his words a little less articulate this time around. "I mean, it's embarrassing, but you're the only actual relationship I've ever had. We dated for three years, and even though we were young, it meant something to me. I didn't date again until sophomore year at Parsons."

I quickly found the bottom of Theodore's Kettle.

"John, I feel like I owe you the biggest apology." I looked from his sunken eyes to the waitress a few booths away. She caught my gaze, and I lifted the drink with a nod before turning back to John. His tan skin had a brightness to it I'd never noticed before. My guess was he still wore SPF 50 every time the temperature went above sixty degrees. I respected him for caring about himself in ways other men didn't. Good skin. Articulation. Crisp clothes with that fresh dryer-sheet scent to them. Overly oiled cuticles. "I never meant to upset you. We just...well, we needed to branch out, you know? See the rest of the world. Like you said, we were so young."

"Did you see it?" he asked.

"See what?"

"The rest of the world." His lips curled into a grin. "If you haven't, I can show you some of it this weekend."

A tiny dimple peeked from the bottom of his left cheek, as if impressed by his own pickup line. Though Emmie would have laughed directly into his face, the thought behind it was genuine—and I was a sucker for every sappy line in the book.

I melted a little, ignoring Emmie's laugh echoing through my brain.

"I think I can take you up on that." I quietly thanked the waitress when she handed me the second drink. Dammit. I should have asked for the smaller version of this thing. Drinking a second one of these would be a death sentence. I hesitantly looked up from the kettle and said, "On one condition."

He raised an eyebrow, lifting the neck of his beer up just the slightest bit. "I never call you Francis again?"

I chuckled into the straw as I prepared to take a sip. "Never again."

After an unexpectedly busy week of surprise meetings, video calls with the corporate office, and failed logo designs, it was reassuring to know Emmie would be on the other side of my apartment door Saturday morning like she always was. I also had about three hours before her slow, dramatic knocks began sounding. She usually arrived around the time Loaf started begging for breakfast and I went for my second cup of coffee.

The consistent routine we'd kept over the last couple of years was impressive.

The fresh brew sat warming my palms. Porridge was sleeping at the opposite end of the couch while Loaf rose from the depths of the dirty laundry piled beside the washing machine. Though Porridge was the social butterfly of the two, Loaf was my spirit animal. We woke with the sun. We only socialized when necessary. We cared too much about breakfast.

If only Loaf were human.

My head fell back against the couch, and I stared up at the ceiling—at the maze of industrial piping that never seemed safe to me but gave me an anxious sort of comfort. Though the television buzzed with some Saturday morning talk show, my brain hummed with thoughts—memories. It had been years since John and I locked eyes on each other before our Monday night reunion. Even after our break-up—a break-up I thought was without forever wounds—he wouldn't look me in the eye. I now knew the truth. His heart had been concretely stuck in his chest at the same time mine had easily wiggled away.

Like us all, he was flawed. I knew well that flaws sculpted us into who we were destined to become. But would I be able to embrace the human behind the flaws? I'd done it once—twice for some. So, this time around couldn't be much harder.

Right?

His high school flaws had been more on the level of petty annoyances: too straightforward; too technical; too obsessed with date nights at Three-Ring. His personality still felt mechanical, but his heart seemed pure. Genuine. Maybe I gave too many people the benefit of the doubt, but this guy had never shown me an ounce of insincerity. Even as we'd passed each other in those crowded hallways as angsty, emotional teens, he'd worn his heart smack on the center of his sleeve.

I'd seen it every time he quickly looked away when I tried to catch his eye.

I guess I thought he was more angry than heartbroken.

I was only halfway through my mug of coffee when knocks sounded, followed by the drag of Emmie's feet clad in the disgusting dragon slippers she wouldn't let me throw away.

They were from 2010 and needed to be set on fire.

The slippers weren't what shocked me; her being an hour early did.

What a weird fucking week.

"I thought maybe I'd meet you in the hallway with your hair a mess after nonstop sexting with John," Emmie said with a voice sounding gruffly hungover without consuming an ounce of alcohol.

Yet.

"Why would my hair get messed up from sexting?"

Emmie paused as she fully stepped into my apartment, closing the door behind her. "I didn't think that one through."

"We've just been texting, Em. I'm sorry our texts haven't been naughty enough to make you want to read them like some smutty romance novel. We've been reminiscing. I'm not just trying to hook up." The thought of sending nudes to John or jumping into bed with him made my stomach churn a little bit. I still needed to reignite the flames. Right now, there was barely an ember glowing. "Coffee is still hot."

"Good. Here's your mail. I still have the extra key from when I watched Loaf and Idge last month." Emmie slid three envelopes onto the counter on her way to the coffeepot, standing in front of it and flailing her arms to waft the scent toward her. "There's something from that cousin you went to college with. James, maybe? Isn't he the one with—?

"Stop snooping, woman!"

She continued to face the coffee pot, conducting a silent symphony with her arms. "Start getting your own mail, bitch."

I laughed on my way to the counter and watched as she finally filled herself a mug. She flopped over the arm of the couch, making sure not to leave a drop of coffee on the beige fabric that was likely older than her atrocious slippers. Emmie curled close to Porridge, replacing my lazy Sunday position, while I reached for the envelope. Across from the refrigerator, on the other side of the island, was my corkboard. Grabbing a faux-wood tack, I pinned the unopened envelope next to four similar-looking ones already tacked to the board.

"Is this some new trend I don't know about?" Emmie asked, looking up over the side of the couch as I walked back around the island. "A place where unopened letters go to die? The Island of Misfit Mail?"

"They're just save-the-dates for next year. My cousin, my college roommate, a friend from the college book club I founded, and the one high school friend I still talk to."

Emmie's eyebrows lifted as she brought the mug to her lips. "Was this friend at that unhinged reunion?"

"She lives in Portugal."

"Oh. Gotcha. And you're hanging them all up on a corkboard because…" Emmie's lips turned up slyly as she watched me reach for the coffeepot, a spark glowing behind her dark eyes. "I didn't take you as some jealous character from a rom-com, but you secretly are, aren't you? That's *really* why you're rummaging through your used baggage, isn't it?"

"What? No. That's not why I'm doing it!" My tone took me by surprise, and I inhaled deeply, fluttering my gray-green eyes back to neutral. "The reunion just made me realize how confident I am about making a relationship, in general, work. Starting from scratch may take too long—especially if our deadline is the My Cup Gala. Then, after I find gold in my *baggage*, I'll have dates for these weddings."

"You think John is the gold you're looking for?"

"He could be a copper piece, perhaps. Do you want some chocolate vodka mixed with your coffee? I think it's about time for chocolate vodka." I reached for the bottle sitting atop the fridge and unscrewed the lid. It wasn't even noon, and the bottle was ready for action. "And maybe he will be. We have a date next Friday at Three-Ring, like the old days. I was hoping we could meet sooner, but he has a busy schedule."

"Well, then you'll have more time to tell me about all the sexts you've been receiving before you dive into details about the next date." Emmie nodded toward the vodka I'd just finished mixing into my freshly poured brew. "I'll take a hefty shot of that with this joe, please."

"Em, I'm sorry, but there haven't been any sexts. No nudes. No dick pics. Nothing," I said, walking over to her with vodka in hand. "And *you* must tell me *your* plans for Monday. Isn't Monday your big day with the *Real Estate Ringleader*?"

"Yes. Yes, it is." Emmie's eyes stared through me as vodka sloshed into her mug. She didn't even break our gaze as she kept pouring. "Let's make it *two* hefty shots."

Jake, 29

Real Estate Agent
Sips with WOMEN
Looking for CASUAL, RELATIONSHIP, MARRIAGE

Hot or Cold

Honestly, I can't say no to a simple cold brew. I also can't say no to a simple cup of hot, black coffee. What can I say? I'm just open to all the simple, good things life has to offer.

Sweetness

I like a little something-something in my cold brew. Hot coffee? Keep it black. Don't change what's already perfect.

With A Side Of

Good conversation and a pretty face.

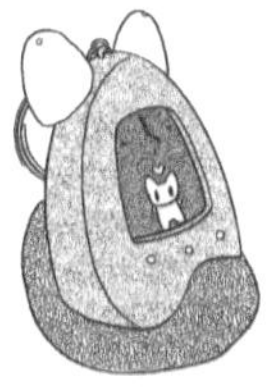

Chapter 8

Emmie

I sat hunched on my bed, wearing a T-shirt from Hot Topic that now pooled around my thighs, no longer sticking to me like latex, as it did in high school. The television across from my bed buzzed with another rerun of *Gilmore Girls*—a show I'd quietly obsessed over during my teenage years mostly because of my fascination with Luke and his diner.

And my secret crush on Lorelei.

I blindly watched Rory bicker with her mother for the fourteenth time in the last twelve minutes, unfazed and wide awake. Growing up, I hated hearing them constantly argue, until I realized how much I silently bickered with everyone around me from the confines of my skull. I'd pushed through a mute battle within myself when discovering Barry—the kid who smelled like weed in geometry class—was the one always putting pieces of eraser in my hair. I'd screamed inside my mouth every time someone shut the locker door over my fingers, trying not to let a defeated whisper escape for their pleasure. I pressed my lips together whenever I overheard someone wonder *why so-and-so was dating the Mixed M&M,* eyes darting toward me then quickly away.

If only I practiced voodoo.

I mean, I could still learn.

My back collapsed over the sheets, and I shuffled socked feet beneath the comforter, squeezing my eyes shut. I didn't need to look at my beloved Tamagotchi clock—a discovery made at a thrift shop during my sophomore year of college—to know it was nearing three in the morning. It was the fourth rerun of *Gilmore Girls*—that in itself told the time. It wasn't the time or the haunting 2000s antique sitting on the desk making my mind bounce inside of my brain.

It was the idea of riding in a nauseating time machine just to prove to those who hurt me that they had never been worth my pain. That sickening ride was both terrifying and necessary if I wanted to keep my job while maintaining an ounce of self-respect.

Even though I'd lose dignity along the way.

The cold, nervous sweat soaking my body when I woke was, in fact, rain spraying in from the bottom of my window. I immediately regretted my weird obsession with wearing socks at night the second my wool-covered feet hit the pool of water beside my desk. Slamming the window shut, stripping off my soaked T-shirt, and throwing towels over the bed sheets, I knew this Monday was off to a terrific start.

Stretching the most comfortable pencil skirt I owned up over my thighs and hips, I ventured outside and questioned every soaking step I took toward my Toyota. When my hand met the door handle, I stepped into a puddle I thought my burgundy suede booties could conquer. I knew now they could not. Perfect ringlets, typically bouncing at the edges of my ears, now mimicked the brushed hair of a dog at mid-groom. I slammed down the mirror when I got into the driver's seat and backed out of my usual spot beneath the oak tree, ignoring the angry rain pellets obstructing my view.

For the first time in the almost three years I'd worked at My Cup, I was jealous of Fern's cozy, cut-off-from-the-world cubicle. We'd started off as clueless researchers two years before the app launched, analyzing relationship data and Googling coffee brands and shops. Once separated into our teams, I'd been relieved to see that the content group was in an open-concept corner. The extrovert in me embraced the ability to speak to whomever I wanted, whenever I wanted throughout the day.

Now, the introvert hiding inside just wanted to huddle behind some stupid cubicle wall.

I parked a few houses down from the one with the big, red sign screaming OPEN HOUSE in the front yard. I thought, maybe, I'd just remove the sign, put it in someone else's yard, and leave, but that wasn't the mature way to go about this project.

Mentally manipulating my ex was apparently better.

"Fuck! Shit!" My ankle twisted as I lifted it out of another puddle outside of the driver's side door. Looking down at it, I set my boot right back into it, slamming the door behind me and feeling the rain flatten down the curls I hoped would magically bounce back to life on the walk to the front door.

All I had to lean on now were my oversized sunglasses, the red lipstick I'd applied at stop signs, and the pencil skirt doubling as Spanx.

Ducking under the awning, the reflection staring back at me from the front door glass told me I would look like a psychopath if I wore these sunglasses inside. However, the reflection also showed someone who looked absolutely nothing like the high school nobody Jake had dated.

Choosing the psychopathic route, I pushed open the door.

The ranch was small, bright, and open—a typical home setup most millennial real estate agents went for these days. Everything was visible from my spot at the entrance: two thirty-something women nodding at the modern appliances in the kitchen; a couple in their sixties continuously stroking the velvet furniture; a red-haired woman leaning against the far wall, taking a packet from Jake, who sat on a metal stool.

He looked identical to the billboards lining the highways and signs picketing everyone's yard. I wanted to see if he'd had Botox to minimize his crow's feet or if that little bump on his nose had been shaved away. However, I knew those details didn't matter.

The people walking around this house did.

He did.

The redhead's heels clicked toward the entrance, and I scooted aside, smiling her way when she reached for her jacket and neatly hung it over her arm.

She'd regret not putting it on once she stepped outside.

"It's a beautiful place," she said, looking out the window. Her lips molded into a grimace. "I didn't bring my umbrella. Is it really *that* bad out?"

I looked from her jacket over her arm—and the hood it donned—back to meet her eyes.

"Not as bad as the last house this Ringleader guy showed." My voice stuck to the back of my throat, and I tried desperately to push down the lingering hesitance. "And the one before that."

"Huh?" She leaned in a little closer, eyebrows raised. "He's the *best* in the Finger Lakes region. What do you mean?"

"Well, he's definitely known for being the *best* at one thing." My brain was working fast, fumbling over thoughts. "I found condoms inside the bathroom cabinets of the last two houses I looked at that he was selling. I bet this one will be a three-for-three."

The redhead looked over her shoulder at Jake, who was now leaning against the wall and smiling into his phone. Her gaze told me she was thinking about whether or not she wanted to be his next real-estate romp, her eyes traveling from his polished Oxfords to the perfectly barbered mane with barely a gray hair in sight. However, she hadn't overlooked his chapped, dry lips and the small potbelly hanging over his belt.

Practically right on cue, he stretched his arms above his head to reveal spotty sweat stains leaking through the fabric of his overpriced button-up.

"Gross," she whispered as she pushed through the front door, leaving the stapled packet he'd handed her on the side table by my hip.

The pen in my coat pocket finally came in handy as I jotted *SMALL DICK* in capital letters across the front page. I honestly couldn't remember the size of his package—perhaps that was a sign in itself. But a surge of adrenaline was taking control of my limbs, forcing me toward the older couple still petting the couch.

I stood beside them, looking below my sunglasses at the velvet furniture that, indeed, was soothingly soft. Being the couch sat in the center of the space, Jake had now noticed my presence and nodded in my direction.

His grin was proof he'd gotten some Botox around his eyes and mouth.

It was also proof he didn't recognize me.

"Mr. Merchant said this velvet was imported from Egypt specifically for *this* house. And the place comes fully furnished. Can you believe it?" The older man spoke quietly, his wife silent with one hand bringing tea to her lips and the other sitting atop the arm of the couch. "All the furniture stays. Do you think you'll bid on the place?"

I lifted my chin with an unexpected air of confidence. "Nope. Not from this guy."

"Why not, dear?" The white-haired woman woke from her trance, her bright-blue eyes trying to see through the dark lenses of my sunglasses.

Think, Emmie. Think.

"Oh, I thought most people knew about the whole *Junkyard Jake* thing."

"Excuse me?" The man leaned in closer, his breath warm on my cheek. I stepped to my left, my hand quickly moving from the couch.

"Oh, yeah. He stalks out junkyards and drives around most nights looking for furniture on the side of the road and whatever. He scrubs it, sprays it with essential oils, and calls it new."

"This cannot be true." The man turned to his wife, who now had her nose touching the velvet. She'd practically faceplanted into the arm of the couch to take a long sniff.

"I mean, I do think that's a hint of tea tree I smell." The skin on the bridge of her nose scrunched. "Maybe some Febreze too."

Holy hell. People believed anything.

"Look at that app Olivia always talks about. Look up this Junkyard Jake fellow," the man urged, stepping away from the couch and turning toward the door with his wife at his heels. "We should tell her folks about this before they go to his open house next week."

His wife nodded, clicking away on her phone with her face far too close to the screen. "I think our granddaughter is too young to use these kinds of apps, dear."

"Don't toddlers use apps these days?"

She rolled her eyes, squinting and practically pushing her eyeball against the screen. "Not apps like the one *you're* talking about."

"Everyone is on some kind of app these days! Just type in his name somewhere. I'm sure he will show up," I said, trying not to sound annoyed as I watched them exit the house, their fingers intertwining before the door hit their loafers.

Old people were fucking adorable.

Even though they smelled a little like musk and cotton balls.

The two remaining women had made their way to the front door as well, reaching for their umbrellas before lifting the packet from the side table. Giggling, they both looked over at Jake, who was now walking in my direction with a curled brow.

Deep breaths. Deeeeeep breaths.

"Ma'am, is there anything I can help you with? It's become an unexpectedly quiet and quick open house today."

My bones froze beneath my skin, and I hoped he couldn't see the wide, uncertain eyes hiding behind my sunglasses. He set a hand on the back of the couch and peered around the house, his Oxfords tapping against the engineered hardwood. The sweat stains had grown from small spots to handprints reaching downward on his button-up, and I could now see more silver streaks sprinkled through his chestnut hair.

Most men aged gracefully, and most men pulled off silver hair annoyingly well.

In this case, I'd aged better.

Way better.

"Well, *Jacob*, I think people are talking." I slowly took a few steps away from the *Egyptian* velvet, which, honestly, probably was imported from Egypt.

The stuff seemed legit.

"Excuse me?" His head cocked to the side, and I finally saw his brow crinkle ever so slightly. Twisting my red lips into a grin, I slowly removed my sunglasses and continued to step toward the entrance, reaching for the packet on the side table and shaking my head.

"Whoever wrote this must have had a really memorable experience with you in high school. Maybe some boob action here or a blow job there when an exam was coming up." I lifted the packet up so he could see the writing across the front page. The words were much bolder than I remembered them being when I'd written them fifteen minutes earlier.

Jake took a step closer, his eyes squinting as they roamed my lightly freckled face and the tan skin hugging it. Those two features—plus the curls—had remained constant over the years, but my hair had been chopped, and my signature frames sat waiting in my jacket pocket. My hips still had a curve to them, which I never wanted to lose, but no longer held that additional hundred or so pounds Jake had cautiously touched over a decade ago.

I reached into my jacket and slipped the large, square glasses atop my nose.

Jake's face went white. "Emmeline?"

"Please. It's Emmie." I wagged my hand his way and turned on my heel, reaching for the door handle. "The house looks great, by the way. You're a real ringleader these days."

He opened his mouth to say something, his hands upturned by his hips.

"There's no need to say anything. Save your breath." I twisted the handle, and rain sprinkled over the half-moon-shaped tile at the entrance. The tile was a good choice on Jake's part—if he'd even been part of the house-flipping process. "It will be a quiet open house for you. Enjoy."

"Why? Why so quiet?" His words came out jumbled, his feet sinking through the tiled floor as his hands remained upturned.

"Oh, you still don't know, do you?" I hesitated for a second, to see if everything would click inside of his brain. I wasn't sure if he was even capable of piecing together what I was saying—clicking puzzle pieces from the past together with pieces from the present.

Either way, fire was pulsing inside of me. Confidence was fueling my adrenaline. Never in my life had I felt so satisfied.

That was a lie. Kyle and Rae satisfied me just fine on a weekly basis.

"What the hell are you talking about? This is my career you're messing with."

I snickered, stepping beneath the awning. "Maybe the next one will work out...but I don't know. I doubt it. *People. Are. Talking.* You, of all people, know how it is."

The second he blinked, I knew I'd won, and the rain weighing down my curls had never felt so good.

Chapter 9

FERN

I'd avoided Three-Ring for almost a decade.

Well, I guess that wasn't entirely true.

I'd been forced through the center's giant double doors for graduation parties and work events over the last decade, but nothing came close to matching the mediocre concerts, nerdy game nights, or beloved appetizer buffets of my teenage years. I'd been part of the team who designed the art déco logo for the small coffee bar inside of Three-Ring—all in the name of My Cup, of course—and still never had a latte from it. Invitations to cocktail nights and stand-up events in the more renovated lounges came my way over the years, but I always declined.

It wasn't that I hated the place. The appetizer buffet was remarkable, surprisingly stocked with vegetarian options, and the place had local art lining the brick inside and out. Three-Ring hosted some of the biggest concerts in the Finger Lakes region and always supported the up-and-coming strugglers—even hosting my sister's band before they hit it big in the pop-worship world—or hitting it as big as anyone can in a genre like that could from Merlin Heights.

After attending Teen Game Hour with John every fucking Friday from eighth to tenth grade, my interest in this place had come to a royal halt.

Instead of Friday night games, we were showing up for happy hour at the newly branded and renamed Booze Buffet housed inside of Three-Ring. The grandiose buffet wasn't stocked with finger sandwiches, salads, and fancy cheeses, but with pre-mixed cocktails, pre-poured wine, locally crafted beer, and even shot glasses rippling at the brim. Several people moved quickly behind the buffet, making sure spaces filled the second a glass disappeared.

"The Bloody Marys look fresh. I grabbed two." John's voice took me by surprise, and I turned away from the busy buffet to see him standing with a glass in each hand. His button-up was loose around his neck, dark hair that definitely hadn't been there during our pre-teen years poking up from between the top buttons. I glanced at the drinks again, squinting casually at the skewers filled with olives, cheeses, curled bacon, and a pickle.

Bacon.

"They do look...*fresh*." I did my best not to cringe as I grabbed the glass he pushed in my direction. Immediately, my fingers slipped the pickle from the skewer, and I popped it between my teeth. I plucked off the bacon with my fingertips before placing the pickle back on the skewer, the bacon crumbling in the palm of my hand. "Do you...like bacon?"

John chugged half of his glass before staring back at my palm, tomato juice sticking to his top lip.

"Do you always rip apart your Bloody Marys?" His voice was hoarse with shock.

"I'm vegetarian, so...kind of. Yeah." Shrugging, I closed my hand and brought the drink to my lips, taking a satisfied sip before spotting a garbage can a few feet away. "What do you want to do?"

"I want to get us those shots over there." John laughed lowly before shaking his head with a smile. "You've gone from Francis to Fran to Fern to vegetarian in fifteen years. That's quite a shot-worthy transformation."

"It's not like it's my identity or anything. I bounce between vegetarian and vegan way too often. I just don't eat meat anymore." After another strong sip, I shuffled to the garbage can and tossed out the bacon, rubbing my palm on my jeans before realizing there was now a trail of grease across my denim-covered thigh.

At this point, I'd need three more of these—*with* bacon—to impress John.

"Let's go sit by the window. I think there's live music in half an hour," John said, nodding toward the large window overlooking one of the few landscaped streets in Merlin Heights. He sat down onto a small, leather loveseat, and I immediately wondered whether I should snuggle in close or sit on the bench across from him.

With a long sip, I squeezed in next to him, the bacon clinging to his skewer near my temple.

"Now that I've apparently *rebranded* myself since we last dated, have you done any rebranding over the years?" I tried leaning on the arm of the loveseat so my legs weren't practically on his lap—and his bacon wasn't practically in my mouth. Though I was sure I looked more awkward than casual, he only shrugged, and a faint grin curved his lips.

He was oblivious to my discomfort.

"Spoken like a true designer." He spun the skewer around his glass before sliding off the olive, pickle, and, thankfully, the bacon into his drink. I watched the bacon hide beneath the crimson surface as the glass met his lips, and he placed it on the side table. "I don't think I've changed much since middle or high school. Maybe I've gotten a little taller, but I don't think I have the capacity to change too much."

"What do you mean?

"I'm pretty sure I'm part cyborg," he said. "It's in my DNA. Change just gives me anxiety, so I avoid it."

My laugh turned into a snort, and I lifted my drink to block the sound.

It failed.

"We're all part cyborg, in some way. It doesn't mean you can't change. Maybe you're just confident with who you are, and you're fine with that."

John laughed lightly, his shoulders awkwardly tensing below his ears. "Confidence has never been my forte."

I envisioned him avoiding my gaze in the busy high school hallway, his glasses fogging as he looked the other way.

"Well, when you say it like that, then yeah, your confidence shits the bed. You can't say that out loud, John!" I said at practically a shout. "Manifest that confidence!"

"It's easier for you to say that, though, Fern." His lips tightly rolled together, as if calling me anything but Francis burned his throat. "You've always radiated confidence."

Another snort escaped as I finished my Bloody Mary.

"That's kind, but I think I'm just living life without a filter," I said, setting the glass on the table in front of our knees. John shrugged, finishing his glass and turning away slightly as bacon slid over his lips. I ignored the roll in my stomach but appreciated the respectful gesture.

"Filtered or not, you speak openly and honestly. I've always loved that about you." He angled his body toward me, the tips of our knees touching as he squared his shoulders. I expected some kind of spark to ignite inside of me, but I felt nothing. Not even the tiniest flicker of fire burned within my chest. He leaned forward, his dark eyes pinned to mine. "I've always loved your unapologetic confidence. Whether or not you see it that way."

I didn't think I could get any closer to the arm of the couch at this point. I was practically sitting on it. "That's so sweet of y—"

"I've always loved *you*, Francis."

Then he attacked my face.

He was inside my mouth within a matter of seconds, one hand tightly gripping my knee and the other pulling my face toward his. His mouth consumed mine, and I didn't even have time to think about how it felt to kiss him without metal brackets clicking against my teeth. I could only think about how nauseating the tomato paste covering my tongue tasted. How tiny beads of sweat were dripping from his forehead onto mine.

How I absolutely did not want to kiss him back.

Though I usually thought about the needs of others before my own, it was time to put myself first. Sitting here getting my throat tongue-stabbed by someone I felt zero emotions for was not my idea of a great time. I wasn't going to feel bad for leaving this make-out session from Hell, even if the tiniest part of my brain was forcing my guilt to grow.

I mentally crossed John's name off the list of exes.

Pressing my foot forward onto the coffee table, I knocked over one of our empty Bloody Marys, glass shattering over the tile and waking him up from the middle school flashback he'd fallen into.

"Oh, geez, John." I stumbled to my feet, walking backward and grabbing my purse as I tip-toed around broken glass on the floor, an olive rolling beneath the loveseat. "Let me go get someone to help with this."

"I'm *not* sorry, Fran. I've always loved you and never won't!" John shouted, his gaze attacking my eyes as powerfully as his mouth had attacked my face. A few people by the Booze Buffet looked over their shoulders before grabbing a drink, watching the scene continue to unfold.

My social anxiety was screaming. "Let me find... That's nice to say... I will..."

Then, for the first time in my dating history, I left. I walked out of the date without hesitation. I didn't turn around to give John a third or fourth chance. Each step carried that confidence John had always seen and I was just now starting to feel.

I stopped around the corner to subtly watch an employee sweep up the glass while a middle-aged man tuned his guitar near the buffet, lights fading to create an intimate environment I was thankfully avoiding. When John stood up to grab two more drinks from the Booze Buffet—expecting my return—I turned on my heel with my face angled down.

I exited the double doors and didn't look back. I'd only return to Three-Ring when I had an actual ring on my finger.

Chapter 10

Emmie

"You *actually* did this?" Al asked, looking above his lopsided frames with a gaze inked in both terror and intrigue. I nodded, reaching for my coffee while scooting back in the chair. His eyes darted back to the tablet, and his finger scrolled across the screen as coffee scorched my taste buds. "And you actually learned *this* lesson from it?" he asked.

"Well, kind of." I couldn't lie. My face would crinkle like a raisin, and my glasses would fog up if I even attempted one. "It was more just fun for me, and the lesson came after. I really had to think about it."

I'd thought about the lesson for hours.

Hours.

"I mean, it makes sense." Al sat back, placing his glasses on the tablet in front of him. "If someone was afraid to date *me*, fearing others would talk about us, I'd be furious. Actually, furious is an understatement. And *you* sat on that anger for, what, close to a decade?"

I couldn't imagine anyone purposely dating Al, but those thoughts hid behind the head nod I was giving him.

"This part, right here." Al lifted the tablet up, squinting his eyes closed as his glasses slid onto the desk. "This is what My Cup subscribers will remember: *I internalized these emotions for years before using them to transform myself. Because of those emotions, I had turned into a person I knew I would be proud of, as well as someone he would be impressed by. But I didn't want him just impressed with my looks, because that shit ultimately doesn't matter. You see, you want to impress people with your confidence. Your aura. Your wit. These really matter when you're facing a past or a present relationship. You can rely on karma, to an extent—but I wouldn't recommend going to the extent I did. Just make sure you're not the one getting burned in the end. Always be the flame.*"

I finished my coffee with lifted eyebrows, my brain slowly remembering what I'd written during the late hours of the night.

"That. *That's* why your blog probably won't be going anywhere," Al said, the tablet dropping out of his hands and onto the desk, barely missing his thick frames.

My heart hit my rib cage as I sat up straighter. "So, I don't have to worry?"

"Well, unfortunately, we *all* must worry a little for the next few months—at least until the gala." Al's words forced my hopeful heart back into its dull rhythm. "With sTEAl My Heart having the powerful release it did, corporate is being finicky with finances."

My eyes rolled into the back of my skull, a migraine pressing against my temples. "That name is atrocious."

"It is." Al reached for his glasses and set them back atop the tablet, mimicking the relaxed posture he'd had before my quote jumped off the page at him. With how thick the lenses in those things were, I wasn't sure how he could sit here without wearing them for so long. "I honestly don't think they're a tremendous threat, but niche dating apps are big right now, and any competition is worrisome. People are becoming more and more visual—making many blogs a piece of the past—even if a blog kicks ass, like yours."

"Cursing before noon? On a Monday, nonetheless?" I dramatically grabbed the edge of his desk, looking over my shoulder toward his closed office door. "I'm appalled."

Al's cracked lips upturned, and he shook his head, twisting to face the monitor overtaking his desk—a monitor I appreciated even though most saw it as an out-of-date monstrosity.

Vintage. I guess the early '90s were officially in that category.

Now *that* was appalling.

"Your humor too. My Cup needs that. We've gotten too serious since breaking so much ground in the last year," Al said. "We need it both in the office and in our content."

"I appreciate that, Al. I'll keep making a fool of myself and finding some deep, profound reason behind my foolishness." I got to my feet and blew some curls out of my line of vision, making my way to the door. "All in the name of My Cup, of course."

But really, I'd had too much fun over the weekend not to make part of this venture purely for my enjoyment too.

Bad karma or not, I was all in.

It was officially fall, and Fern was in her fucking glory. Her face held this permanently cheesy grin when the air finally grew crisp and flavor shots of pumpkin and cinnamon and apple were available everywhere and anywhere. It made me both jealous and disgusted that someone could be as happy about wearing layers and decorating a cubicle with oversized gourds as she was. She scooted her boots through fallen leaves, leaving an outline of dirt on the sidewalk behind them, hugging the fresh latte we'd snagged from Spellbound after work in her gloved hands.

"How can you be so damn joyful when you and John didn't work out?" I asked.

Fern's smile widened. "Did I tell you I kicked a glass onto the floor? *On purpose?*"

"And then you left the poor guy alone on the couch," I said, remembering the discussion we'd had over lunch. "You shattered the glass *and* that goofy man's heart. You're becoming as bad as me."

"I mean, I gave it a valiant effort. He was just...well, a little too obsessed. You, on the other hand, are walking into your little dates with a *much* different mindset," Fern said, the shrug of her shoulders barely noticeable from inside her thick jacket. It was barely sixty-five degrees, and she was dressed like a damn Eskimo. "Plus, he practically face-planted onto my mouth. He was giving me CPR with bacon breath."

"So, John is obviously out." I pushed away the excessive imagery Fern was known for painting. Not that I didn't appreciate it. I was always up for hearing anyone's dirty details. However, this was not my preferred flavor of spice. "Are you going to keep dating these guys you know won't work out?"

"Where's the positivity, Em?" Fern kicked a small pile of oak leaves from under the tree where my car was parked. It had been my day to drive, but she insisted we walk the half mile to the office this morning. I should have never agreed. I was not made for anything but the summer heat. "Everyone changes. I know someone will click. We clicked before, and now that we're more mature, we're likely to click even better now."

"Is that a researched fact?"

"Probably. I'll Google it." Fern added an extra hop to her step before stopping in her boots and reaching into her pocket, lifting a vibrating phone to her ear. "Marian, hi."

My heart palpitated when she spoke her sister's name.

Marian hadn't visited for a weekend since leaving for her big, statewide tour with Thea and the Thunderclouds that summer. Before the ministry band grew from little to a little bit bigger, she'd regularly leave an imprint on Fern's couch alongside Porridge and Loaf. She was a Sunday school teacher and the marketing manager at Two Mighty Pillars—and the ideal offspring in the eyes of the Powers family. With Marian now spreading *Godly* awareness as lead guitarist, Fern knew the recent salary increase My Cup handed her wouldn't trump her sister's purity.

The thought of her sister as "perfectly pure" was laughable.

As long as Fern wore clothing that showcased her inked skin, colored her hair vibrantly, and worked at The Devil's Cup—as her mother called it—she could never win.

Nor did she really want to.

"Well." Fern's voice heightened, and she shuffled quickly through the leaves to catch my stride. "The whole family is visiting this weekend."

"They'll stick around for more than just a coffee?" My eyes widened, and I tried to hide the excitement fluttering behind my ribs. "Is Marian staying the weekend?"

Fern lowered her lids and pursed her lips knowingly. "Probably. Yes."

I threw my hands up with way too much enthusiasm. "So much for scheduling your next date. We'll have Marian to entertain!"

"I was already looking for a way to accidentally bump into Davis. Their visit may help," Fern said, raising her eyebrows while taking a quick sip of her latte.

"*Davis?* He can't go by Dave? Or maybe Big D? It has to be *Davis?*"

"You know better than to judge a person's name," Fern spat, tossing her latte into the trashcan by the apartment entrance. "Did you judge me when you found out my name was Fern?"

"I judged you when I discovered *why* you'd changed it," I said lowly, remembering the weekend-long *FernGully* marathon she'd forced me to sit through on repeat.

"That's fair." Fern shrugged, twisting her key and shoving the door with all her little body could muster. This door had never been kind to her tiny frame.

"So, how long is Marian staying? Just Friday? Maybe until Sunday?" The question made Fern walk up the stairs backward, her lips pursed and eyes narrowed.

"Oh, stop that," she said, turning back to face forward once making it to the second floor. "My parents just *love* watching you flirt with their innocent, angelic child. Focus on your next blog. Not getting into my sister's pants."

Fern got to her apartment door, and I crept toward the next staircase. Her door opened, and Porridge greeted Fern as usual, pawing out into the hallway to rub against her denim legs.

"I have all week to figure out how the hell I'm going to make this next blog work." Giggling to myself, I climbed onto the first step of the stairs leading to my floor and peeked over the railing, giving my hair a quick fluff. "I only have a few days to convince your *pure* little sister I'm worth her time."

"And Rae and Kyle won't care?" Fern's head shifted to the side, Porridge using her knees as a scratching post.

"Please. I'm their fucking unicorn. I come and go as I please." My eyebrows danced above my glasses as my lips curved into a sinister grin. "Get it?"

"Yes, Em. I caught that one," Fern said, looking down the hall to make sure no one else had. "Documenting your love life would probably get you just as much attention as The Cheater Chase will."

"The Cheater Chase. That title flows beautifully off the tongue every time we say it." I took a couple of steps up the stairs before clearing my throat to make sure it would echo perfectly against the concrete walls. "Now onto chasing your sister."

"Shut up!" Fern shouted before snickering and slamming the door behind her.

MY CUP ' JOE
@BrewMeUpGood
ESPRESSNO
STIR & COME BACK
LET'S BREW IT
Kyle, 27
Blogger
Sips with WOMEN, MEN, NON-BINARY
Looking for CASUAL
Hot or Cold
I'm open to all types of coffee. I don't judge.
Sweetness
I'm always up for a little sugar (and spice), but I probably lean more toward the spicy side. Not in my coffee, though! You know what I mean.
With A Side Of
Honesty, communication, and a cold, hoppy IPA.

Chapter 11

FERN

The kiln was cool, and three mugs sat perched on the windowsill, the morning light giving a natural glow to the glazed sheen. I had stayed up until four in the morning, finishing the mugs and making sure they were free of chips or knicks. I'd also painted and glazed them in styles I knew my parents and Marian would appreciate: one had a verse from Romans, one had a verse from Psalms, and one had multicolored outlines of cats painted on the clay.

Marian was asked on a weekly basis to foster a new cat.

She rarely declined an offer...even though her neighbor watched them whenever she was out on tour—which was all the damn time.

The coffee was still dripping into the carafe, and the Keurig was warm and ready as backup. The plants were watered, laundry folded, and the countertop was spotless. My hair fell damp over my shoulder in a single braid I knew would leave a lovely—and probably phallic—shape on my shirt. Leaning against the countertop and adjusting the braid, I quietly hoped it left an uncomfortable mark behind.

Every visit with my parents was just that: uncomfortable.

I heard an abrupt knock on the door, followed by a creak. Without looking up, I reached for a mug on the shelf and set it near the filled carafe. "They're not here yet. Coffee is hot."

"Hot and ready. Just how I like it," Emmie laughed, scuffling toward the kitchen in oversized sweatpants and dragon slippers.

I faced her with a snicker as she reached for the carafe and began pouring. "Sexual jokes first thing in the morning *and* right before my family arrives?"

"Are you surprised?"

"Impressed, if anything," I added.

"That's my girl." She brought the mug to her lips and inhaled the scent—something she always did before taking a sip. "Have you reached out to that Davis guy?"

"Well, he is *actually* lead production engineer at Willow Center of the Arts...or at least that's what his My Cup profile says." I looked down at my damp sweater and readjusted the braid again. "I got us all tickets to the *Brigadoon* Brunch they're doing today on their small stage."

The thought of running into Davis made my stomach lurch into my throat.

"Clever plan. I'll go get ready." Emmie started toward the door before stopping near the couch and looking over her shoulder, lifting the mug to her upturned lips for a sip.

"You're hilarious. I hope your humor is contagious, because I may need some," I said, rethinking my plan to sit through a musical all morning alongside my parents.

My positivity needed to make a grand entrance before my family did. I'd put on my usual façade the second my mother embraced me—the same mask I'd worn two weeks earlier during our coffee date. My father would tell us ministry stories over beignets or discuss the next retreat he was planning. Marian would text me jokes from under the table, regarding the mediocre acting on stage or how many times our father referenced a bible quote.

I was looking most forward to my parents leaving, Marian staying the night, and wine being poured.

Religion wasn't something I loathed. I respected spirituality and everyone's choice to choose what they wanted to believe in. My parents made it seem as if they embraced everyone's right to believe as they liked, but over time, I realized I was the only one not allowed to do just that. I decided long ago that the magical, incredible stories I heard every Sunday were just that: fiction and fantasy.

I preferred *FernGully* and *The NeverEnding Story* to Noah's Ark and David and Goliath.

The knock on the door made Emmie jump, one of her slippers sliding off as coffee dripped over a few of her fingers. She frantically pointed to her sweatpants and slippers while shaking her head, obviously wishing she'd changed before making her way downstairs. My shoulders hit my ears, and I pinched my lips together, walking around her to open the door.

They stood in the hallway like a framed family photograph straight out of the '90s.

I took a deep breath and prepared my plastic smile. "Hey, guys, come on in! The coffee is hot and ready."

I heard Emmie snicker from behind me as I realized what I'd said.

Marian flung her arms around my neck, lifting onto her toes as she squeezed tight. Even with her annoyingly perfect persona, two weeks was too long without it. Before Marian could back away, my mother wrapped her arms around the both of us, and I knew my father was next in line.

We were a living, breathing family sitcom.

I wanted to vomit.

"It's so good to see you, Frannie." My dad released his grip, which allowed the rest of them to step away, giving me the chance to breathe. *"How good and pleasant it is when God's people live together in unity."*

Marian's eyes caught mine, and I brought my hand to the back of my sweater, unfolding my index finger from my fist.

He'd been in my apartment for forty seconds, and already, we'd heard our first verse.

My mother set her hands on my shoulders before cupping my chin. "Oh, Psalm 133:1. It's so nice having the four of us together. Getting coffee together is always great, yes. But this is better."

Was it, though?

"Well, it's been about two weeks, Mom, since we met for coffee. Six months for Dad," Marian added, stepping into the living room and noticing Emmie on the arm of the couch. Marian's eyes widened, and coffee dripped off Emmie's lip before she adjusted her glasses. "Emmie. Hi."

"Coffee anyone?" Emmie lifted her mug into the air, wiping the corner of her mouth on the sleeve of her slouchy crewneck. Her eyes darted from Marian's to mine and then back to my sister's again before Emmie's slippered feet shuffled into the kitchen.

"Of course. Yes." Marian brushed by me, following Emmie, who reached for a mug and filled it up for her before finishing her own.

"So, what's the plan for today, kiddo?" my father asked, running fingers through his newly darkened locks. For a man who only cared what God thought of him, he sure cared a lot about keeping his hair as dark as it had been at eighteen.

This was proof that hair-dye addiction was genetic.

"I got us tickets for the *Brigadoon* Brunch at Willow Arts. We have just enough time to sip some coffee in our *new* mugs over here." I turned on my heels and led them to the windowsill where I gently pushed aside Mr. Monstera who was hovering over the three mugs. "I finally felt inspired."

Inspired was an overstatement.

My personal, creative projects were practically nonexistent with all the projects taking over my brain at My Cup. I'd felt obligated to gift my family something as a *thank you* for visiting, forcing whatever creative energy lurking inside of me to escape.

My mom clasped her hands together and hopped in her little flats as I handed over her mug, my father reaching for the one I pushed in his direction. Marian gingerly walked over to the window with her jaw dropped, setting down her coffee on the side table before reaching for her gift.

"If I'd waited five minutes, I could have had my coffee in this beauty." Marian shook her head and looked over her shoulder at Emmie, who casually leaned against the kitchen counter, the oversized dragon heads of her slippers nodding as she wiggled her toes. "*Ms. Impatient* over there should have waited because, Fern...this mug is gorgeous. Your work gets better and better each time."

I saw Emmie's grin from the corner of my eye and knew she would count Marian's jab as flirtation.

"*I can do all things through him who strengthens me,*" my dad said, bowing his head and looking down into the mug in his hands.

"Oh, yes," my mother whispered, reaching for my father's arm. "It's the perfect time for Philippians."

I beg to differ.

"I can see your work is improving, Fernie." My father's words were quiet and kind even with a low ache already buzzing in my head. "But I can also tell you haven't trusted yourself in Him. Once you do, your work will be flawless."

"Once your heart is fully given to Him, true love too will also find you." My mother's eyes brightened just the tiniest bit as she rubbed her index finger along the soft, smooth rim of her mug. "Oh! How was that date, dear?"

"More coffee anyone? Here, I'll bring it to you." Emmie quickly reached for the carafe and shuffled over to the window where we all huddled, pouring coffee into the mugs my parents were holding. She always said she had been a barista in another life. "Sugar? Creamer? I'll go grab some."

"I'll help." Marian squeezed my arm gently before fleeing behind Emmie, leaving me to stand and smile at my parents.

All I really wanted to do was smile at the fucking liquor cabinet.

The small auditorium brought flashbacks of high school field trips and back row make-out sessions to the forefront of my mind. Ironically, the one I'd been making out with during most of those field trips also worked somewhere in this building. Back then, Merlin Heights only had a few places to escape to when that rare freedom was granted. There was the movie theater and the bowling alley, where most high schoolers frequented, but even as a teen, I was a *small-business snob*. The Willow Center quickly became my teenage go-to when Three-Ring was too busy or when traveling to Greyport's ice skating rink was too far of a drive.

Though the room and stage were identical to their original construction, the seats had changed drastically. Gone were the squeaky, plastic chairs that pinched the skin of your thighs and left embarrassing sweat marks behind. Circular tables scattered the room instead with evenly numbered chairs to meet the millennial brunch crew's needs.

"I've never seen *Brigadoon*," my mother said quietly, lifting the menu. "Have you seen *Brigadoon*?"

"I haven't seen *Brigadoon*. Have you, Marian?" My father turned to face my sister as she flattened a napkin over her skirt that practically overflowed onto my own lap.

"I haven't seen *Brigadoon*. Nope."

"*Brigadoon*." The three of them peered at me as I twisted my mauve lips into a grin. "I just wanted to say it one more time."

The lights began to blink when a waitress walked over to our table, and I thankfully ordered a mimosa, Marian mimicking the order, and my parents ordered water with lemon. During the minutes it took for her to mix our drinks and pour some water, my parents asked Marian about where Thea and the Thunderclouds were going next on their fall tour. I listened. I smiled. I quickly reached for my mimosa before the waitress set down any other drinks.

"We're almost done with all our shows in the Finger Lakes region. We're hoping to get booked near or in New York City next. Thea's assistant is sending media packages out this week." Marian pulled her mimosa toward her and spun the straw around the outside of the glass before lightly clinking it against mine, our eyes meeting. "Fingers crossed."

"I know it'll all work out. You deserve it," I stated.

I wasn't lying. I wanted the best for my sister and the band she worked so damn hard to make a success. She had always been musically gifted—along with always acing her statewide tests and getting on the Dean's list in college every single semester. Though my envy neared jealousy, I couldn't be mad at her. Anger wasn't really something I had inside of me after being conditioned by my father to always give people the benefit of the doubt. If anything, I was angrier with my parents for priding her triumphs over mine when mine were equally as impressive.

Mine just didn't line up with *His* standards.

The lights dimmed, and the curtain rose, my mother scooting closer to my father and slipping her hand into his. I wanted to focus but couldn't help thinking about the real reason I was at The Willow Center.

Had Davis been the one to dim the lights before the curtain rose? Was he backstage wearing all-black attire like he had during his drama show days in high school? Was he sitting home, relaxing on his day off?

"Bathroom break," I whispered, my voice carrying more than I'd meant it to.

"Ten minutes in? Frannie." My mother shook her head, turning to face the stage while setting her cheek on my father's slouching shoulder. Trying not to add the percussion of heels to the musical number on stage, I slipped out the double doors and into the hallway.

Mid-morning sun was my favorite, just not when it dove directly into my eyes after being in a dark room. My eyes strained as I skittered down the hallway, not entirely sure where my body was leading me.

And then my heels were in the air.

My ass slammed onto the hard tiles below—tiles that were covered in water.

"Dammit!" I would have done anything to have the ass Emmie had—the one she always rolled her eyes about but knew would make a much cozier cushion if she were in my shoes.

She never wore these kinds of shoes, though.

Nor did she ever fall to the ground like a drunken fawn on ice.

"Fern?"

The second I heard his voice, I knew it was him. The singsong voice that had entranced me nearly a decade ago still put me into an otherworldly stupor. My head was spinning, my jeans were soaked, and my ass was a bruised, deflated balloon.

"Hello. Hi." I slowly lifted my head to look him in the eyes—something I wanted to both avoid and do desperately. "Davis?"

"Fern fucking Powers. Let me help you. Here." He reached down, and I placed my hand into his as he heaved me up to my feet before I realized there was a mop in his opposite hand. "I'm guessing the sun got in your eyes."

"Yes. Yup. It sure did," I said with an excessive nod.

"Brunchers fall on a weekly basis. If people would read the fine print when they buy tickets, they'd see it's mentioned...but no one ever reads that stuff. This auditorium wasn't made for mornings." Davis stepped back, placing the mop against the wall. "I also wasn't made for cleaning up spilled mimosas, but here I am."

"So, here you are." I smiled up at him, hoping my lipstick hadn't smudged during the fall or from when I'd chugged my mimosa. He looked different, but I couldn't exactly pinpoint how. Maybe it was because he wasn't wearing glasses, his hazel eyes shining a little brighter with sunlight falling into them. Maybe it was how his uniform fit him ridiculously well in all the right places, pushing the years of scrawny legs and arms far into past memory.

Or maybe it was his fucking voice—a voice that should be on stage, not behind it.

"How've you been? I'm surprised this is the first time I've run into you since graduation." He softly pressed his hand to my shoulder, pushing me out of the line of bright sunlight still blinding us both.

"I'm just as surprised. Yeah, I've been pretty good. Things have been good," I said. In the hall's shadow, I could see the outline of formed biceps beneath his black T-shirt. When the hell did he start caring about working out? He'd never wanted to hike the trails along Claus Lake or bike ride to Rockberry Park with me in high school.

"That's great. You look the same," he said with that stupidly perfect mouth of his.

"How's Beth?" The question came out suddenly but not unex-pectedly. I expected Beth to come into the conversation, just not this early.

"Beth O'Malley." His voice lowered, laughing to himself as he scuffed his shoes on the damp floor and reached for the mop. "We ended things several years ago. Have you heard of Bette Ohm?"

My eyes widened. "The YourEyesOnly star who sings opera while doing dumb yoga poses in lingerie?"

And now he knew I watched softcore porn.

What a great start this was turning out to be.

He laughed, the sweetest flush brightening his cheeks. "Yeah. That's her."

"That's *Beth?* You're kidding me." My jaw practically hit the ass imprint I'd left on the damp floor.

"I'm not," Davis said, doing a final few sweeps with the mop. "She wanted to pursue her singing career on a more public level and move out to Los Angeles. I guess, in a way, she did all that...and more. If she'd asked me to go with her, I might have gone, but I found a good job and house here."

His voice was sullen, and his eyes were thin, but his posture still held the confidence I'd fallen in love with at fourteen. Emmie didn't believe me when I told her love could happen at such a young age. Love was unmistakable when you knew. For me, the cliché held true. The butterflies. The excitement. The attraction. The spark you felt when his hand accidentally brushed yours.

That spark returned when he'd shifted me into the shadows moments ago.

I hadn't felt a spark like that in years.

"I'm glad you're happy. I mean, you *are* happy, right?" I asked, cocking my head to the side and slowly running my hands over my sore ass. He looked up, and his eyes settled onto mine, soft dimples warming his cheeks.

"I am. I mean, how often do I see an ex-girlfriend fall on her ass and she sticks around to talk after?"

"I'm *that* person." With my hand raised into the air, I almost knocked the mop over, which made him clutch it even tighter. "Yup. I'm *that* ex."

"You are. That spunk still looks good on you, Fern." He stepped away but hesitantly rocked side to side before walking any farther. "I'm so glad I ran into you."

"Or slipped into me." I immediately regretted the word-vomit and pressed my lips together, taking a few careful steps back toward the door. "I should probably get back to that mimosa...and the show too."

"You know where you can find even better mimosas?" Davis asked before I booked it back into the theater. The mimosa I'd had inside these doors hadn't been all that impressive, but a few extra seconds listening to his voice was worth missing another scene for.

"Thirsty Theodore's?" I whispered, my hands clutching the large auditorium door handles.

Did Thirsty Theodore's even have mimosas on their menu?

"Wine Thyme. They opened a few months ago down off Main Street." Davis leaned the mop against the water fountain and took a step in my direction, scratching the back of his neck before meeting my gaze. "Why don't we go try them out sometime? Maybe Wednesday? It doesn't necessarily have to be for mimosas.

"Absolutely," I responded, my voice echoing. Before another fall occurred, I pulled open the double doors.

"We're friends on social," he said softly. "I'll message you tonight."

"I look forward to it." With a smile, I snuck back to my seat, relieved he'd been the one to ask me out.

Bruised ass and all.

Chapter 12

Emmie

The second Fern texted me saying her parents had officially left the parking lot, I grabbed a six-pack from the fridge, and my feet fell back into my slippers. Saturdays were often days I didn't change out of my pajamas. Oversized sweatshirts and slippers were my go-to attire, unless there was a party or we were meeting friends at Thirsty Theodore's. Since there was a visitor in the building, I decided to change things up and put on pajamas I hadn't yet slept in.

I mean, I had *some* class.

Most of the day was spent stalking social media and staring at the Merlin Community College's activity calendar until my eyes started crossing. I'd been trying to nail down the message behind my messing with Manny Longo's head for the next *Cheater Chase* blog. Al had texted me twice since Jake's blog went live to rave about the engagement statistics behind the post, stating how eager he and corporate were for the next one. Though pleased my writing was still hitting a high note with supervisors, I wondered how the previous weekend had affected The Real Estate Ringleader's popularity.

The fact that I genuinely cared so much made me reach into the six-pack I was carrying down the stairs and open one beer before even knocking on Fern's door.

"It's open!" she shouted as I stepped inside. The smell of General Tso's chicken smacked me in the face.

It also was a kind reminder to call my mother before Monday came around.

"You didn't waste any time, did you?" Marian said, snickering from the couch where both Porridge and Loaf lay curled against her.

I wish I could be those cats right now.

"I never waste time." The ale tasted of fall—spice and cinnamon dancing on my tongue. "Plus, my day was boring as hell."

"Did you get any research done?" Fern asked from the kitchen, opening the tops of all the containers. Steam curled from the boxes that sat atop the kitchen island, silently beckoning us over. "Come get the goods."

"Never say *that* on a first date," I muttered as I shuffled over and set the now five-pack on the counter. "And research is slow-moving. I'm not sure how to approach Manny. I never wanted to see his scummy face again...but here we are."

"What research are you doing, Em?" Marian appeared at my side, reaching over for a plate before piling white rice and Kung Pao chicken onto her plate. She turned to face me as she stepped aside, her short, dark hair falling over her face.

I took a long swig of beer as butterflies head-banged against my stomach.

"I'm just screwing over my exes and trying to make it mean some-thing." The words felt both sour and satisfying to say aloud. "So far, so good."

"Wow," Marian said, rice sticking to her upper lip. I had to force myself not to lick it off. "If Dad were here, he'd have a biblical verse to throw your way for *that*. I'm sure I could throw one your way too if you really need that extra push of guilt."

"Oh, please do. I need all the Jesus I can get." I carried my bowl of General Tso's over to the coffee table, hovering above it and wafting the scent toward me before stuffing a forkful into my mouth. "You fill your life with Sunday school and Thea's band these days. I'm sure you have a few quotes up your sleeve, merging God with rock and roll."

"He is all I want without the drama; He is all I'll ever need for love," Marian quietly sang, her voice wrapped in satirical lightness. Rolling her eyes, she took a bite from her plate. "The lyrics don't really have anything to do with your research, though. It was the first quote that came to mind since we've been playing that song all month."

"Want one?" I nodded toward the beer on the counter, and Marian dramatically nodded in return, widening her light eyes and slouching down onto the couch beside me. Fern, while also trying to carry her plate and a bottle of wine safely beneath her arm, brought the beer to the coffee table.

In typical Fern fashion, the balancing act was a messy success.

"Are you actually enjoying the band, though?" Fern popped off the wine cork and scurried back into the kitchen, grabbing three glasses from the cupboard.

"Yeah, Thea is great." Marian opened the beer and smiled against the can, the satisfying sip loosening her up a bit. "I love traveling and playing guitar—that's a no-brainer. The marketing work I do for Two Mighty Pillars is also great…even if it's from whatever hotel couch I'm on that night. Even though everything is good, I miss having a home base."

"Don't you still do the Sunday school stuff too? You do all that *and* make it back every Sunday?" Fern crossed her legs beneath her on the ground while pouring wine into a glass, her eyes never leaving her sister.

"If I stopped teaching Sunday school, Dad would murder me." Marian swiftly finished her beer, and I watched in awe as she set the empty can on the table.

Either she was stressed, or she could do amazing things with that mouth of hers.

Or both.

"But this is *your* life. Not theirs. You know this," Fern said softly, her brows lifted.

We'd had this conversation before. Actually, we'd had it the last three times Marian had come for a weekend visit. Marian would smile while complaining, occasionally roll her eyes, and go back to living the life she knew her parents were proud of. Fern paved her own path without worrying if it matched the path built by her parents.

But Marian was too much of a people pleaser to pave her own way without getting distracted by the one already constructed for her.

"Maybe someday I'll quit Sunday school and just do the band and marketing. Maybe that's a goal I can accomplish in the next year." Marian sighed, picking at a few pieces of rice on the edge of her plate with her fingers. "I love my students, but I hate rushing back every weekend when we're hours away."

"Your parents won't disown you if you do your own thing, you know." I turned toward Fern who sat cross-legged on the rug, a bottle of wine in her lap and a full fork in her hands. "I mean, they haven't completely disowned this one yet, and look at her. She's living the dream. Dating her exes and all."

"You never *did* answer how that date went with John." Marian's eyes grew wide as she continued to pick at the rice on her plate. "So, how'd it go?"

"He's still obsessed with me. But not in the *hot* way movies make it out to be," she said. "So, I'm onto Davis."

"Davis the drama nerd? Talk about *obsessed*. You were obsessed with him, Fern." Marian leaned toward the coffee table, her hands flat on either side of her plate. "For reasons I'll never understand but obsessed nonetheless. "

"It was love, not obsession," Fern corrected, lifting the bottle of wine into the air. "Do you guys want wine too?"

"I probably shouldn't mix. You don't want hungover Emmie strolling into your apartment tomorrow morning."

"I'll mix. Pour me a strong one." Marian crossed her arms and leaned back against the couch, Porridge jumping onto her lap. Immediately, a grin crossed her pale face. "*Give strong drink to the one who is perishing and wine to those in bitter distress.*"

"And there it is." I leaned in closer to Marian, clinking my beer against hers as Fern slid the wine bottle in her sister's direction.

Fern went to sleep after drinking half the wine straight from the bottle. I wasn't sure if it was because we kept bringing up her past relationship with Davis or if she was too lazy to pour herself more glasses. Either way, watching her devour two more plates of Mao tofu before hobbling off to bed was something I hadn't seen in months.

"She screams into the microphone. Raspy and loud. It's like metal meets Jesus with a hint of folk," Marian said, opening her fourth beer of the night after finishing another glass of wine. For a little thing, she sure drank a lot while still standing her ground. I hated how much her confident control turned me on. "It's what the people want, and Thea gives people what they want. We all do."

"I dig it. Metal. Folk. Punk. R&B. I'll try it all." I realized I'd have to get up to get another beer, and my lazy ass wasn't having it. Instead, I caved and finished Fern's bottle of wine, hoping she wouldn't wake up furious to find it gone. "Metal mixed with Christian rock means you're screaming to the heavens and, in return, screaming into the hearts of your fans. Am I right?"

Marian began a slow, dramatic clap from her cozy corner of the couch. "That was deep. You're *obviously* a writer."

"*Blogger*. There's definitely a difference," I said, shaking my head as lukewarm wine slid down my throat. "I'd cry if I tried writing a novel."

"You? Cry?" Marian laughed, sitting up and crossing her legs beneath her. "Impossible."

"Fuck you. I have feelings," I laughed, reaching for a crusty piece of rice and forcing it in my mouth simply because it was in front of me. "You should express yours to your parents more often."

"I know, I know." Marian sunk back into the oversized pillow wedged against the arm of the couch. "I will in time. Once I save enough to buy a house, I'll spill some secrets they won't enjoy hearing. They deserve honest children over perfect ones."

"Secrets? Do you need practice spilling some of those now? I can absolutely help." I shifted closer to Marian, setting my chin on the top of my hand as my head tilted to the side. She looked down at the beer between her palms and giggled, the corners of her eyes creating the sweetest laugh lines.

"Well, legal or not, my parents would kill me if they found out I smoke a little weed from time to time. I'm actually more of an edible fan. They nearly disowned Fern when they discovered her high school stash—which is another reason I keep my mouth shut." Marian snickered, biting her lip slightly before meeting my gaze. "Oh, and I've made out with Thea a few times."

My jaw dropped.

Damn you, Thea.

"Girl, you do you. Once your parents open their eyes more to the world outside of Two Mighty Pillars, they'll see all they're missing." I was trying my best to stay calm after hearing her last statement—a statement I wasn't even sure Fern knew anything about. "Then they'll feel guilty for all the life you guys missed out on growing up—even though Fern is going back and reliving some of that life now."

"I honestly don't think they would forgive us as easily as we hope," Marian said, taking a quick sip before placing the beer on the coffee table. "We were taught to forgive, but they struggle to follow their own advice. On the topic of forgiveness, you'll forgive me for the last time I visited, right?"

I narrowed my gaze, crinkling my brow. "Forgive you for what?"

"For not doing this." Marian leaned forward, and her hand cupped the back of my neck, easing my body toward hers until her lips hit mine.

I expected her lips to be soft and her skin to feel flawless beneath my touch, but fuck, this was proof her dermatologist was Jesus himself. Confidence radiated from her pores, and her body fell over mine, my back sinking into the meticulously propped pillows Fern had arranged that morning. If Fern walked out of her room right now, I would immediately get blamed for this.

I'd take the blame any day.

I just didn't want this to stop.

"Practice, right?" Marian's voice came out hushed, her lips meeting the nape of my neck as straight, black-blue hair covered her face. "Just a little practice spilling some secrets. Is that okay?"

My focus was fading, but I would not let a chance like this fade too. I slid my hands down to her waist, sneaking my thumbs into the waistband of her sweatpants.

I leaned in closer, her breath hot on my skin. "Just call me coach."

MY CUP O' JOE
@davIS_geek
ESPRESSO NO
SIP & COME BACK
LET'S BREW IT
Davis, 28
Lead Production Manager
Sips with WOMEN
Looking for RELATIONSHIP, MARRIAGE
Hot or Cold
I drink iced coffee all year round. No hot coffee for me, thanks! Well...unless it's offered to me. Turning down caffeine is a crime.
Sweetness
I'll take a little cream and sugar. A little almond milk? Even better.
With A Side Of
I'm a sucker for good, live entertainment. Coffee and a show? What could be better?

Chapter 13

FERN

After Marian left suspiciously early Sunday morning, I spent the rest of the day at the lathe, sculpting some holiday gifts. Most family members expected a new mug or planter wrapped in gold ribbon come Christmas morning. Some friends hinted at needing a new home for their growing succulent stash or even matching platters for their growing family. I felt honored creating these items for those who genuinely appreciated them.

Unlike my father.

If he appreciated the handmade gifts I gave him almost every time he visited, he only showed it through biblical verses and passive-aggressive remarks.

Porridge lay on my right foot while Loaf lay in a patch of sunlight hitting the hardwood, both becoming startled whenever I started or stopped the wheel. Three mugs were formed by the time I finished my second cup of coffee, an hourly reminder to get up and stretch while walking back into the kitchen for a refill. My phone sat blinking on the counter, and once my hands were dry and fresh coffee was dripping into my mug, I saw two new messages in my inbox.

Davis.

I didn't expect him to forget to message. He'd always been true to his word with saint-like honesty that my parents adored. Unlike John, who often fibbed and adjusted his glasses before looking away, Davis was one to wear his words on his sleeve.

Though this was a trait I respected, it also was one that had bitten me in the ass when the break-up happened—when he told me he was in love with Beth.

Today, his message was quick, clear, and to the point—making me wonder if men thought about their words as much as women did when it came to texts and emails. Emmie often spoke strictly in emojis, and when I dug deeper into her text messages, she always told me I was being a cliché female.

My response to Davis was just as precise as his:

Wednesday is great! Wine Thyme at eight.

The unplanned rhyme made me wish I could delete and re-send—something I knew I could do but would regret even more than my surprise attempt at Shakespeare. Instead, I filled up my mug and sat behind the wheel, clay climbing beneath my nail beds until that fourth refill was needed.

And there would definitely be a fourth refill.

"I've never seen this many gardens before. Like, inside of a restaurant."

"And on every wall too," Davis said, reaching for the opposite chair and gesturing toward it. My shoulder brushed his chest on my way to the chair, and goosebumps slammed into the fabric of my blouse, my stomach lurching into my throat.

"I would love to know who built all these wall planters. I mean, look over there. Someone built those out of window frames." Trying to ignore how overstimulated I was—in all the best ways—I pointed to the wall behind the bar where there looked to be cherry tomatoes and basil curling out from planters set on repurposed farmhouse frames. "Oh, and above the doorway. Lavender. That's *real* lavender flourishing in those teeny, tiny panels."

"*Flourishing*, huh?" Davis's lips twisted into that familiar grin I hadn't seen since we were sixteen. "You haven't changed a bit, Fern."

"I would live in a greenhouse if someone let me. I practically already do." Shrugging, I slid the menu closer. I eyed the empty glass again, wishing water would just magically appear. If I were in the real *Fern-Gully*, it would be possible. "I'm also vegetarian now."

"That doesn't surprise me—both the greenhouse thing and being a vegetarian." Davis flipped the menu over. "The mojito has mint in it. Throw in some strawberries and you've got yourself a meal."

I laughed and lifted my eyebrows. "Not a bad idea since mojitos are a favorite of mine. This fishbowl thing could be an actual meal, though."

Obviously, I also had a thing for extra-large cocktail bowls.

"It doesn't have actual fish in it, Fernie." Davis peered above his menu, his lips curling into a dimpled cheek.

That dimple. That grin. Memories flooded my mind, and I tried focusing on the menu instead of the ping of pain resurfacing inside my scarred heart.

The server showed up right when I needed her to with a water pitcher in hand.

"Mini fishbowl with extra Swedish fish and extra pineapple rum, please." I pushed the menu aside and sat back, crossing my legs beneath the table and attempting to mimic Davis's eyebrow lift. I realized the attempt had failed when he shook his head and laughed.

"I'll try out the thyme bourbon cocktail," he said, lifting his chin in my direction before the server booked it to the bar. "Make sure this one over here gets those extra Swedish fish."

"*All* the fish, please." I reached for the lemon wedged on the rim of my water, squeezing it into the glass. As water hit my tongue, those hazel eyes of his powered right into my own.

Fuck. Those eyes still had such an addictive charm.

"So, you know what I do—well, when I'm not cleaning up spilled drinks. What do you do to make the big bucks these days?" Davis shifted closer to the table. "I'm guessing you're either an art teacher or a detective."

He wasn't far off.

"Nope and nope," I said, clearing my throat and mimicking his shift toward the table, my elbow nudging the lemon water. "I'm a graphic designer at My Cup."

"My Cup O' Joe? The dating app?" Davis asked. "That must be a fun gig. I'm not gonna lie; I have a profile on there."

davIS_geek. I'd scrolled through his profile pages more times than I wanted to admit.

"It's fun, yes. I just do a lot of behind-the-scenes stuff to make it pretty. I don't *really* do a ton with the dating part of it."

Besides having full access to everyone registered on the site.

"I'd use that to my advantage if I worked there," Davis said with a laugh as he leaned back, the drinks sliding onto our table. "I'm surprised you're still single, having access to all the singletons of the world and all."

"My profile isn't active on there right now, actually." The fishbowl in front of me was neon blue with approximately ten gummy fish hovering above triangular-shaped ice cubes. With a deep breath, I took a long sip. "Well, my profile *is* on the app. I just keep my inbox closed most of the time."

Davis's eyebrows pinched together as he leaned closer. "Really? Why?"

"Well, it's *recommended* that new hires make a profile if they're single, just to get an idea of how everything works…which, yes, is a little controversial. But mine has been on *Snoozed Sips Mode* since spring." My throat burned as I remembered my request for extra pineapple rum. "I guess it was too much trying to work for the app and constantly feeling obligated to respond to messages on there too. Many of us switch over to the *Snoozed Sips* mode after making our profiles. Shit, this is strong!"

"Can I?" Davis reached for the straw, his fingers brushing mine as I released my grip and watched the straw slide between his lips.

My gaze was locked on his mouth, and I didn't care if it was obvious.

And it definitely was.

"It's a little sweet and *way* stronger than expected…but save some for me!" I tugged the straw back, plucking it from his teeth.

"Just like you," Davis said softly, watching as I popped the straw back into the drink.

"I'm just a *little* sweet?" My head leaned to the side, auburn locks falling over my shoulder as I delicately slipped the straw between my dark lips.

Davis lifted his hand and, with squinted eyes, motioned his thumb and forefinger together, leaving a small space between. "Just a little."

Cliché and Corny would have been the names of my cats if Loaf and Porridge hadn't fit them so perfectly. I was a sucker for anything cheesy, and Davis was still all about the cheese.

He hadn't forgotten the key to my poor, nostalgic heart.

Davis finished two thyme bourbons and most of my yellow Swedish fish by the time I was halfway through the fishbowl. The oversized pretzels from the appetizer bar were quickly devoured but not without some hot German beer cheese dripping onto my chest right above my cleavage.

I did my best to ignore the pain as I wiped it away, biting my lip before placing my finger into my mouth to subtly suck the cheese off.

Our eye contact never broke.

It was hotter than the burn from the cheese.

Davis paid for our drinks and pretzels, allowing me to argue with him for only a few seconds before tossing me another compliment to shut me up. He helped me put on my jacket, even though it was just my raggedy denim one, and opened the door as we walked into the brisk, fall night.

"I'm definitely going back to try the ginger thyme mojito." I kicked at a few damp leaves with the tip of my boot before peering in his direction. Either he had gotten taller, or I had shrunk over the last decade. The latter seemed more realistic. "The fishbowl was great and all, but you probably felt like you were bringing some seven-year-old out to their birthday dinner."

"I asked you out. I expected nothing less than you fumbling over your words and picking at gummies all night," Davis said, turning to face me with a growing grin I couldn't look away from. A neatly trimmed, five o'clock shadow had appeared since the previous weekend, showcasing his growth from boy to man over the course of a decade.

That and those unexpected biceps straining through his button-up.

I had to touch them.

Touch him.

Before we turned the corner to where my apartment building was, my hand gripped his upper arm, yanking him closer until there wasn't a breath of air between us. In the blink of an eye, his soft lips fell over mine, and my back pressed against the brick wall behind us. Both of his hands cupped my face, forcing me up onto my toes as we both drank each other in, desperate to taste these new versions of each other. My fingernails clawed into his biceps, and though I wanted to feel what laid sculpted beneath, I knew a street corner wasn't the place for that.

My apartment building was only a block away, and though morals were weighing me down, I had to taste more of him.

I was starving.

MY CUP O' JOE
@man.oh.MANNY
MERLIN STUDENT LIFE CENTER
ESPRESSNO
STIR & COME BACK
LET'S BREW IT
Manny, 32
Student Life Manager
Sips with WOMEN
Looking for CASUAL
Hot or Cold
I don't have much of a preference! I like caffeine in any form.
Sweetness
A hidden sweet side never hurt anyone, right?
With A Side Of
Whatever makes you happy. My treat.

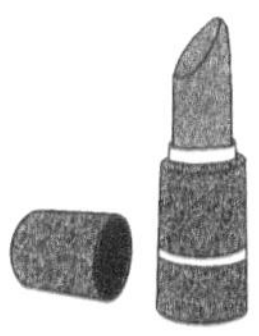

Chapter 14

Emmie

"**B**lack iced coffee. Large."

"*Iced*?" Oliver looked up from his phone and shot me a bewildered expression before setting it inside his apron. "Who the hell are you? Fern?"

"Did I ask for almond milk, pistachio syrup, and sugar cubes? *That's* Fern. Even though she does prefer that fake sugar crap." Though I was about his height already, I shifted onto my toes to scrutinize the glass as iced coffee slurred inside of it. "Hurry. I have shit to do."

"Doubtful, but okay," he said, filling the glass so the coffee sat even with the edge of the mason jar. My fist wanted to meet his smug fucking face. "Enjoy the walk to your table."

"You're a dick." I looked down at the glass and thought about leaving it there on the counter. However, I knew that would mean he won this little battle, which was something I could never let happen. Instead, I bent my knees, put my mouth on the lip of the glass, and practically swallowed down two full ice cubes so it was easier to carry.

I slid a five-dollar bill onto the counter before wrapping my hands around the jar and standing up straight.

We both knew the drink cost over five dollars.

He shrugged and ripped his phone from the pocket of his apron, delivering me the tiniest bit of triumph because he had officially finished bickering.

The second my glass safely sat on the table, Fern rushed through the door and placed her hand on the counter in front of Oliver, asking for her usual before dropping her bag on the chair in front of me, her breath heavy and her brow beaded with sweat. For one of the smallest humans I knew, Fern sure grew tired without doing too much.

"I'm sorry, I'm sorry," Fern said, her voice raspy. "I haven't been here on time in, like, over a month."

"I'm going to *obviously* tell HR about this."

Fern flicked my shoulder before stepping back to the counter to retrieve her drink from Oliver without facing his foolish pouring skills. "I'm sure Najma would love getting a complaint from HR on a Friday morning."

"Better your supervisor than mine," I said, slowly lifting the iced coffee to my lips. I wasn't sure why I'd chosen iced coffee today. It was a rare choice for me, and it tasted glorious. I just could never tell Oliver that. "Al would verbally kick my ass if he got a complaint. At least Naj would smile the whole time she tells you off."

"Thankfully, neither of us has dealt with this." Fern crossed her fingers and shut her eyes tight before opening them wide while reaching for her mug. "Oh, and I slept with Davis."

"Holy shit, Fern!" My glass hit the table, throwing dark, icy drops onto my keyboard. Swiping them away, I stared at her with unblinking eyes. "You hooked up after your first date? Who are you? Me?" I dabbed the ENTER key with my thumb before licking off the coffee from it.

"Well, it *really* wasn't our first date. It was just our first date in nearly a decade."

"Were you drunk?"

"Do I have to be drunk to have a one-night stand?" Fern asked, lifting her eyebrows and desperately trying to make her serious façade fit better than it did.

"Usually *you* do, yes," I said, finally opening the tab I needed to focus on for tomorrow's assignment. Centered on the banner of Merlin Community College's student life page was Manny. His stupid tan skin. His stupid teeth. His stupid, unruly locks.

I wanted to knock those perfectly bleached fangs from his face.

"That's fair," Fern said with a shrug, dragging her finger across her tablet and leaning back in the chair with a proud smile. "We may or may not see each other again Saturday night."

"Did you guys even have a chance to talk?" I asked.

Fern's head snapped up from her tablet. "Of course. I'm not *that* naïve."

"Well, if he's visiting your place tomorrow night, just be ready for a knock on your door. Kyle and Rae are gone for the weekend, so I can't turn my emotions into orgasms after I fuck over Manny." I flicked my gaze back to Manny's dark, shaggy eyebrows and his toothy, forced laugh that was vandalizing my laptop screen. "I'm going to walk into a gym of horny, drunk college students on Saturday and hope Manny looks at me instead of all of them."

"Well, damn," Fern said, twisting her fingers together atop her tablet. "That's your plan? Just walk in and hope for the best?"

"Well, he cheated on me with two sorority girls during my freshman year, and I heard, through the grapevine, it was because *I just wasn't hot enough.*" Heat bubbled in my blood when I spoke the truth out loud. "I'm hoping to grab his attention somehow and maybe flirt with him a little before confessing who I am. The details are still fuzzy."

"Well, he deserves whatever you hand him, and I know you'll hand him a shitshow," Fern said confidently, sitting up straighter with a slight shimmy to her shoulders. At least she believed I could get away with this. "I hope you fuck him up."

I laughed into my coffee, sitting back against the booth. "Just like Davis did to you the other night?"

"That was good," Fern said, rolling her eyes.

She'd grown too accustomed to my crude retorts over the years.

But I wasn't going to stop anytime soon. "That's what you thought the other night too."

"You're a piece of work, you know that?" Fern shook her head, looking down at her fingers before angling her gaze back up to meet mine, the edge of her lips twisting upward. "But that's definitely what I thought."

Bodycon dresses were not made for women who had junk-in-the-trunk and power-thighs. I wasn't sure if millennials still used the phrase "junk-in-the-trunk," but that was the only explanation for what was happening back there. I couldn't make it over thirty seconds without yanking the edge of the red elastic down to mid-thigh before it inched back above my comfort level. They also should have had a disclaimer on the tag saying something along the lines of *Only for College-Aged Students Hoping to Get Laid.*

Or those trying to seduce their asshole exes.

Blending in came easier than expected. I thought I'd stick out like a sore thumb in the college gymnasium, as if a strobe light was following me to ensure students I wasn't their eighteen- or nineteen-year-old hook-up for the night. Instead, I was pretty sure I had the same dress on as several other girls who tripped by me, Bacardi on their breath and some drunken stranger on their arm. Even my seven-year-old, go-to leather jacket looked like some I saw in the crowd.

The door between the hallway and gymnasium that I casually leaned against had the perfect view of the space's layout. The three stages were getting their finishing touches tweaked when I arrived at my station in the doorframe, applause igniting every time metal clinked together. I didn't want to stay long enough to have my own Battle of the Bands memories smack me in the face—memories including too much boxed wine poured into a plastic bottle hidden in my coat. My goal was to watch the venue fill up with barely dressed college that students I knew Manny would have his filthy little eyes on.

If only I could scoop those eyes out with a spoon and get away with it.

That wasn't the plan, and really, I wasn't sure what my plan was. All I knew was I wanted to get his attention in a way I never could during our little college romp. Walking into these scenarios felt like a murder-mystery party—you never truly knew how the event was going to play out until the ball started rolling.

Then I spotted that rolling ball.

Manny walked into the gymnasium through the central doors with his hands on his hips, laughing alongside some middle-aged blonde. There was a slight jiggle to his belly when he laughed, something I never expected to see on someone who once cared way too much about appearance—both his own and the looks of his hook-ups. He still had that flawless, tan skin and dark hair that mimicked Mario Lopez during his prime *Saved by the Bell* years—a show most of these students had never heard of. I had quietly hoped they'd photoshopped some extra hair to his hairline in the staff headshots I'd seen, but he remained genetically blessed.

I rubbed my matte-red lips together and slipped my glasses into the pocket of my leather jacket before rustling up my hair a bit. I wanted him to see me as a colleague or a student, not the ex-girlfriend he'd recognize the instant he saw my signature glasses and awkward posture.

Except, my posture had transformed from awkward to confident since our last interaction.

Maybe he wouldn't instantly recognize me, but I wasn't taking any chances.

He nonchalantly patted the blonde's shoulder, and she returned the goodbye with a nod before walking toward the front stage. Manny stood there, grinning at the familiar students who stumbled by. For several minutes, he remained in the same general area. He would point to this and that when someone asked him a question, check a few things off occasional clipboards when someone put one in his face, and hug slurring students as they fell into his embrace.

Seconds before the lights faded, he returned to that central doorway, and our eyes met.

His double-take made my stomach drop through the gymnasium floor. I wanted to run out of the building, tripping over my heeled boots as I crossed the parking lot. However, when he leaned against the doorframe and coolly scanned the bleachers, I realized that look my way was what I was there for.

The double-take wasn't because he recognized me. It was because I looked fine as hell.

Small groups of students took each of the three stages, setting up their equipment as a woman in a glittery green pantsuit welcomed the crowd and explained the rules. Two redheads careened through the hallway doors Manny stood by, one throwing her arms in the air before wrapping them around his shoulders with a squeal. When she released her grip, he pointed to some empty space on the bleachers, and they made their way in that direction, bumping into other students who still scattered the floor.

Right as the gymnasium burst into applause and hysteric shouts, Manny looked my way again.

It was showtime.

My crimson lips turned up, and I wiggled my fingers from their spot near my thigh. I hoped my subtle hello gave him another chance to check out this new, healthier body he'd never had the chance to touch. He faintly lifted his chin into the air, his eyebrows raising, before turning back to stare at the stage. I hoped he would keep nodding to the music for a few minutes longer, allowing me to brainstorm a detailed plan, but as I yanked my phone from my jacket pocket, our eyes met again.

With my face angled down at the phone in my hands, I gestured toward the hallway as some curly bangs fell in front of my eyes. I was just as surprised by my own actions as Manny when he looked toward the double doors and then back at me in question. I nodded, puckering my plump lips together and sliding my phone back into my jacket. When he pushed through the doors near him, I did my best to cavalierly strut to the hallway doors closest to me.

Tense breaths clouded my throat when I saw him walking my way, and I twisted on my heel with a grin, turning us down a hallway and away from clashing guitar chords and drums. I wedged myself into the doorframe of a locked lecture hall, taking a deep breath and stretching the top of my dress down so the edge of my lace bra outlined my cleavage.

My cleavage was already covered in beads of sweat.

"Well, hello." His voice was raspy and confident, as if he'd done something like this before—and I'm sure he had. When he removed his hands from his pockets, I caught the dull sheen of a tungsten band on his left hand. Color drained from my cheeks, and I hoped my suggestive smile masked the guilt crawling up my throat.

Fuck. I hadn't even thought about the possibility of him being married.

"Well, hi," I whispered. His familiar cologne was already on my skin, his Oxfords barely three feet away from the heels hiding my trembling toes. "I'm guessing you work at the college, huh?"

"I do. Yes." Manny took a step forward, his breath emitting a mixture of peppermint and Hendricks. "Can I assist you with something?"

He took a step closer, his eyes shifting from my lips down to my thighs and back to my lips again.

"Oh, yes." My voice was wavering, and I leaned onto one hip, trying not to focus on the ringed hand reaching around my waist. I wasn't sure if I was sucking in my core to look thinner or because I just didn't want him touching me—or both. "Maybe you could update me on some college events coming up. I may apply for that open position in admissions."

"There's a position available in admissions, huh?" Both of his hands sat on my hip bones, tugging me toward something very solid between us. I tried to push away the vision of his ringed hand still interrupting my thoughts and swallowed down the vomit climbing up my throat. "Are there any other *positions* you're interested in? I may be able to help you out."

He was even closer now. His hot breath hovered below my ear, his lips brushing against my neck as he began his slow dive downward. I swallowed hard and said, "Just like how you helped those sorority sisters out with some positions?"

His mouth halted above my clavicle, his grip tightening the second the memory shot into his horny brain.

"What was that?" he mumbled, his lips turning my blood to ice once they touched my skin again. Him trying to ignore the reality behind my words was infuriating. I reached for his left hand and whipped it into the air, shoving him away as my blood completely turned to lava.

"First off, you *obviously* haven't changed." I released his left hand, throwing it against his chest as he stumbled back a couple of steps. Yanking out my glasses and setting them on my nose, I shuffled my fingers through my hair again. "And second, those stupid, skinny sorority sisters you cheated on me with? Word was going around that I wasn't *hot* enough for you. Do you recall any of that?"

"Em...Emmie?" Manny whispered, his pupils dilating. He even had the nerve to very obviously look me up and down again. "But you...you're just—"

I took three steps into the middle of the hallway until I was nose-to-nose with Manny Longo, an electric guitar and snare drum vibrating the walls surrounding us. I lifted his left hand into the air again, tilting my head to the side before looking directly at his wedding band.

"Hot?" The word slipped off my lips like caramel. "Am I *hot* enough for you now? Obviously, I'm worth ruining a marriage for. Maybe I'll reach out to that poor wife of yours and let her know what you've been up to."

He looked from my hand wrapped around his wrist to the ring on his finger before finally meeting my gaze. His lips opened just to close again, words not forming the way his mind hoped they would. He always had too much to say in college. Now, his mouth couldn't form a single damn word.

"That's what I thought," I said, looking him directly in the eyes. "Now I'm confident. I'm self-aware. I'm healthy. I'm fucking proud of the person I am. There was no reason *not* to be proud of who I was back then too, but I see my worth now. You fucked with my head a little bit back then. So, I thought I'd fuck with yours a little too."

The soft sound of heels on tile shot our eyes toward the hallway corner leading back to the gymnasium. One student bent over a water fountain while the other leaned against the wall with hands hastily rushing to their pockets, turning to watch their drunk friend's face get plastered with water.

I released my grip on Manny, keeping my hand in the air as I backed away from him. My heels clicked against the tile, and my hand stayed put in the air as I desperately tried to keep it from shaking. I wanted to run. I wanted to kick my heels off and watch a shoe nail Manny directly in the balls.

I didn't have that kind of coordination, though. Instead, I lifted my middle finger into the air as I backed into the door leading me away from Manny, his ringed hand, and wilting boner. Once the door closed and I stood trembling in the bitter night air with my finger still raised, I turned on my heel toward the car and into a world I was both running away from and running back to.

Chapter 15

FERN

"And then you told your parents we were going to a church retreat. Remember?" Davis's hand squeezed my thigh as the other reached for the neck of the beer on the side table.

"It was the only way they'd get off my ass." I playfully pushed his shoulder away just as he attempted to slug some of the beer. My uncanny way of doing things at the worst possible time pulled through as droplets fell down his lips onto the neck of his T-shirt. Shaking his head, he attempted the drink again.

It was a success.

"Wasn't that the first time you ever *really* lied?" Davis asked.

"I mean, sort of." We were digging deep into the vault with this one, and after two glasses of pinot, my thin frame and thinning memory were not prepared. "I think we watched a couple of prerecorded sermons on my laptop. That only counts as a teeny, tiny white lie. Right?"

"I clearly remember us watching a viral video of a drunk pastor falling offstage during some huge conference out west."

"Holy shit, yes!" I sat up straight, wine flying from the top of my glass onto the chest of his shirt, leaving a few damp splotches beneath the ones on his neckline.

He looked down, shaking his head with upturned lips. "You're still as smooth as you were in high school, huh?"

"Unfortunately, yeah," I said with a shrug, reaching for the napkin on the coffee table and leaning onto his thigh. Gently, I dabbed the blotches on his shirt, one knee sliding to the other side of his thigh so I coolly straddled his leg. "My parents would say it's God's way of showing me I need to trust in Him more. I say it's genetics and karma."

"I'd say it's probably a good mix of all the above," Davis said, watching my fingers press harder against the damp cotton tee, my thighs tightening around his. His hands cupped my nonexistent ass, the tips of his fingers pressing through the thin fabric of my leggings and pulling me in closer. My body naturally sunk into him—onto him—as I set the napkin aside, my weight pressing down and my hips circling subtly as I reached for my wine. I brought my other hand around the back of his neck, his chin almost sandwiched between my cleavage.

I brought the wine to my lips, watching him from the corner of my eye as he nuzzled closer to my chest. "That's a very Christian answer. My parents would approve."

"They always liked me," he said with a snicker. "They appreciated my ability to toss a Corinthians verse out there once in a while."

My head shot back with a laugh. "That was all such an act!"

"The act was worth it."

Goosebumps grew the second his lips brushed my chest. He released one of the hands gripping my ass to gently lower the hem of my shirt, his tongue circling and his teeth nipping until his mouth tickled the edge of my bra. Heat spiraled between my legs, and my head fell back, the wine glass miraculously staying put in my grasp.

I took a quick and cautious sip before setting the glass back onto the side table, arching my back into the whitened knuckles of his fingers digging into my meager backside. At this moment, I didn't care how insecure I was about my ass—and I was pretty damn insecure about it. His touch, his taste, his body growing hard below mine was all it took for my insecurities to dissolve.

He tenderly pulled down the fabric of my bra, his lips melting over my peaked nipples, his tongue rolling against me in swift motions that sent a jolt of heat directly to my clit. I rotated my hips over the hard ridge growing inside his jeans, my movements becoming hungrier with every flick of his tongue.

We hadn't taken a single piece of clothing off yet, and I already felt myself trembling against him, desperate for release.

A gasp exited my lungs just as the apartment door flung open, slamming into the wall behind it.

"I'm sure you guys are doing the dirty, but you *were* warned." Emmie's heels clicked over the hardwood, one boot flying toward the coffee table as the other slid off by the refrigerator door that quickly opened. She stood in front of the fridge, the light silhouetting her figure as she propped her hands on her hips. "Damn, did you guys drink my IPAs?"

"I mean, a warning closer to your grand arrival would have been nice," I said, quickly shoving my nipple back into my shirt. "This is Emmie. We work together, and she lives upstairs."

"What's up, Davey?" She snapped the beer against the countertop, foam dripping over the rim and onto her fingers. "I've heard a lot about you."

"Oh, really?" Davis adjusted himself quickly and snagged a pillow to cover his very obvious bulge.

"Well, I mentioned to her we'd be hanging out tonight," I said, setting my hand on his thigh, opening my eyes wider and gently squeezing his jeans.

"I also mentioned I was coming over." Emmie strode into the living room, pulling at her dress that was definitely two sizes too small. "Holy shit, how do people wear these without seven pairs of Spanx and spandex shorts under them? Fern, were you a Bodycon girl in college?"

"Is that an actual *thing?*" I asked, twisting toward Emmie as she collapsed onto the sofa across from us. Loaf climbed up from the depths of the couch to curl into her lap as I jealously watched. I'd sit on that couch for hours waiting for Loaf to climb out from wherever he was hiding, just for him to stare at me and dart away most of the time. It was like Emmie had this uncanny, magnetic energy Loaf couldn't ignore.

I couldn't envy a cat right now, knowing how aroused Davis had been moments before.

My mind was still humming from being so close to orgasm during the shortest dry-hump session in history.

Clothes on. Nipples out. Boners hidden. Edging until interrupted.

Adulthood intimacy at its finest.

"Answer the girl's question, Fernie," Davis said, nudging his elbow into my waist, finally removing the pillow from his lap apprehensively.

I looked down to see well-fit jeans hugging his body, free of tension just below the belt.

It was still a beautiful sight.

"I think most girls went through a *Bodycon* stage—or some kind of self-discovery phase—in college. Skin-tight dresses at nineteen years old are just part of self-discovery, I guess." I twisted my legs beneath me, leaning into Davis. "I mean, I tried out acrylic nails, blonde high-lights, cigarettes, and tanning beds. That, right there, is proof we all go through some inner-exploration phase."

Emmie clenched the pillow next to her and leaned over her knees. "You were tan once?"

Davis leaned forward as well, his brows hitting the ceiling. "Ciga-rettes, Fern? Really?"

"I mean, they were hand-rolled... and the tobacco was from the reservation." Davis's eyes held the sadness of the world's loneliest bas-sett hound. I'd never felt such guilt. "It was almost healthier, in a sense. Right?"

"Nope. Not really." Emmie took a swig of beer, petting Loaf and pinning her dark eyes against mine. I could tell she both had a *lot* she needed to say and a *lot* she wanted to hear from me.

"The phase only lasted, like, a month...and it was only during my freshman year at Merlin." My fingers walked up Davis's arm, and I felt his muscles tense beneath the plaid button-up hiding his stained T-shirt. "I stick to wine and mixed drinks these days. Maybe the occa-sional beer when I'm feeling a little saucy."

Emmie sunk further into the sofa with a grin, obviously giving up on yanking the edge of her dress lower the more it snuck up her thighs. "And the occasional joint when you want to feel even saucier."

I would not deny the fact, but I *was* going to deflect it.

"Hey, Emmie, how was *your* night?" I dramatically grabbed my wine, cocking my head to the side and giving Emmie all my attention. For someone who wanted me to get laid just as much as she did, she sure showed it in odd ways.

For example, not texting me before barging into the apartment.

"I almost hooked up with a married guy tonight." She promptly finished her beer, shaking it in the air before returning to her feet. "Well, I guess since he had his hands all over me and mentioned nothing about being non-monogamous, I'd say he cheated tonight. I wish I'd flung my heels directly into his nuts."

"I'll take one of whatever you're having!" Davis shouted over his shoulder, Emmie peeking above the open refrigerator door with a satisfied smile.

"Because you're terrified of me or because you're impressed?" Emmie asked, shutting the fridge and shaking her hips as she carried a beer in each hand.

"A little bit of both," he admitted, flicking the bottle top with his thumb and swiftly catching it. I thought that little move was only possible in movies. How was the tip of his thumb not bleeding all over the place? He glanced at me from the corner of his eye, subtly smiling and bringing the beer up to his lips. Fuck. I wanted to be on those lips. "If anything, this is entertainment I've never had before. Bring it on."

"You just asked for a death wish, sir." I snuggled in closer to his side, hugging his arm closest to me. His hand climbed onto my leg, and heat bled through my leggings when his fingers pressed down.

"Can't be too bad," he whispered. "I'll die a beautiful death sitting next to you."

My heart dropped, and his lips found my forehead. Emmie shook her head in front of us, stroking Loaf, who'd returned to her lap. She lifted her beer into the air with raised eyebrows, her mouth silently mouthing *I like him* before taking a drink.

His likability was only one of the traits that had driven my heart smack into the wall I'd built up since high school. Over the last week or so, I'd led my heart straight into the crimson blaze that engulfed it for years before any trace of it came crawling to the surface. I wondered if my heart could handle falling in love with the same person twice.

Which led me to wonder what the heck happened between him and Beth.

Excuse me. *Bette Ohm.*

"You can start the logo drafts early if you want," Najma said. Her body gracefully floated in my direction while she dipped a tea bag in and out of one of her many precious China cups. The scent of her office and the sound of her voice always sent me into a state of serenity.

This week, Najma was using her great-grandmother's second favorite tea set with lavender florals etched into the enamel. The week before, it had been her great-uncle's beloved perse clay set. The week before that, she'd sipped cautiously from her mother's fine silver.

Najma had originally pitched the idea of adding more beverages to My Cup. At first, corporate did not take the idea well, wanting My Cup to strictly stay in the coffee and espresso niche. The moment her presentation brought up sTEAl My Heart's newfound success in the dating realm only months after My Cup went live, the supervisory committee agreed to add tea, kombucha, and hand-squeezed juice to the app.

Hand-squeezed juice was quickly dismissed from the line-up.

I mean, come on. The name itself was begging for inappropriate profiles to be made.

"I've actually already started working on a few sketches." I positioned the tablet on her desk, sliding it toward her. She lowered herself into the chair and reached forward, blowing steam from her drink away from the screen. "I also jumped the gun a little bit on the new profile picture placements. I know you wanted to think about that this month, but I just got too excited."

"I did, I did." Najma looked up and her tiny, pink lips curled upward. "You're always ahead of the game. Well done."

My fingers tapped the edge of the desk before I set them on my knees, sitting back in the chair. I swear I was smiling like a satisfied puppy, even though I was doing all I could to force away the giddiness I felt. Her compliments—her aura—was the purest of medicine. I knew I was lucky to have Najma as my role model, my supervisor. Not everyone reported to someone who magically distinguished the imposter syndrome dancing around in your skull just by being in your presence. I knew I was lucky.

I mean...Emmie had Al.

Enough said.

Whenever I met with Najma, which was typically once every few weeks, I found myself walking into My Cup's very own Zen garden. Najma never turned on the overhead fluorescent lights. She always clicked on her spirit tree lamp—a thin, silver fixture shaped like a willow tree with tiny, circular bulbs clinging to the branches. The top of her desk was naked except for the Himalayan salt lamp sitting in the left-hand corner, the computer monitor placed slightly to the left, and the desktop serenity fountain on the right-hand side. A taupe, shag rug sat centrally beneath her desk, and the one other chair she allowed in her office was her great-grandmother's velvet wingback.

She believed less clutter in your world allowed for more creativity in your mind.

I thought she was brilliant as hell—and probably a cyborg.

"I like the second option," she said, finally taking a sip of her tea as she slid the tablet back in my direction. "Perhaps, a little more detail on the outside of the mug and some shading may make the font pop a little more. The colors are on-brand, which corporate is finicky about. Everything else is exquisite. You're on the right track. You're *beyond* the track, really."

"Thank you, Naj. Number two is my personal favorite." I set the tablet back on my lap and took a deep breath. I closed my eyes for what felt like more than two seconds and comfortably released the air from my lungs. The second my eyes opened and my fingers spread across the screen of the tablet, Najma's dark eyes hit mine like a cautious dagger.

She was the only person who could make you feel both at ease and on edge with a single stare.

"You've been working hard," Najma said, scooting forward after setting her teacup onto the ceramic platter. "But I sense some anxiety."

Damn her and her therapeutic sixth sense.

"I've been working hard, yes." In more ways than one. "But...well...my parents did recently visit. That usually brings some angst into my life."

Angst was an understatement.

Najma nodded, braiding her fingers together and setting them atop the mahogany desk. "I remember you mentioning your sister a few times in the past."

"*She*, actually, doesn't cause too much stress," I admitted, slipping my hands beneath my thighs so my quivering fingers wouldn't knock over Najma's fountain. Why was I so fucking nervous? I had no reason to be. I had the right to be proud of my work and how far I'd come. Those two things mattered the most. My family could officially disown me for all I cared. "I mean, it's stressful how unintentionally perfect Marian is in the eyes of my parents. But I'm used to that. I'm perfectly okay with being the family misfit."

I embraced that title more than anyone probably should.

"This seems to still quietly bother you." Her head tilted curiously to the right while the light from the salt lamp turned her tawny skin to silk. "I'm glad it doesn't affect your work. In fact, you've been asking for more work, it seems. If you ever need to lessen your workload, you know I'll approve. You deserve it."

I also deserved a raise.

As I adjusted myself in her velvet wingback, I glimpsed my reflection in her China cabinet. Sunken pouches clung to the skin below my eyes, and even though I thought I was sitting in perfect alignment, my shoulders look like weights were yanking them toward the floor. I took pride in what I fed my body. I scheduled two self-care alarms a day where I stretched and refilled my water bottle. All my planners had self-care stickers I stuck on the days I needed to give myself extra attention. Hell, I'd had more orgasms in the last two weeks than I'd had in over a year.

That was a self-care milestone to be damn proud of.

"I appreciate you, Naj. I really do." My shoulders squared to face the flawless woman in front of me. "I will always keep you in the loop with my wellness. Things have been oddly wonderful lately, though."

"I'm glad to hear that, Fern," Najma said kindly. She nodded, and I exited her office when she gestured subtly toward the door, lifting the tablet from beneath my arm and swiping across the screen.

The last couple of weeks truly had been wonderful. There'd been drinks with alcohol-infused Swedish fish, make-out sessions against brick walls, and a few all-night romp sessions I never expected would come from the geek I had dated in high school. Just thinking about the time we'd spent together over the last few weeks caused heat to trickle into my cheeks and to others places absolutely not appropriate for work.

I immediately crossed my legs tight when I sat back down at my desk, inhaling deeply as I reached for my cell phone.

If things were so wonderful, though, why did I find my index finger hovering above the My Cup O' Joe search bar? If I genuinely felt like I could trust the past enough to bring it into my present, why was I typing Beth O'Malley's name into the database?

"What research are you doing today?" The sound of Chase's voice forced my phone to fly across my desk, bumping into the framed photo of Loaf and Porridge sitting beside the computer monitor. If it had slid even the slightest bit farther, the thin planter holding my eight-year-old bamboo would have tumbled over.

If that happened, I'd take the day off.

"Research? None. I'm...I don't know, just scrolling...like all of us millennials mindlessly do. We can't even stop ourselves once we start, you know?" I stood up and yanked down the bottom of my blouse, leaning over my desk and eyeing the cactus on the cubicle ledge we shared. "Did you hide anything behind Spike today?"

Chase shook his head, white teeth matching the ivory button-down he was wearing. Today, black cats clad in oversized sunglasses scattered his shirt. "Nah. I haven't found anything worth buying over the last week. It's your turn, though. Stop at The Vintage Press and see what you can find. That place is a gold mine."

"I haven't been there in months. Thank you for the reminder to get my ass back there!"

"You've been busy, huh?" Chase crossed his arms and leaned on the ledge, setting his chin on top of his wrist.

I swallowed deeply with a shrug, my fingers going from the hem of my blouse to wrap around the uneven ends of hair hitting my shoulders. My hair was getting too long. "I guess. Sort of." I looked away from the cactus to meet Chase's dark eyes. For being the monstrously tall human he was, he looked so soft and small leaning against the ledge like this, his chin propped on his arm. "Have you ever—I don't know—researched ex-partners of the person you're hanging out with before? Hypothetically, of course."

Chase bit the inside of his cheek, his eyes darting away from mine. "I think I'm probably one of the few workers here who rarely goes on My Cup unless forced to fix something. I've probably done some accidental social media scanning, but I also haven't had a *hang-out person* in a while. Is this guy your boyfriend?"

"Not really. I mean, kind of. Honestly, I have no clue what to even call it," I admitted, shaking my head and sinking down into the swivel chair. I began slowly spinning in the chair. "Adulthood makes dating terms so much more confusing than they should be. Why can't we pass notes to each other like we used to in middle school? You know, when you would ask someone if they liked you and they'd have to circle *yes* or *no*."

"I guess social media is just the upgraded version of that," Chase said, his gaze falling back onto mine with a kind smile pursing his lips. "I would, personally, love a hand-written note snuck to me."

"Right?" I threw my hands into the air, my hair catching on my silver thumb ring before I awkwardly shook it out of the tangle. Yeah, my hair *definitely* needed a trim. Shoulder-length hair was just too much for me to handle. "It probably doesn't happen anymore because no one can handwrite anything these days."

"And here we are," Chase said, standing up straight and forcing my eyes to follow his rising frame. "We work for the digital version of middle school note passing. This version just involves fewer hormonal outbursts and way more coffee."

"I should probably get back to editing the logo for our caffeinated note-passing platform." I tapped the darkened screen of the tablet, reaching for my phone and setting it on my lap. "Are you going to Emmie's Halloween party again this year?"

"Chicken costume and all. I'll be there." Chase eyed the cactus, nodding toward it. "I live near The Vintage Press if you're ever near that part of Merlin. Hanging out around candy buttons and comic books could get your head out of the funk it's in."

I pressed my dark lips together, a smile falling naturally over my face. The pale skin of my cheeks grew crimson, and my fingers caressed the warmth. "I will definitely let you know. You're the best cubicle neighbor a girl could have."

"It's only because I bring you candy and listen to your problems."

I snickered, rolling my eyes. "I mean, obviously."

Chase lowered into his seat with a smirk, disappearing as I heard him click away on his keyboard and lift the phone from the receiver. Even as I focused on line work and logo drafts, occasionally refreshing my email inbox on the monitor, my fingers found their way back to my phone screen.

And to the app.

And to her name.

My head and heart collided as I clicked her My Cup profile. She had signed up using the name I connected my ex-best friend with and not some character's name she had concocted for show.

A show I wondered if Davis still watched with a hopeful heart.

MY CUP ' JOE

Chase, 33

Senior IT Manager
Sips with WOMEN
Looking for FRIENDSHIP, RELATIONSHIP, MARRIAGE

Hot or Cold

I just like good, strong coffee.

Sweetness

A little cream and sugar is fine. Basic, I know.

With A Side Of

Humor. Coffee tastes better when you go in for a sip, laugh, and it flies out of your nose. Okay, honestly? Humor, a comic book, and someone who doesn't take themselves too seriously.

Chapter 16

Emmie

Fern didn't throw hot coffee in my face when I finally told her about my hook-up with Marian. Even with Fern's naivete, she sensed that her sister's quick departure the next morning had something to do with late-night activities going on once her bedroom door closed.

Yes, Fern was naïve, but she wasn't oblivious.

She knew I thought Marian was one of the classiest, sweetest, most naturally attractive people I'd ever laid eyes on. She saw how Marian giggled easily at my quips and nudged me when passing by for another bottle of beer or plate of Kung Pao chicken. Whether or not she wanted to acknowledge it, Fern knew something was humming below the surface with the friendship her sister and I had created over the years.

What Fern didn't know about was her sister's sexuality and her relationship with Thea.

Until I swung by her cubicle at lunch time.

"She's being a complete moron," Fern whispered from her desk, hands flexed on either side of her head. It looked like she was trying to crush her skull in. "My parents will disown her."

"Because she's fooling around with girls...or because she's specifically fooling around with Satan's spawn? That's me. I'm the spawn." Leaning further into Fern's workspace, I heard Chase's swivel chair whistle as he stood up, his fingers curling around the cubicle ledge and peeking over. "Of course, *that* would grab your attention."

"Don't mind me," he said, popping up to stand at his full Hulk height. "I'd rather snoop on this conversation than code the new profile layout. Coding isn't even in my job description, and they throw shit like this at me because I won't say no."

Fern sat forward on the edge of her chair, and if she shifted forward any farther, she was sure to fall flat on her face. "No, no, no. She's a moron because she's fooling around with her career *and* her heart. She's worse than me with breakups. When she breaks, she is forever shattered."

"Me too," Chase added, his low voice shocking against our whiny ones. "I cry. I'm a crier."

Fern eyed Chase and shook her head, reaching up for the cactus sitting on the ledge and tipping it to poke the top of his hand. He stepped back, flinching dramatically and bringing his hand to his cheek.

"Well, maybe her and Thea will actually last. Maybe they'll be more than just make-out buddies," I said, snagging the cactus from Fern and lightly poking one of the spikes against my index finger. I pressed the spike a little harder at the thought of Marian with Thea—her short, auburn hair falling over Thea's face and her soft, strong hands pulling her in against her chest.

If I couldn't be the one with Marian, maybe they'd at least let me watch.

Maybe Marian had hidden voyeur tendencies I could work with.

"Marian could fall head over heels for you, leave the band, and end her career all while breaking the hearts of both Thea and our parents."

"Challenge accepted," I whispered with thin eyes while rolling my lips together. Watching my best friend squirm was pure bliss. When Fern's head fell to the side and I saw the emotion sleeping deep in those gray eyes, I placed the cactus back on the ledge and set a hand on her shoulder. "I'm kidding. I am *kidding*, Fern. It will all be fine. Marian has a good head on her shoulders...like, the best one I've ever seen. She won't mess things up."

"But I also don't want her to live some life that isn't hers just for the sake of being what our parents expect her to be." Fern took a deep breath in, and as she exhaled, she sat back into her chair while squaring her shoulders toward the computer monitor. "She will make the right decisions. If she veers away from her true self, I'll talk to her. I just want her to please both her head *and* her heart—and not choose the one she feels obligated to please."

"You've always followed your heart rather than your head, Fern." My words didn't seem to surprise or offend her as she nodded, clicking a few letters on the keyboard. "She may follow your lead."

"That's because I'm an awkward romantic with anxious tendencies."

Chase laughed, adjusting the top button of his striped polo. "Say that with confidence, dammit. I have a thing for anxiously awkward romantics."

"Anxiously awkward romantics who win sour candy competitions?" Fern lifted a brow, showcasing a sliver of the personality we'd missed during this meltdown.

Chase shifted his hands back and forth with open palms. Holy shit, his palms were the size of basketballs. "Eh…you *may* need to take back the *winning* part of that sentence."

"Never." Fern's phone began buzzing beside her wrist. She grabbed it and shook it in the air, twisting in her chair so she could extend her legs. "Well, it's time to stretch and refill this water bottle."

I quickly snagged the bottle from her clammy little hands and backed away from the cubicle.

"I got this. You do your weird wellness ritual, and I'll make sure your water is at room temperature."

Fern's smile was grateful as fuck. "Thank you, Emmie. You really are a good friend."

"Yeah, yeah." I walked a few steps backward before turning around to face the kitchenette, running my index finger beneath the tap water until it was lukewarm.

Lian Wu Garfield had worked as the receptionist at Neville's Family Practice since completing ESL 101 at Merlin Community College years before I was even a sprinkle of existence. Once receiving her GED after being homeschooled off and on for almost two decades, she knew she had to improve her English to be taken seriously as the career-driven woman she aspired to become. She understood just enough English to pass the classes necessary to get that GED, but she wanted to be more than a housewife or laundress—career paths her parents expected her to take. Lian adored her mother, but she couldn't imagine scrubbing foul stains out of other people's clothes for the rest of her life.

One month after getting a B+ in ESL, she began working as a receptionist. Three months after that, clad in his camouflage jacket and trousers, Elton Garfield limped into Neville's Family Practice, and Lian couldn't look away from his dark eyes and even darker skin. He had a magnetic pull on her, causing her skin to flush at every hint of a joke and her heart to pound whenever he walked through the door for post-surgical scans. When Elton's hip didn't require weekly exams anymore and he was given a script for Greyport Physical Therapy visits, Lian got to her feet the second he began threading his rugged arms into his jacket.

The moment her lips parted to speak, Elton asked her to dinner.

One year later, after my mom almost hemorrhaged herself to death, I was born.

"The carrots keep falling out today. We should try Hen Hao Chi next time," my mom suggested, picking up a tiny carrot stick with her chopsticks and nibbling at the end. I twisted myself side to side in one of the unsteady office swivel chairs, lifting an entire roll with my fingers and stuffing it into my mouth. Though my mother was always hesitant of the prepackaged sushi I obsessed over, she still ate every piece of rice rolling around on her plate. "I'll try the spicy salmon next month."

"I won't give up this rainbow roll. I'm a basic bitch over here." Another piece collapsed into my mouth, and I licked each finger and watched as my mother shook her head in my direction with her tiny lips curved into a crescent.

"You eat like your father. He never stopped to taste."

"Genetics," I said with a shrug, my boot pressing against the floor to restart the side-to-side swivel motion which seemed to pause with every bite. "I taste what I'm eating way more now, though. Compare my eating habits now to the ones from my childhood. That's a picture you may not want to imagine."

"Messy and fast. Just like Elton." Her thin shoulders lifted with a laugh. She took a deep breath before robotically readjusting herself in her chair as if a puppeteer had a thread hammered to the top of her head. Catching my gaze, her face grew still and serious. "The thinner you get, the more you look like him."

"I prefer to say I'm getting *healthier*, Mom." I raised an eyebrow, her comparison sinking in as I leaned back with a devious grin. "Are you saying I get blacker with each pound I lose?"

"Emmaline, no!" My mother set her hands on the desk by her side, looking up as if the entire waiting room had heard my comment.

Being uncomfortably offensive around my conservative mother was always the highlight of my week.

Dating outside of my mom's culture was taboo when my parents began seeing one another. My grandparents didn't like it, but they also didn't scorn her for following her heart—something rare among Chinese parents during that time. My father's parents lived in New Jersey and were not even aware my mother was in his life until they'd visited a year later. He'd walked through their New Jersey entrance-way alongside a small, dark-haired woman holding a sienna-skinned newborn bundled in her arms.

Instead of becoming outraged with shock, the way my mom expected them to be, his mother stood up and asked to hold me. As she slowly swayed me in that all-knowing maternal fashion mothers' bodies naturally do, his father hugged my mom before even learning her first name.

If only the world had grown more accepting as time passed.

In ways, it had. But those tiny pieces of progress were hard to focus on when the world was constantly shaming you, belittling you, and tearing you apart for what you believed in, who you loved, or what you looked like.

"Sorry, sorry." I emphatically wagged my hand and reached forward, patting my mother's skirted knee. "Also, this is as thin as I'm going to get, Mom. I'm a proud size ten."

After two years of mostly eating plant-based meals, early morning walks, and consistent cognitive-behavioral therapy sessions, I deserved to show off these newly toned curves.

And damn, did they look good.

"Don't get as small as Fern," she said, her eyes peeking above thin frames balancing at the edge of her nose. "There's nothing to that girl."

"Nothing but anxiety and phenomenal hair. She's just genetically a tiny human." I crunched the plastic container into the garbage by my mother's foot, poking her shoulder with my index finger as a snort-like laugh snuck out. "You're in this boat too, Mom. You need to eat a freaking box of Twinkies."

"*Twinkies*?" Her brow line furrowed for a few seconds before a spark livened up her eyes. "The fuzzy banana slug sandwiches you ate as a kid?"

My feet found the floor, and I cupped her fragile face in my hands, lifting it gently and kissing the center of her forehead. "Yes, Mom. The fuzzy banana slug sandwiches."

Chapter 17

FERN

His fingers pressed firmly against my hip bones, one hand gliding up across my skin until it fell over my right breast. I arched my back, and a hiccup of relief escaped, feeling his warm breath brush against the goosebumps covering my inner thighs. I clawed at his husky shoulders, and from the hungry growl escaping his lips—lips humming ferociously between my legs—I could tell I was causing more pleasure than pain.

His tense muscles looked sculpted from marble.

His dewy skin made my fingers slip as I dug them deeper into his shoulder blades.

His fingers gripped my breast as he plunged in deeper between my legs.

His tongue circled my clit, and I thrust myself against him, letting out a shrill moan, causing Porridge to race out from his sanctuary beneath the bed.

Davis giggled into my damp skin, hovering himself above my sex as he kissed my belly, my chest, my neck.

"There were never cats hiding beneath your bed in high school," Davis whispered in my ear before his teeth softly tugged at it. My relaxed muscles tensed again, and I forced my body to unwind against its will.

"Or so you think." My fingers walked down his back until his brawny backside filled my palms. Fuck. Why did every single part of him feel so good? "Maybe I was secretly hiding a family of Siamese kittens under there, and they were just too scared to run out."

"If that were the case, I feel bad for the earthquake we gave them every time we hung out." Davis lowered himself over me, casually looking along the side of the bed for more cats while pressing his stiffness against my bare skin. I tugged at the elastic of his boxers, slipping a couple fingers beneath so I could hug his hard cock in my hand.

Just touching him made me crave another orgasm.

"I think we're safe," I whispered, slowly lowering the fabric down his thighs. It was obvious he was ready to add even more fire to the evening, and after our nonstop teasing and foreplay, I was more than ready too. "I still can't believe *this* is you. I mean, you were good in high school. But *this?* This is a whole new level."

"Well, we're not really sharing firsts anymore. We played a little trial-and-error back then." Davis kicked his boxers onto the floor, holding himself in a plank position above my body as I reached around him, digging my nails into his back and yanking him down closer. "I do like this more advanced version of trial-and-error, though."

"I haven't yet experienced the error part of this game."

With his body still hovering above me, my hands stroking his glorious erection up and down, I greedily pushed my hips up toward him.

His smile was playful, taunting, but he caved the moment my bare sex grazed his. He lowered his body and thrust himself into me, my body completely at his mercy as my nails returned to digging craters into his shoulder blades.

The second he was deep inside of me, my back arching as I cried out his name, Loaf angrily pounced out from beneath the bed, following in Porridge's lead.

We spent the rest of the evening in the kitchen, chopping water chestnuts and scallions while clad only in aprons. He hadn't only visited the farmer's market at his own will, but he also brought over two aprons his little sister had sewn for him during her high school Home and Careers class. He'd carefully tied the apron around my naked body, his hands sliding down to pinch the *barely there ass* he kindly reminded me was *cute.* My bare nipples poked against the fabric as I wiggled around the kitchen island, trying to accidentally pull his apron loose while he sautéed vegetables.

"I've never been a fan of tofu, but this is pretty damn good." Davis nodded and stabbed his fork into another square of tofu, grabbing some broccoli and bok choy along with it.

"It's amazing when you find the right mix of seasoning and oils," I explained, angling my legs so the apron fell over my knees and the straps were barely covering my nipples, leaving him the tiniest bit distracted with each forkful. Even though I had a small dining table in the corner of the living room, dinners were usually eaten at the coffee table. This was partially because the dining table was covered in fallen leaves, potting soil, and the reaching limbs of pothos.

It was also partially because I preferred sitting on the floor in front of the TV like the millennial I was.

"You ate salmon and shrimp all the time when we dated. Is that all out of the picture now?" Davis reached for a napkin and dabbed masala from his bottom lip.

"Honestly, the smell of seafood makes me nauseated." Saying the words aloud forced my stomach into a somersault. "I think we ate too much of it in high school."

"Beth was obsessed with grilled salmon. Like, *obsessed*. Grilled salmon wraps, grilled salmon salads, grilled salmon with a side of fries." Davis laughed, shaking his head and looking at the ceiling. "I'd take *this* any day over another damn grilled salmon rice bowl."

Silence bit into my skull. Though Davis continued digging into his stir fry as if the name was any other household one, my insides churned. The pain in my gut wasn't out of jealousy or anger. It wasn't even out of frustration from losing both a boyfriend and a best friend at the same time, all those years ago.

Maybe it was curiosity stinging the pit of my stomach or all the *what ifs* dangling in the air.

From the widening of Davis's eyes and the gentle slump of his shoulders, it was clear the wall of tension had made way across the coffee table. He finished chewing and set the fork down on his napkin, walking his fingers across the table and tapping my thumb with a playful twinkle in his eyes. I snapped my face back to neutral, grazing his forefinger with my thumb.

"You and Beth," I whispered, the name stinging my tongue. "Have you guys kept in touch?"

"Honestly..." His response was quick, and he leaned back onto his free hand, wriggling his other away from my grasp so he could adjust the apron over his upper thigh. When he cleared his throat and brought the other hand behind him for balance, my breathing slowed. "We usually talk—I don't know—on a weekly or biweekly basis."

There was no *slowing* of breath. My breath completely turned to ice in my chest.

"Oh," I said, reaching for the wine with one hand and adjusting the apron so it hung over my sneaky left nipple. "That's nice, though. I mean, staying friends with people is great. Like, what we're doing. Right?"

Word-vomit. So much word-vomit.

"I guess it's kind of the same thing—in a way." He shrugged as color flooded back into his face, and he reached for his glass. "We just talk about things. She always asks if I'm planning to move out that way, and I tell her repeatedly that my job here is fine."

"Is it *just* your job that is stopping you?" I asked, scooting closer to the coffee table. "I bet you could find a similar job out in LA and make, what, triple what you make at Willow Center."

Unfiltered, vile word-vomit.

I stuffed a huge forkful of stir fry into my mouth just to shut myself up.

"I've thought about that, actually." Davis scooted closer to the coffee table as well, edging around the side of it and walking his hand toward my knee. His touch sent lightning through me, but nothing like the sparks from earlier.

"You have?" I asked, smiling down at his hand as I folded mine over his.

"A few times, I've looked into jobs out there, and like you said, they do pay ridiculously more."

"So, what's holding you back?" I pressed my hand against his and slowly slid it upward on my thigh, his fingers relaxing as I took control and deflected us away from the conversation at hand.

If I couldn't control the words spewing from my lips, maybe I could control what was going on below his apron.

"I mean, *this* has been a nice distraction. That's for sure," Davis said, his voice low as he slipped his hand below the hem of my apron, his fingers crawling up my thigh.

"I'm glad I can help," I whispered.

Before I could take another breath, the wall of ice melted inside my lungs as Davis's fingers shifted inside of me. The rug bit my bare back, forcing my eyes shut as I did everything I could to focus on his hardening cock and the gasps escaping my lungs.

But I couldn't.

My brain just wouldn't let me.

While my body was trembling at his touch, desperate for more, my brain kept forcing the word *distraction* to the front of my eyelids, begging to be seen.

Chapter 18

Emmie

Not only did I wake to find my Tamagotchi clock face down on the bedroom floor, I also woke to three text messages and two emails all before nine o'clock. Though the clock randomly falling onto the hardwood seemed eerie, the messages and emails were right on cue.

Well, sort of.

After the editorial team reviewed my most recent *Expresso with Emmie: The Cheater Chase*—the subtitle being *MANnY Still Like it Hot*—they scheduled to publish it at the usual Friday morning time. Though it was recommended that we start our workday at eight o'clock, even with our remote freedom, I almost always pushed snooze on my phone until the damn Tamagotchi clock buzzed from my desk at quarter-to-nine as my final reminder. It had never fallen onto the floor or missed a late-morning wake-up alarm before. Even on mornings when I wanted to chuck it out the window because it followed directions so well, I could somehow control my anger and exhaustion.

This morning, however, felt different.

I didn't like it.

I knew I'd get a few interesting reactions to this most recent blog. Some opinionated emails, comments, and reviews were bound to happen. I'd faced criticism—and praise—many times since starting at My Cup. The inappropriate comments and jabs at my writing came with the territory. My skin had become the best of armor, both protecting me and toughening me up for whatever shit the future smacked me with.

One text was from Fern, asking where I was. This made me do a double-take at the fallen clock before my socked feet slid me across the room and practically into the closet door. Yanking a hooded sweatshirt over my baggy T-shirt, I clicked the next text to see it was from Izzy, who often was the first member of the team to read my work: *Holy shit, did you see how many Beans you got for this one already? Congrats on outranking!*

I paused and stared at the screen with one arm in the air, still pushing through the sleeve. My second month writing content for My Cup was the first and only time I'd ever outranked on a blog, and that was when, well, we were brand spanking new. I'd written a very honest piece about my unfiltered poly lifestyle that went viral and drew such interest from those wanting throuple, open, and poly relationships that new buttons and codes were immediately added to the app to support more users.

I typically got around one-thousand Coffee Beans—My Cup's version of the *Like* button—per publication. For Izzy to congratulate my outranking this early in the day, the beans must have been literally overflowing.

And that was a design element Fern added the week after my blog *Expresso with Emmie: More Fun with More People* went viral.

Finally tugging down the sweatshirt and pulling black leggings over bristly skin, I clicked the final text before realizing it was a number I didn't recognize. The area code was familiar, but the numbers after it were a jumbled mess. I kept staring at the numbers as I slipped my laptop into my leather bag and lugged it over my shoulder, my hands reaching for the keys dangling by the door.

As my fingers hugged the jagged metal, the tightening grip forced bite marks into my palm.

"Shit," I whispered, slamming the door behind me.

"So, what are you going to say?" Fern asked, setting down her tablet and braiding her fingers together. Fern had the voice of a trained, tranquil therapist this morning. She usually had two personas. It was either this therapeutic, calming presence or the anxious, energetic creature we'd grown to love.

"I don't fucking know." I rocked back and forth over my hands laying squished below my thighs. "Probably text him an apology?"

"But would it be a *genuine* apology?" Fern asked softly.

Fuck. She *was* my counselor this morning.

"I'm not really sorry about what I did. No, I didn't mean to mess up a marriage or a career—even though I'm sure I've messed up two careers in the last month." I gave my fingers permission to wriggle away from beneath my thighs specifically so I could chug down some of the black coffee staring up at me. I genuinely feel great after how the last two little scenes unfolded. Those guys treated me like shit. They deserved every bit of it."

"You've embraced karma in the most respectable yet foulest of ways."

"Karma is my religion, and weirdly, I'm believing in it more and more." I hated admitting this truth aloud, but it felt so good rolling off my tongue. Everyone had a little bad hiding inside of them. I'd played the role of *The Quiet, Perfect Student and Girlfriend* for far too long when, really, that had never been the role I needed to play.

The only role I'd ever wanted to play was one where I could be wholeheartedly myself. These blogs took me out of my comfort zone. With each blog written, I felt closer to the role I was meant to play—if not *the* role. I also knew how ridiculous it sounded that these blogs increased my self-esteem all while tearing down others.

The candle was lit at both ends.

"So, you really believe that..." Fern lifted her tablet, scrolling and clicking until her eyebrows lifted. "'*Call it selfish, but if doing the right thing means doing a little bit of the wrong thing to bring yourself mental closure...it's worth it.*'"

I sat back with a confident nod. "I sure do."

"Even after his text?" Fern asked, eyeing the phone near my hand.

I swiped my finger over the screen until Manny's text sat clearly lit before me. I'd read it several times on the way to Spellbound and several more times over the last hour. Hell, I could probably recite it at this point:

"*Thanks to the shitshow you pulled off, two students have come forward, saying I sexually assaulted them during my time as student life manager. I'm not sure if it was your plan all along to make our hallway charade go viral, but not only did I lose my job, I'm also losing my wife. I'm sorry for pissing you off sophomore year, but this is the real world now. Not some college prank. Grow the fuck up."*

We'd already gawked at the video five times since walking into Spellbound Beans. We watched it two more times at our own discretion and three more times when messages were sent my way with the video linked, as if I hadn't seen it already. Even Oliver had shouted from across the counter, flinging his phone into the air so that customers could watch as Manny squeezed my ass and kissed my neck.

I wanted to vomit.

After that, I decided not to watch it again for at least the next twenty-four hours.

"His wife and those students didn't deserve to live with some hidden secret weighing them down. In a way, I think what happened was a necessary evil. I just want to know the names of those two drunken assholes who spotted us in the damn hallway," I said through gritted teeth. "The music was so loud I could barely even hear Manny's disgusting comments. Those two students had probably been hanging at the water fountain since he'd left the gym for all I know."

"I do think what you did was ballsy as hell." Fern's tiny plum lips turned up slightly. "I could never do it. I mean, maybe I could. After a few drinks. This takes guts I don't even think I have when I'm angry and blacking out on too much cabernet."

"It feels both amazing and nauseating all at once," I admitted, clicking the laptop back to life before taking a deep breath. "It just means this next venture must be planned better since more eyes are checking out *The Cheater Chase.*"

"And I'm sure Al and corporate are pretty impressed by the series since you outranked before nine o'clock."

"How do that many people even see a blog that goes live at six in the morning? Do people really scroll and stalk *that* much before getting their asses out of bed?"

Fern lifted an open, ringed hand beside her ear. "Guilty. I'm a major before-bed and before-work social media scroller. I've also probably been social media stalking Beth-Betty-Bette-Beatrice a little bit *too* much lately."

"Is that Davis's ex-turned-YourEyesOnly star you've talked about?" Rolling my eyes, I finally found the courage to click onto the tab I'd been avoiding, the screen filling with a photograph of a serene, sterile waiting room that was obviously set up perfectly before the professional picture was taken. At the bottom, right-hand corner of the screen, five portraits stared directly at me.

There she was.

"Yes, yes. That's Beth. Maybe I should just suck it up and call her Bette Ohm from now on. That's the name she wants the world to know her by." Fern's snicker became a snort, and her hand raced to her mouth, the couple at the table beside us glimpsing up over their coffee. "It's just so weird. All of it. It's just so weird."

"Stop," I spat, sensing her therapeutic mask slipping. "Davis obviously has a thing for you since he stays over so often."

"He said he still talks to Beth. Bette, I mean. They still talk." Fern was hiding behind the quick laugh that turned into the clearing of her throat. "You're right, though. He texts me all the time, and the sex... Emmie, the sex. It's insane."

"How often does he still talk to her?" I scooted closer to the table, my chest practically knocking over the empty mug.

Fern shifted closer to the table as well, dramatically shuffling her eyebrows flirtatiously. "Emmie...I've never been with someone *this* good."

"Fern," I said, pulling her away from the failed deflection. Her wide, circular eyes became hollow, and she slouched her shoulders even more.

"They talk on a biweekly basis. Sometimes more."

"Okay. It's time we talk about *your* little dilemma." I shut my laptop so *her* portrait wouldn't leer at me for the rest of the morning. I would face the dark, cold eyes from the portrait later that night. I still had to concoct some kind of gutsy plan that would exceed the last two.

"Is it really a dilemma, though?" Fern was asking a question she already knew the answer to—a performance she put on when she needed to step aside as therapist. "I mean, I haven't done anything wrong. I don't think I have yet, at least."

"I feel like stepping on the toes of a mending relationship can be just as shitty as sticking around to create your own," I said. "It seems like Davis may still have some mending to do."

MY CUP ' JOE

Marian, 24

Musician
Sips with EXPLORING
Looking for CASUAL, RELATIONSHIP

Hot or Cold

Does a cortado count? It's definitely a tie between a
simple cup of coffee and a beautifully bitter cortado.

Sweetness

I honestly like my coffee black and my espresso
strong. Something is wrong with my tastebuds...but
wrong in the best of ways!

With A Side Of

Christian rock, a beer, and the Bible. I am friends with
Jesus...but I also appreciate some loud music and a
good Kolsch.

Chapter 19

FERN

The tips of my fingers drumming against the windowpane mimicked the rain pouring down onto the sidewalk outside. October was nearing its end, and despite the impending snow, I found solace in the gloomy weather. My brain was as gray as the fog wrapping around the orange and gold leaves barely clinging to branches, taking in one last breath before their final exhale.

Though I lived for weather like this, part of me was pushing down emotions I needed to bring to the surface. However, tonight wasn't the night for that. The feelings would have to hide a little bit longer. I was a professional at slipping into costumes radiating certainty even when they were clumsily stitched. I wore those costumes with grace, hiding behind insecurities bleeding through the seams.

Only an unlucky few saw the rips I tried to hide.

I turned around to face the dim apartment, lukewarm coffee keeping my clammy hands cozy as my back hit the window. The overgrown spider plant—the one I'd named Legs—tickled my forehead, and I let the ascending limbs reach toward my nose. My brain was too engrossed in My Cup's design relaunch, Emmie's yearly Halloween party, and Davis's recent confessions to care about the attention Legs begged for.

I let my discussion with Emmie at Spellbound simmer for the rest of Friday, not letting emotions climb through my fingers and into texts with Davis. I forced myself away from social media and threw my energy into making an unusually shaped planter I wasn't sure I'd ever use once the kiln was finished with it. Even when Emmie knocked on the door to see if I wanted to order Chinese or talk about costumes, I quietly declined—all while wearing a believably artificial grin.

Even after falling asleep quickly Friday night, I woke in a haze. My head ached even with caffeine suppressing the pain. My heart was nudging me to text Davis, to casually remind him of when the Halloween party started that night. However, my head was screaming to wait for him to ping a text my way instead.

Bitter, black coffee slid down my throat as I listened to the angel and devil bicker on my shoulders. The mere fact that I was drinking my coffee black without complaint meant my brain and body were nowhere near in sync. I swiped Legs out of my vision and grazed Loaf's ears from atop the couch, wondering if I just needed some of that pumpkin oat milk sitting in my fridge. Hell, maybe I needed to stir in some hot chocolate—or vodka—and *really* take myself over the edge.

Fuck. I was losing it.

Popping open the oat milk, pumpkin flavor dripped into my coffee. It was October, after all. I'd slip into an orange leotard come nightfall and slip out of reality. Becoming a character seemed better than dwelling on Davis all afternoon.

"Really?" My eyebrows rattled the jagged bangs covering my forehead—a spur-of-the-moment decision I'd made after overdosing on pumpkin oat milk that morning. After watching crimson hair fall into my bathroom sink that afternoon, my mood immediately skyrocketed. It was a little scary how quickly hair impacted my mood. "You can't host a yearly Halloween party and re-costume. It's practically forbidden."

"Well, people can suck it." Emmie attempted to zip up the back of the giant pickle costume she'd lazily decided to wear two years in a row. As her fingers grazed the zipper, she looked over her shoulder with a grin. "Get it? Because I'm a pickle. And a pickle looks—"

"I get it, Em. Your comic relief is appreciated," I said, reaching for the glass of vodka-cranberry calling my name on her desk. "Even though I don't appreciate the two-year pickle you're in."

Smiling, Emmie finally got the back zipped and flattened the bubbling fabric around her center as a knock sounded from the other room. "Plus, some people haven't seen my pickle yet. Come in!"

The cold, stiff vodka rubbed my throat raw as my sister walked into Emmie's bedroom, practically causing the alcohol to resurface all over the unmade bed. "What the hell? Marian?"

"Surprise?" Her voice was timid, but her embrace was warm—a quiet wish for forgiveness.

"Aren't you on tour right now? And what about Sunday school tomorrow?"

"We had a Friday night show this weekend, *Mom*," Marian said, laughing before gently squeezing my upper arms and backing away. "I got Kyla to sub tomorrow's class. I said I would video chat in and say hello to the students."

"Wow." I took a quick sip of my drink, this time enjoying the burn. "You must have *really* wanted to surprise your *sister*, huh? Because *I'm* obviously the reason you're here."

"Oh, please. You love that we hooked up." Emmie stepped forward, wrapping her arm around Marian's shoulders and playfully tugging her close. "It makes your sister seem a little more human, right?"

Marian shrugged. "Thanks?"

"First off, I don't know exactly what the hooking up entailed, nor do you need to tell me. Secondly," I said, pausing to look at my little sister's soft features as she leaned into Emmie's embrace, "I support your humanity in every shape and form. That will never change."

"I'll just safely say thank you again," Marian snickered, shaking her head. "Plus, we have an understanding. Emmie and I are nothing more than playmates."

"Marian also understands I have various other playmates too." Emmie's eyes peeked over my shoulder for a quick second, glancing toward her apartment door. "A few who should be here any minute."

"Again, I fully support all the playmates and friendships and whatever." I lifted my glass from Emmie's desk, my knuckles sweeping the side of her clock and catching it before the relic rolled off the ledge. That thing was always so touchy. "If you get way too drunk later and start spilling your soul to me about how attached you are—either of you—I won't stop you, but I will say I told you so."

"Fern. Our soul-picking pumpkin," Emmie said as a knock sounded at the apartment door. "That's probably Kyle and Rae."

The three of us left the bedroom as Emmie welcomed Kyle, Rae, and two other My Cup employees inside while Marian opened the fridge for a fruity sour. Leaning against the far wall with my sister opening her drink beside me, I anxiously waited for Davis to arrive after refilling my glass and finally receiving an *I'm on my way* text.

This kind of anxiety was supposed to come from those *new relationship* nerves or the *maybe he's the one* possibility. My irritability was supposed to be from butterflies flitting around in my stomach or growing goosebumps when imagining his skin on mine.

Instead, nerves were forcing down bile biting my throat.

I sensed a hangover brewing even before drink number two had been poured.

"Does this pumpkin befriend chickens?" Chase's voice smacked away some of the nerves clouding my mind. His soft, subtle smile was the familiar relief I needed.

"Are you a grass-fed chicken?"

He nodded in my direction and set a hand on my shoulder—a hand clad in a yellow glove with golden feathers very obviously hot-glued onto it. "Organic, ma'am."

"Then, of course we're friends." I reached for his feathered hand, lifting it so I could see what he was holding. "What the fuck is this?"

Chase raised what looked like a jug of maple syrup with a faded rooster scrawled across the front. "The Crying Cock?"

"Excuse me?"

He let out one of those chesty laughs I always heard from his side of the cubicle wall—the kind of laugh you desperately tried to keep from coming out. "The Crying Cock Brewery. It's a microbrewery near my brother's place in Rockberry Park. He visited last weekend and snagged me their newest IPA. Try it."

I wrapped my fingers around the little handle, my eyes staring down at the illustrated rooster as the hoppy ale flowed into my system. I could hear Marian giggle from my side, knowing very well that IPAs were not my cup of tea. "That's...uh...it's got some hop to it."

Chase teasingly pulled the jug back toward him, hugging it against his feathered chest. "Sorry you're not feelin' the hop, Fernie. I'll gladly keep all the hop to myself."

More knocks sounded and more costumed bodies made their way inside. Davis walked into the apartment behind a cluster of three people dressed as mice, immediately catching my gaze and scooting around the group of blind rodents. Marian's hand gently wrapped around the free wrist hanging at my side, a gentle reminder to relax as my breathing obviously heightened at Davis's embrace. His hands lingered at my waist, and his lips brushed my cheek—two motions I would have been completely smitten over weeks before.

My brain rattled in my skull, forcing snapshots of memories to the front of my eyelids.

"Perfect costume," I said, placing my hands on his shoulders and leaning back against the windowsill. I watched Chase take a swig from his cock jug and walk toward the living room, finding myself oddly wanting another hoppy gulp the farther he strode away.

"Someone needed to be in charge of the pumpkin patch." Davis shoved his thumbs beneath the denim straps covering his chest, nodding his straw hat downward. He wore one of those grins, bringing me right back to the many high school make-out sessions we had against his corner locker.

Then her face sketched its way into another snapshot.

I couldn't push that fucking memory away.

"Cheers…to that. Yes, cheers," I quickly said, fumbling over my words and pushing my glass forward before realizing it had nothing to bump into. As I emptied my drink, I heard Marian clear her throat from my side. "Oh, this is my little sister. Do you remember Marian? You guys may have met a—"

"Wow, yes. I honestly didn't even recognize you," Davis said, lifting his eyebrows. He pulled an unexpected can of beer from one of the pockets of his overalls, flicking the top open. "You got *tall*."

"Well, I was much smaller when you guys dated." Marian giggled, shaking an empty can in the air while reaching for my glass. "I'll bring over a refill and then wander around. Emmie is starting a card game that may just be calling my name."

Her departure stung my gut as Davis took her spot beside me, his proximity bringing an apprehensive glow to my brow.

Her blonde hair. Her radiant smile. Their fingers locking together.

"What did you do today? Did you do anything? Talk to anyone?" My voice came out hoarse as I grabbed the full glass from Marian, watching her walk to the couch and sit down beside Emmie and Kyle.

"Are you asking me or your sister?" Davis wondered before realizing I was completely avoiding his gaze.

"*You*, silly." I took a long sip, swallowed, and turned to look at him. Most of my lipstick had rubbed off on the edge of the glass. Even as I rolled my lips together in hopes of spreading out whatever color remained, it only enhanced my nerves.

"Yeah?" Davis asked, bringing the beer to his lips. "You alright?"

"Of course. Yeah. Why?"

I was so fucked.

And not in the way I preferred.

"The last week or so, you've been—I don't know—jittery," Davis said softly.

"I'm always jittery."

"Well, that is true." Davis twisted to face forward, scanning the room of laughing adults clad in childish costumes. "Just more jittery than usual."

The bile was back in my throat.

I couldn't avoid the sour taste. The sting of truth was climbing up my throat. "Do you miss her?"

"And there it is." Davis brought the beer back up for a long drink before pressing his lips together with a nod. "And don't ask *there is what.*"

He knew me too well.

"Okay, alright." I squared my body so I faced his perfect profile. He didn't shift, keeping his gaze forward and the muscles in his jaw clenched. "Bette."

"Beth."

"Beth, yes," I corrected, the glow on my brow turning damp beneath my bangs. I was grateful I'd chopped them when I did. They were the perfect umbrella for my nervous sweat. "Do you miss her? You guys had a good thing going. Since you still talk, I just wonder if you miss her?"

The roar of some alternative hit from the early 2000s switched to an acoustic version of a recent radio favorite. His chest rose and faltered before he turned to face me, both of us staring directly at one another for the first time since his arrival. "I do."

"You do?" I repeated, each word trembling a little more than they'd sounded in my head.

"To be completely honest, Fernie, I really do." Davis laughed and leaned the back of his head against the windowpane. "You're right. Beth and I had an awesome thing going, and I have *you* to thank for that. I also have you to thank for my never having a single bad relationship I can think of because, well, you and Beth were the only real girlfriends I've ever had."

"But wasn't it a bad breakup? You and Beth?" I imagined her telling him of her cross-country move while Davis became an emotional wreck, falling to his knees and begging her to stay.

Instead of wrinkling his forehead at the question, he shrugged. "It sucked, yeah...but I admired her grit. She was leaving all she had ever known behind to follow her dreams, as cliché as it seemed. We never fought or got angry about it. We've kept in touch."

"So, why don't you leave?"

Davis's eyes doubled in size. "What?"

"I mean, why don't you go to California?" I wanted to snatch all the words falling from my tongue, but I rarely took anything back. It was both a blessing and a curse—like most of my traits.

And though this time around was proving to be a curse, I hoped for some hidden blessing to come my way.

Any blessing was welcome—even the teeniest, tiniest one.

"I can't just up and leave my job," Davis said with a hollow laugh.

"To find a better paying one in LA? No…you could never do such a thing." I furrowed my brow playfully. "Davis. You've never been one to fail at a mission, especially missions of the heart."

"Why are you saying all of this?" Davis took another sip of beer before opening his eyes wider and pouring their darkness into mine. His body shifted closer, minimizing the inches of air between us, and I felt his fingers gently wrap around my waist. I couldn't ignore the sting of heat his touch handed me, even if I was doing all I could to wash the sting away. "Haven't you had fun over the last month?"

"I've had more fun over these weeks than all the other weeks and months of this year combined," I said, pausing as my body veered toward him. It felt so painfully natural to fall into him. I hated how perfect it felt. "Probably more fun this month than in the last few years, actually."

His hands tenderly pulled me closer. "Then why fight the fun we're having?"

"Because you're still in love with her, Davis." I felt his fingers freeze at my waist, and I fought the urge to lean into him. Instead, I set my glass on the windowsill and pressed my hands against his that sat frozen at my waist.

Davis was slow to respond, but when he felt my hands on his, it was obvious why they were there. Instead of watching his glossy eyes stare down into his beer, I looked up at Marian, who was snuggled into Emmie's side on the couch. Emmie's hand sat on my little sister's thigh, and their laughter echoed across the table before them flooded with cards. When Rae slammed a card on top of another pile before throwing her arms above her head, Emmie shouted, "No!" and took my sister in against her chest. Emmie kissed the top of Marian's head and corrected the cat ears she was wearing.

My sister had always seemed perfect, but I was learning she was just being perfectly herself. She wasn't hiding the truth from our parents; she just wasn't bringing it all to the forefront. She wasn't trying to please any clichés by teaching Sunday school; she actually enjoyed it. She wasn't trying to stick to any of the guidelines our parents set; she was just walking slightly off the paved path.

Though her eyes were tawny and mine matched the gloomy afternoon sky, our genetics held true for one thing: we couldn't help but be unapologetically ourselves.

Davis stood there, feeling as hopeless and gawky as I felt whenever I walked through the doors of My Cup or Spellbound Beans or, hell, the fucking Merlin Grocery. It was moments like these when I finally felt at ease with my social qualms. Knowing I wasn't alone when it came to feeling reality's unease made my nerves settle a bit.

But the look on his face brought those nerves back to the surface. I hadn't just kicked the puppy; I'd forced him to realize everything he'd buried years ago was worth digging up.

And though I wanted to sauté sprouts with him only wearing an apron and watch him laugh about some juvenile argument we once had, I knew it was best he saw the truth he'd been sitting on for years.

When the apartment door closed at his heels, right before he gave me that final nod, it was obvious he knew what ex was worth leaving behind and which one he needed to chase.

Chapter 20

Emmie

I t was the end of my sophomore year at Merlin Community when I finally started going to college parties. Instead of being looked at as the quiet girl from study group, I became known as the not-so-quiet girl who knew how to shotgun a beer. At first, I'd only attend these parties as the designated driver to help my roommates safely get their asses into bed. Once my unexpected party skills emerged, my title as Designated Tucker-Inner and Puke-Cleaner was replaced by Shotgun Wizard and Queen of Keg Stands.

This transition started after a very dark, very tall, and very beautiful senior asked me to take her friend's place at the flip cup table. I'd stood with my glass of water in the kitchen corner of the baseball house, adjusting my glasses and smiling at whoever walked in for a refill. The second this senior started talking to me, white noise took over. My head nodded without my brain's command, and I followed her without knowing what the hell I was doing.

And without knowing how horrible Keystone Light tasted.

That night, I fell in lust with Pricilla "Cici" Greene.

I also became a force to reckon with at the flip cup table.

Now, seven or so years after she asked me to stand beside her at the table that night, her photo on the Lyra Center for Skin website was staring up at me. Of course, she sat smiling between two photographs of ridiculously gorgeous blondes who were pinched and prodded to perfection. She, on the other hand, was blessed with the plumpest pucker and silkiest black skin imaginable without ever being touched by a needle or scalpel.

Bitch.

I'd scrolled through her impressive list of credentials several times, surprised she actually followed through with all she said she would do after graduation. She'd gotten all the degrees and certificates needed to become the top-notch dermatologist she'd always wanted to be. She'd followed in her father's footsteps, co-owning her own skin and aesthetics business while winning numerous awards and statewide recognition.

She'd even ended up between two blondes like how I'd found her the night we broke up.

I sat back in my swivel chair and ran a hand over my face, removing my glasses and setting them on my thighs. I hadn't gotten anywhere with the direction of this next blog, and between the chatter on the other side of our content corner and the flickering light above my desk—the one maintenance promised they'd fix—I'd never progress forward. Her dimpled grin was still mocking me from the bottom of the screen, her hair without a trace of silver and her complexion still unnaturally perfect.

I wanted to vomit.

"She's cute." Fern's voice should have caught me by surprise, but I expected her at this time of day. The mid-afternoon slump was when we wandered the office and made unnecessary conversation with co-workers we didn't even like. She reached for my empty coffee mug, looping the handle around her index finger so her rings clinked against the ceramic.

"She's an asshole."

"Tell me more, tell me more," Fern sang, continuing to dangle the mug on his finger. "What did she say or do to make you add her to the list?"

"She cheated on me with some volleyball players...and probably a couple lacrosse girls too—I just wasn't lucky enough to catch her and the lax ladies doing the dirty," I said with a sigh, slumping back into my chair as the light flickered above me.

Cici had been a regular at all the athletic houses at Merlin Community College, the baseball house being where she frequented the most. We'd snuck into one of the back bedrooms later that night to make out drunkenly against an unsteady closet door as her soft hands climbed into my sweater. I should have known then she was one to jump from sports house to sports house and girl to girl. I'd instead focused on her flawless body when she threw her T-shirt onto my dorm room floor later that night and her delicious mouth as it explored my body. Back then, it had been a body I'd desperately tried to hide from her until the night I found her cheating.

I turned to Fern and pinched a fake smile on my face. "'You don't really look that good naked, but your personality is bangin'.' That's what she said before I heard giggles coming from her bottom bunk."

Fern stopped swinging the coffee mug around on her index finger, her ashen eyes pinned to mine. "Wait, she actually *said* that to you?"

"All these assholes actually said the unbelievable things they said to me." I scrolled up on the Lyra Center for Skin website so her face wasn't gawking at me. "I mean, a few other hookups said similar things, but they made the smart choice of moving far, far away."

"Very smart, indeed," Fern said, leaning onto my desk so the light flickered off her newly brightened locks. "Most people are too scared to say shit like that out loud. I mean, I wouldn't have the balls to say anything *that* bad. I'd probably be petty and hide behind a text message or start crying on a voicemail."

"No texts. No tears. She said the words right to my face." She'd whispered them to me in the hallway outside of her dorm room way back when with a comforter wrapped around her body like a cocoon. "Manny and Jake hid behind text messages or emails most of the time. Cici is a class act."

"Well, shit. I'm getting you more coffee," Fern said, backing away from my desk.

"Fern. Hey." Before her footsteps were too far from my cubicle, I caught her eye. "Are you okay? I mean, after everything that went down on Saturday?"

She stopped backing away and dropped her shoulders, forcing her tinted lips into a meager grin. Though she was wearing her favorite mask, I could see through it—this time more than ever. She'd actually felt something for Davis. This was obvious. She'd wanted him to be The One—even over a decade later.

"I'm okay. Yeah, I'll be alright." Fern shuffled back toward my desk, placing the cold mug against her cheek. "But what would *really* make me okay is if you fuck over this Cici character. Like...*really* fuck her over. Because if she could see your confidence—and body—now, she'd feel like the biggest bitch for doing and saying that shit to you."

"You're too kind, Fern...and I agree." I tried to flip my hair over my shoulder but barely could get some curls to shift over the tips of my ears. Fern shook her head and frolicked toward the coffee corner like the fairy her brain believed her to be, leaving me to stare blankly at the screen.

Then, my fingers found their way to the phone keypad beside the computer monitor, and before my brain could catch up, a ringtone filled my ears.

"Hello? Hi. I'm great, thanks. I'd like to schedule a visit with Dr. Greene, please." It was ironic how upbeat my phone voice had become over the years, masking the terror hiding behind each syllable I spoke. As the receptionist checked Dr. Pricilla Greene's schedule, I sunk down into my chair and watched Fern's ringed fingers slide a steaming mug into my free hand. Between realizing what I was doing and the coffee warming my palm, my dread turned into fire fueling my plan forward.

Maybe it was my adrenaline or Fern's excited yet sad, gray eyes staring at me, but I suddenly felt an urge to hand Cici a taste of her own medicine.

"Is that her office?" Fern murmured, kneeling down by my swivel chair. I nodded just as the receptionist's voice interrupted the piano playing in the background.

"Oh, yes. This is urgent, for sure. It's an emergency only a trained, experienced dermatologist like Ci—Dr. Greene...can help with." I eyed Fern, the corners of my lips shifting upward. "It's something she *really* needs to see."

I expected Fern to twist on her heel and run far away the second we walked inside the entrance of Abandon. I'd somewhat guilted her into checking out this risqué event after scheduling my skin scan with Cici that afternoon. With all these emotions stirring inside of me, I didn't want to just grab drinks at Thirsty Theodore's or visit one of our co-worker's lofts for a few cocktails and some petty office gossip.

I was craving an escape from the norm.

And maybe some half-naked men and women playing with sex toys in public.

I'd ended up telling Fern about Rae's new gig being the marketing guru at Abandon Arts Center and attempted to describe what the event would entail. Fern applauded Rae for bringing her provocative, engaging visions into the community without holding anything back—something I personally knew Rae had a hard time doing. Fern also mentioned it could be a learning experience with My Cup's rebranding launch and update right around the corner. The changes would explore more sexualities, lifestyles, and pronouns than any other dating app yet had, and this could be good research.

She was right, even though I hated her mixing work with play.

And play was definitely what this night would consist of.

Fern's eyes curiously widened as she unbuttoned her peacoat, staring as the crimson-clad aerialist descended a black silk in the far corner.

Men, women—whoever and whatever—strolled by in spiky heels and flashy unitards, handing neon-colored shot glasses to visitors. Two performers sat inside a metal hoop hanging behind one of the bars, where they poured glasses of champagne, and a Chinese swinging pole shimmered at another bar, a performer mixing a cocktail as her body practically floated mid-air.

"Rae is a fucking genius," Fern whispered, her peacoat falling over her forearm.

"You're into this stuff?" I asked, eyeing a fire-breather only a few feet away who was handcuffing a giggling woman to a chair. "It's mostly to market SteamyCirque's spring tour and some of the local products and...uh...furniture being sold in Greyport at some new sex toy cocktail lounge called Velvet."

"Emmie, I get it." Fern turned her shoulders so she was directly facing me. I couldn't avoid her eyes any longer, and when I saw them, they were absent of fear. I was oddly fascinated by this—and surprised. "BDSM. Kinks. Fetishes. I may seem naïve, but I'm not as clueless as you think."

"You know what...this is?" I pointed to whatever product was on my right while walking toward the central hub of Abandon. As I turned, I realized my finger was inches away from a Clone-a-Willy castle. I stepped backward but furrowed my brow at the product description as a couple giggled and reached for a box.

"The title pretty much sums this one up," Fern said. "I may not be like you or Rae or Kyle or, like, that couple over there trying out that four-point restraint. But I do know a few things."

Nodding, I clapped my hands slowly, dipping my head in time with my hands. "I thought the moment you walked in here you were going to puke all over yourself."

"What she's doing up there is the only thing that would make me puke." Fern pointed to the aerialist at the top of the black silks in front of us who was expertly wrapping fabric around her thigh and then around her torso. The performer kicked her leg away from the silk and tumbled down like a chaotic, beautiful falling star, smiling and stretching her arm above her head when she landed.

"Holy shit." I watched in awe as the performer skillfully untangled herself from the knotted silks without a single bead of sweat smudging her makeup. "I want to do that."

"We could take a class, but I bet it's so hard to—"

"No. I want to do that *human*." Something about the way she effortlessly climbed and careened down the fabric brought goosebumps to my skin. Her smile glowed against the vivid makeup painting her face, covering a shade of olive I saw hints of when her tights grew thin near her ankles and where the silver unitard ended at the wrists.

I hadn't consumed a single drink yet, and my vision had already begun to blur as I watched her exit the performing space, walking toward the bar where we stood. At least we weren't back by the Clone-a-Willy Castle because I probably would have already backed into it, finding myself in a pile of penises.

And that wasn't my preferred pile these days.

Kyle was the exception.

"What about my sister?" Fern asked, leaning in my direction as the aerialist grew closer.

"We are playmates. No monogamy right now."

Or, most likely, ever.

"And Marian is actually okay with that? Like, for real?" Fern stood in the middle of the aisle, the aerialist walking by her as another routine began on the static trapeze to our right.

"The lifestyle works for more people than you think. Hey, hi." I stepped away as the aerialist from the silks set her fingers atop the bar, tapping them gently and turning toward me with a red-lipped grin. "You were great up there. Ridiculous, really. In all the best ways, of course."

"That's sweet of you to say. Thank you," she responded, the corners of her lips twisting to reveal two dimples through the shimmery hues of greens and purples shading her face. "I'm glad you enjoyed it."

"We did. It was amazing." Fern stumbled closer after grabbing three glowing glasses from a unicyclist balancing a tray of shots on each hand. She set a shot in front of each of us, the aerialist looking down at the glass with a smile before wrapping her fingers around it. "Cheers! To your fearlessness!"

"Should you drink before climbing back up there?" Before I finished my question, the aerialist's head fell back, and she swiftly emptied the glass. Turning toward Fern, she too had downed the shot and was rolling her dark lips together before sliding the glass my way with a shrug.

"I bought these for you two. Go flirt. Play. Do your thing." Fern stepped back, looking around the event center with wide eyes. "I'll walk around a little bit."

"What? You're going to leave me?" I gazed over my shoulder, and my jaw practically hit the floor as the performer took her hair down from the tight bun it was sprayed into. Her dark locks flowed to the middle of her silver unitard, and I swear every movement she made was happening in slow motion.

Damn, that fabric left nothing to the imagination.

"You're fine. I'm fine," Fern whispered.

"Wait." I reached for Fern's wrist, and she blew a few strands of dyed hair from her eyes. "Are you sure you're okay? You just ended things with Davis, and I know it was something you wanted to make work. I just want you to be okay."

"It wasn't *really* a relationship. We never called it anything concrete. I'll be alright." Fern's eyes dimmed, but her lips perked into the confident grin she constantly hid behind. "I want to take in all of this event. It'll be good to see some different lifestyles in action—especially since you and my sister and 90% of the people here just live their lives however they want to. I need to do that too, in a way."

"You can live your life however you want to, Fern. I mean, you have been. You've been dating guys most people want to completely forget about. Don't think you're not stepping outside the box just because you aren't into those bondage tables over there or polyamory or whatever." I cupped Fern's pointy, pale little chin and lifted it. "You can still be true to yourself without doing extravagant things to prove it."

"Thanks. Now go flirt with that extravagant thing standing next to you," Fern said softly, nodding toward the bar. She took a few steps back into the crowd as a trapeze performer hung from his elbow, and a couple took turns on him with a set of paddles. "I'm going to go educate myself...and maybe buy some furry handcuffs too."

Chapter 21

Fern

My eyes couldn't look away from the woman strapping a ball gag over the volunteer's mouth, blowing fire inches above his bare belly mere seconds later. The audience ooh'ed and ahh'ed every time the performer made fire appear over the helpless—and horny—volunteer.

I wasn't sure what distracted me more: the fire, the ball gag, or my wandering, overthinking mind.

Since Emmie was preparing her next plan of attack, I also started brainstorming who to reconnect with next. Following the first breakup with Davis, I experienced an unforeseen rebellious phase. In a way, I'd blended right in with all the other sixteen-year-olds at the time: sending dirty texts on my Motorola Razr; dying chunky, black streaks into my hair that took years to fully disappear; and drinking too much UV Blue at parties hosted by strangers. The Sisters at St. Merlin Academy definitely weren't fans of these abrupt changes. I'd been able to hide most of these antics from my parents—and even Marian most of the time—and though I grew out of this phase once college hit, those freeing emotions could never truly disappear.

Now they often switched from feelings of freedom to ones of anxiety more than I hoped they would. You'd think college would be the time when independence grows. Instead, college put me into a constant state of apprehension.

The studying. The deadlines. The random hook-ups. The early mornings.

Most of college was with imposter syndrome rather than self-discovery.

As fire breathers took a break and the trapeze artist started gliding through the air, I stepped out of the aisle and grabbed my phone from my pocket. Clicking open the My Cup app, I began nonchalantly scrolling the database. I wasn't expecting anyone from my final high school years to magically show up on the screen—I'd see their coffee mugs and café preferences before realizing who the person behind those pictures was anyway. Maybe I hoped to find someone worth reopening my inbox for, or maybe one of my exes would find *me* this time around.

I wasn't even sure if them finding me was a smart idea.

If Emmie was going through with her plan, I wouldn't give up on mine this easily.

I shoved the phone into my pocket and began walking through the aisle, stopping to look at bottles of edible massage oil and try on some plush wrist cuffs that felt way too comfortable hugging my tiny arms. Forcing my wallet further into my purse and avoiding eye contact with Emmie—who now had her hand at the small of the aerialist's back, I slipped on my peacoat and made my way toward the exit doors.

Two men stepped in front of me to deeply kiss one another in front of the exit with tote bags dangling from their wrists, people quickly walking on either side of me so that I couldn't budge. It was hard ignoring the boxes inside of their bags when words such as BED BONDAGE SYSTEM and COLLAR AND CUFF SET were screaming up at me in bright, bold lettering. As I tried to shuffle around them, the heel of my boot scuffed a damp spot on the tile, and the wall caught me before I slipped forward, face-planting into the make-out session.

"Whoa, whoa, guys. You *must* take this outside or into one of the back privacy booths," a voice said as the men's feet slid out of view and a new set of feet appeared. My eyes scaled up, and I found myself staring at someone from my past—someone who was a regular fixture during my junior year, to be exact. Isaac had blond, coifed hair, high cheekbones, and the slightest outline of ink peeking out from beneath his jacket.

My wandering, anxiety-ridden mind had brought me to the feet of the one person who had introduced me to the world of rebellion all those years ago—a world much like the one we stood in.

Just at a high school level.

What were the fucking odds?

"Holy shit," I whispered in a tone that obviously wasn't as muted as I'd hoped. Isaac clipped his radio back onto his belt where I couldn't help but get a glimpse of that tan skin I used to touch during our six-month dating stretch. Every time one of my fingertips grazed his flawless figure when I was sixteen, a searing spark dove right between my legs. He'd brought out some kind of demon hiding inside of me, just waiting to turn savage.

No wonder my parents hated him so much.

"No way. Fern?" He laughed, shaking his head and stepping back. "Wait a minute. For real?"

"I'm real, yup." For some reason, my hands had flown to my chest—cupping my boobs, to be exact—before awkwardly sliding down to my hips. Why were my anxious reactions always so embarrassing? "It's me, and you're you. I don't believe it either. I was just thinking about you, actually. Well, kind of. Not really."

That didn't sound creepy at all.

Dammit, Fern.

"I can't believe this. Come here." His giant arms encompassed me, and his fingers pressed against the small of my back, which made me release a sound mixing a giggle and a moan. "How the hell have you been?"

"I've been good. Yeah, great," I said, backing out of his grasp. "Do you work here? Or do you, like, work for Velvet or another one of these frisky businesses?" I eyed the Clone-a-Willy stand a few feet away, but this time, I kept my tongue still.

"Oh, you wish I worked for one of these businesses, don't you? Unfortunately, no. I get contracted out here often for security. I'm just working the door tonight." The smoothness of his voice at the beginning of the sentence made me almost black out. I hadn't heard a thing except for something about *contracting* and *a door*. He was sex in a security jacket—of course he would get contracted to work an event like this at Abandon. "What brought you here tonight? Just similar interests?"

"Similar interests to who, Isaac?" I raised my brow and rolled my lips together, leaning onto the wall that should have caught my fall earlier. Isaac let out a hearty laugh and ran his fingers through his hair before stepping closer.

I could watch him run his fingers through his hair all night.

Or he could pull mine.

I needed to fucking focus.

"You're still cute, you know that? You still got that weird spunk. Not that I expected you to change or anything. After all these years, it's kind of expected people will, you know?"

"You look identical to how I remember you." I eyed his wrist, and my fingers pushed up the cuff of his jacket to reveal the colorful markings. "Except you didn't have these back then."

His eyebrow lifted, his lips curling in a way that forced my thighs together. "I have more."

"I'm not surprised." The second our eyes met, our brains clicked too. I was sure his mind had already gone to *hook-up mode* rather than *date mode*, but I tried to push away that possibility—or at least save it for later. I could flirt all I wanted, but I needed to remember my end goal.

He eyed the phone peeking out from my coat pocket and slowly reached for it until the light on the screen brightened his exquisitely blue eyes. "How about I put my number in here, and you text me tomorrow."

"Are you sure I don't still have your number saved in my contacts? Maybe I've had the same phone since sophomore year."

Nope. All my original contacts were washed away during the Motorola toilet plunge of 2007.

"I'd be impressed if you still did," he said, rolling his lips together. "But I've had about three different phones over the last decade. If you have my old number, you've probably sent sexy panty pictures to some horny stranger who hasn't had the balls to admit he's not me."

I hated the word panties. "What? I have not!!"

After a chuckle and his thumb and forefinger gliding across the phone screen, Isaac handed the phone back to me. "Well, now you can."

When Benji mentioned he was going to start offering weekend brunch specials at Spellbound, which would include bottomless mimosas, Emmie and I were the first to offer ourselves up as guinea pigs. When he said the first trial run would be half price, we asked him what time he wanted us to show up.

Of course, this all seemed too good to be true. When we walked into Spellbound on Sunday morning, in our cutest brunch attire—even Emmie was clad in a sweater-dress with some cute ankle boots rather than her usual oversized sweatshirt and jeans—Oliver's face was the one to greet us.

At his sight, Emmie immediately turned to the garbage can by the door and started gagging dramatically.

"Are you surprised?" Oliver asked, chuckling as he set a tray of warm muffins on the counter. "I do work here, you know."

"But this was Benji's idea. He has way more class than you, and you need to have some class for brunch." Emmie's voice echoed through the empty space. "You're going to scare customers away."

"If anything, I'll bring more in. Just you wait and see." As he began walking back toward the kitchen, Oliver turned toward the shelves to his left, reaching for one of the drawers and wrapping his grimy little fingers around the handle. "Oh...and Emmie? You may want some of this before drinking your mimosa. I got some Imodium tucked away in here. You know, you don't want to end up—"

"Shut your fucking mouth, Oliver," Emmie shouted, adjusting her glasses to hide the crimson growing on her freckled cheeks.

It infuriated me how he used Emmie's moody digestive system to his advantage after their incident last year.

Oliver wagged his hand in front of his nose as he let go of the handle and walked backward into the kitchen. "Now *that* would scare away customers."

"Oh look! Our table!" Interlocking my arm with Emmie's, I dragged her toward our usual table and pulled the chair out for her before sliding into mine. "Menus are even here already! This was definitely Benji's hospitality."

Emmie's eyes were stuck on the kitchen entrance Oliver had walked through seconds before. "Oliver is a fucking asshole."

"Ignore him," I whispered, watching as her gaze finally broke. "He purposely tries to get under your skin every time he sees you."

"I think it's his kink. He gets turned on by tearing other people down." Emmie's eyes lifted from the menu back toward the corner bathroom. "I think our shitty bathroom breakup also turns him on in some weird way—pun intended."

"What happened between you and the aerialist on Friday?" This conversation desperately needed redirection. "When I left, you two seemed...cozy."

"I went back to her place," Emmie said, relaxing her shoulders. "We had a few more drinks and fooled around. It was innocent fun."

I waited, staring at her as I held the menu in my hands. "That's all?"

"That's all what?"

"That's all I'm getting?" I asked, setting the menu down. "Where are my dirty details? How were her boobs, or how good was she at going down on you? You always give me specifics even if I don't ask for them."

That got a laugh out of her. It was a short-lived one, but a laugh, nonetheless. "Well, her boobs are A+ in my book, and she was down there for most of the night. I'm also pretty sure she doesn't have a spine."

"There you are! I knew you were in there somewhere!" When I wildly pointed at her, my index finger almost knocked my glass of water onto the floor, save for my cat-like reflexes. For being so damn clumsy, I had an uncanny knack for catching almost-failures.

"You're hilarious, Fern." Emmie rolled her eyes, widening them when Benji walked over to our table. I ordered a strawberry mimosa, Emmie ordered a Bloody Mary, and Benji set down a complimentary muffin—one I'm sure wasn't complimentary for everyone else. Emmie dug into the warm banana-blueberry pastry with her fork as I used my index finger and thumb like the classy dame I was.

The moment Emmie opened her mouth to say something, Oliver appeared. He placed his hand on the table and slid a packet of Imodium toward Emmie's glass.

"There you go, Em," he whispered before dramatically whipping a pad of paper from his apron and turning in my direction. "Now, what meals will I be spitting in today?"

Emmie's shoulders grew just as tense as they had been several minutes before.

In the three years Emmie and I had been best friends, never had I seen someone get a rise out of her as horribly as Oliver.

I dearly hoped that when it was his turn to pay, she got him good.

Pricilla, 32

Dermatologist
Sips with WOMEN
Looking for RELATIONSHIP, MARRIAGE

Hot or Cold

I'm always up for a hot cup of coffee. If you slide a full mug in front of me, i will drink it. Whether it steaming hot or I have to microwave it five times...i'll consume it.

Sweetness

A little sugar here and a cup of bitter brew there. Both are beautiful.

With A Side Of

Confidence and a solid skincare routine.

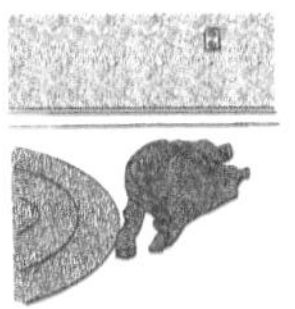

Chapter 22

EMMIE

My eyes were practically picketed behind my dark frames, absorbing every tapping foot and uncomfortable adjustment patients made in the waiting room. I made sure to sit away from the three others in the office but nearest to the door leading to the examination rooms. I wanted to dart into the back hall once my name was called and sit my sweaty ass on the thin, paper-covered cot calling my name before Cici saw me.

The thought of both my sweaty ass and the fact that I'd lay my eyes on her within minutes made my skin itch from inside the peacoat cocooned around me.

I'd never realized how coarse heavy wool felt against bare flesh until now.

"Emma Jane."

For a moment, I forgot that was the name I'd given the receptionist, and in truth, it wasn't too far off from what the insurance cards I'd given her read. I wondered how they would charge me after my visit and whether they would even question the name difference.

I also wondered if I could get this visit reimbursed, seeing as it was work-related and all.

It was a good thing Dr. Pricilla Greene rarely called me anything besides Em during our dating days. I was sure I'd never mentioned my middle name to her, and I honestly wondered if she'd ever learned my full name.

Emily. Emma. Emmerson. Ember.

They were all possibilities.

Wobbling up onto my heeled boots, I pulled the buttoned peacoat closer against me and followed the woman through the doorway and down the hallway to room 34C. I gave the room number a double-take before realizing it was, indeed, my exact bra size. I wondered if they'd purposely named the rooms after cup sizes since there definitely weren't more than seven rooms in the office. How had they possibly gotten all the way to 34C within a few steps down the hall?

Stop thinking about boobs, Em.

Think about revenge.

"Dr. Greene will be with you shortly," a Botoxed blonde, with the longest damn legs I'd ever seen, said. The second she shut the door behind her, the room began closing in around the papered cot I sat on. My throat felt thin, and my breathing tensed within my chest, my fingers fumbling with the top button of my peacoat. My dry eyes scanned the walls of the room where square, metal frames sat centrally on each of the three open walls. One frame held a black-and-white photograph of a hand, another of a chin, and the other of a shoulder.

As someone who appreciated art of every kind, my brain wasn't letting me focus enough to appreciate these body parts.

And I sure did like body parts.

A scuffle of feet outside the door shot through my ears, and I held my breath as a quick knock sounded. A muffled humming noise escaped me that I hoped sounded like a confident, wordless, "Come in," and the door clicked open. One heeled loafer slid into the room, followed by another, and my eyes scanned upward.

The high-waisted, tailored pants.

The indigo blouse dipping a bit too low.

The plump lips.

The dark, stunning skin.

I wanted to place a hand on her face and feel that stupidly soft skin against mine. I wanted her to nibble her bottom lip before her mouth covered my own.

"Emma Jane, is it?" Her voice forced my eyes to align with hers, a hand outstretched in my direction. I stared at it until registering that I needed to confidently shake it rather than shove it down my coat so her palms could caress my naked breasts. Of course, her velvety touch instantly made my hand feel clammy, and when she released her grip, she took a step back and looked down at her clipboard. Her eyes shifted from the top sheet back to my gaze, and her glorious lips twisted faintly. "Have you been a patient of mine before?"

"You could say that." The words came out soft and hoarse. "We've met."

"Have we? You must have been a patient of mine during residency. I was at St. Merlin's then."

I shook my head and smiled, leaning onto my left wrist and unbuttoning the second peacoat button with my free hand. "No, I don't think that was it. Do you recall a timid girl you met at a baseball party? Maybe you pushed aside memories of bathroom hookups and drunken sex'capades with her because—I don't know—she wasn't up to your beauty standards back then?"

The second her eyes floated up and away from her clipboard, I did everything in my power not to book it out of the room at full velocity.

Deep breaths, Emmie.

In and out.

My fingers loosened the third button and then the fourth, my right nipple peeking out as I unbuttoned the fifth. That fifth button was all it took for my bare chest to reveal itself, my fingers hovering over the final button once my soft, tan stomach was fully present.

Cici stood stiff as a board. For a medical professional who saw naked bodies on the regular, I didn't expect her cheeks to grow rosy atop her dewy dark skin or for her breathing to hitch a bit before taking a step back.

"Holy shit. *Em*?"

My peacoat fell to the floor, and I smiled subtly, stepping over the coat as my heeled boots clicked closer to Cici. With absolutely nothing but my boots on, I stood directly in front of her—directly in front of this goddess of a woman who I easily could push against the corner desk and straddle right then and there.

And dammit, I wanted to.

I ran a finger down the side of her tense jawline, outlining it gently before caressing her thick lips. "You got it."

Cici's voice was hushed, but her eyes were screaming into mine. "This...this isn't really the time or place. Could we—"

Her words vibrated against my finger. "My interrupting your little romp session with that volleyball chick probably wasn't the time or place either, right? I should *never* have just showed up and expected you'd invite me inside your dorm, huh? How foolish I was back then...catching you cheating. How rude of me."

"Wha...what? Are you seriously talking about college right now?"

My hand lowered from her lips to her neck, feeling her throat shift as she swallowed hard. My hand continued to explore lower, my palm hovering over her chest and then a fingertip sliding into the elastic hem of her waistline. This little game of touchy-feely had *not* been part of the plan, but fuck did I like it. I also hoped I wouldn't get a call from the police later for violating a medical professional. "Dr. Pricilla, is my personality still *bangin*'?"

"What?" Her vocabulary was as stiff as the nipples staring through the thin fabric of her blouse. I wouldn't allow myself to go any further with her—even with my hand gently tugging at the elastic of her trousers. I couldn't twist this into some sick form of what Fern was doing, no matter how stunning she was and how badly I wanted to rip the stupid hem of these pants off.

"My personality. When we dated, you said it was *bangin'*." I stepped back, trying not to slip on the coat by my heels. "You know what else is bangin', Cici?"

She took another hard swallow, her eyes shifting to the clock above the door before fully focusing on my lips as I spoke. I tipped the corner of my lips upward and bent one knee the slightest bit, sticking my ass into the air as I folded over to snag the coat from the ground. I slipped my arms into the sleeves with raised eyebrows, silently asking her the question again and waiting for a response other than, '*What.*'

Still, she stood silent and unmoving.

When the second-to-last button was secure, a little cleavage peeking out for wandering eyes to skim over, I walked up to face her again.

Our noses were practically touching. "No answer? Hmm...that's too bad." I reached for the door handle, twisting it but not opening it just yet. "Because my body was bangin' back then too. *That* body and *that* person was worth your time. It's too bad you didn't see my worth, Dr. Greene. You fucking missed out."

Opening the door, my heels clicked away from the room, leaving Cici to stand shocked and confused—and maybe the slightest bit horny—in room 34C.

MY CUP ⊙' JOE

Isaac, 30

Security
Sips with WOMEN
Looking for CASUAL

Hot or Cold

Hot chai latte is fine...but make it hella dirty.

Sweetness

I don't know what goes into a chai besides the espresso part...and that's not usually part of the chai. Maybe some spices? Some water? I'm cool with whatever goes into it.

With A Side Of

Submission.

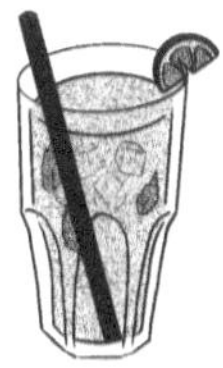

Chapter 23

FERN

It was hard convincing my feet not to wander into The Vintage Press where I could track down the latest edition of *PoisonEye* or find the next sour candy to hide behind Spike. Instead, I knocked on the metal door leading up to Isaac's apartment, which sat only a few steps away from the shop's entrance. When the door clicked, creaking open, Isaac answered in a black tank top and gray sweatpants, snagging my attention away from the swinging door at The Vintage Press.

Isaac reached for my elbow and gingerly led me up the steel stairway. "Right on time. I'm not surprised."

"Not much has changed over the years," I muttered.

His laugh was low and throaty behind me, his hand gliding to the small of my back for just a second before letting it fall. "We'll see about that."

We walked up the stairs, our feet echoing with every step, until we got to an open doorway leading into a large, open-concept loft. It wasn't fancy, by any means, but the large windows overlooking Merlin Heights and Claus Lake brought in light that made the space double in size. When the door closed behind me, zesty, citrusy scents mixed with the sting of tequila beckoned me into the kitchen where I noticed our dinners were already out of the plastic containers and set onto plates. A blender of margaritas sat next to the platters, and Isaac reached for the Jose Cuervo, twisting the top off.

"I feel like I just walked into a Mexican restaurant." I pulled a stool away from the small kitchen island and swung myself up onto it, my eyes staring at the blender while my fingers walked toward a glass beside it. Snickering, Isaac pressed the glass against my palm and wrapped his hand around it so our fingertips touched. He grabbed the pitcher with his other hand and poured some into the glass, our eyes connecting.

"It's better than a restaurant because it's just us. No wait, no crowds." He reached into the fridge for a few ice cubes he then tossed into an empty glass before lifting the bottle of tequila so it hovered above the rim.

"You're drinking straight Jose?" I asked before letting the crushed ice of the margarita cool my throat.

Well, burn was more like it.

Had he used an entire bottle of tequila for these margaritas?

After pouring himself a sufficient amount, he brought the glass to his lips and sipped. "I like getting right to the good stuff. I don't need the fluff."

"I love the fluff," I said quickly, trying to push the conversation in the opposite direction of where I sensed it was leaning. "Just like this margarita...I want *all* the fluff. Give me the blackberries and some crushed ice and an over-the-top glass! Add some sugar or salt around the rim too, while we're at it. Make it *real* fancy."

I was officially talking too much.

Isaac reached into the fridge for a single blackberry, and he walked around the island until he was directly behind me, the scent of citrus and stale cigarettes on his breath as he placed the blackberry atop my drink. Though the Newports brought back some below-par memories, his warm breath on my neck and his fingers as they trailed up my arm made those memories dissipate. His hand landed between my neck and shoulder, and he pressed softly into the sensitive skin, my head falling gently to my shoulder.

"Should we cheers to this unexpected reunion?" he whispered into my ear, a light growl in his tone. I opened my mouth to respond, but instead of words coming out, a sigh escaped my lips when I felt his teeth nibble on my earlobe.

Trying to maintain focus, I lifted my glass and plucked the blackberry off the crushed ice. Twisting away from his touch, I took the blackberry between my teeth and closed my lips around it. I realized how unsexy it would be if seeds ended up between my teeth. Hoping for the best, I grinned. "I think a cheers is a great idea."

The intimate attention felt so fucking good, but I couldn't focus on that.

I was here to rekindle the fire of once was...but through the power of conversation and margaritas—not orgasms.

Yet.

I bumped my glass against his, but before I could go in for a sip, his mouth fell over mine. Instead of tasting ice and fresh berries, I tasted tar and a tequila-coated tongue. My gag reflex abruptly jumped to life, and part of me wanted to kiss him back, but the taste was just so sickening.

I guess I could push aside the cigarette thing. I mean, I'd be a hypocrite to judge him on that since I, too, had had my run with the good ol' cancer sticks.

Did people still call them that?

But this was not my goal. My goal wasn't to add more one-night stands to my list. My goals weren't to expand my sexual knowledge. Hell, my goal wasn't even to orgasm within the first hour of a date—something I knew would happen if I stayed on this route with Isaac.

My goal was to get into a serious relationship by March.

And the gala was only a few months away.

I placed my palm on Isaac's chest, and once his tongue stopped snaking down my throat, I took in a deep, fresh breath of air. "Isaac, the food's gonna get cold. Aren't you hungry?"

"Yeah, I'm hungry." His mouth slid to my collarbone, his warm breath causing my skin to burn with goosebumps. "I'm hungry for you."

I should have seen that coming.

What I didn't expect were his hands to cup both of my thighs—they would have cupped my ass if I had something there to grab—and lift me up so I was forced to wrap my legs around his torso. His face dove into my chest, my crewneck falling low and his lips finding their way to my right nipple and then the left. He started walking, carrying me through the kitchen and into the living room.

With each step away from the wall, I questioned what the fuck I was doing.

I had to focus on what my head wanted over what my heart did—or what my lady bits wanted, in this case.

Passing his shut apartment door on the way to the living room, I wrapped my fingers around the handle and pulled him to a stop. "Isaac. Really. Why don't we just—I don't know—eat and catch up?"

"This isn't what you wanted?" He lifted his eyes, and I couldn't help but feel like, yet again, I was staring down at a kicked, depressed puppy sitting alone in a storefront window.

Why did he have to be such a beautiful jackass?

And why did I always think of sad puppies?

"I mean, yeah. Obviously, I really enjoy this. I mean, like, I *really* do." My feet finally found the floor, but his grip tightened around my waist, and he pulled me in against the firmness poking through his sweatpants. I did my best not to look down, but his mouth was back on my neck, causing my focus to blur. "But I'm not really looking for a hook-up or a one-night stand."

He stepped forward, and his lips found their way down my chest and back into my bra, his tongue flicking at a nipple before lifting his gaze. He'd found my weakness. "Well, this wouldn't really be a one-night stand, would it? It's barely nighttime, and we've hooked up many times before."

"Touché." The pleasure escalating from the quick flicks of his tongue against my hardened flesh was hard to ignore. Taking a deep, muddled breath, I twisted the door handle and pulled away from him. "I should probably just go if this is all you want."

"But I know you don't hate this." He stepped in closer as one of my feet stepped outside of the apartment and into the hallway.

My eyes couldn't help but glimpse at the massive erection pointing directly at me.

It was true what they said about gray sweatpants.

"You're right. I don't hate this," I admitted. Well, the taste and smell of his breath I despised, but he could just make out with my chest all day. I'd have been absolutely okay with that—if we'd at least talked for a solid twenty minutes before he pounced on me. "I just... I want more than this. I need more."

He leaned his waist closer, and his hardness met the fly of my jeans. "I can definitely give you more."

He pulled my hand off the door handle and placed it on the outside of his sweatpants, my palm feeling him with full force. I wasn't sure if I felt flattered or if this was leaning a little too close to sexual coercion for my liking. Before I could get further into my head, I pushed him away and slammed his apartment door behind me, racing down the echoing metal stairs and onto the sidewalk outside. The moment the heavy door slammed at my heels, I leaned my throbbing head against it with heaving breaths bruising my lungs.

Then, my eyes snapped open wide, and my heart faltered.

"Shit. Shit. Shit!" I shouted, kicking the heel of my boot against the metal door. I closed my eyes and hit the back of my head against it, waiting for my headache to turn into a bona fide anxiety attack and wake me from this mess.

"Fern?" A familiar voice forced my eyes toward the entrance of The Vintage Press. There, with one hand in his coat pocket and the other clinging to a thin paper bag, stood Chase.

"Oh, my God. Hi." My breath slowed, relaxing more into its normal rhythm—or as close to normal as I could get it to.

"Are you okay? What, uh...are you doing?" Chase asked, walking in my direction until his recognizable scent calmed me a little bit more.

Ground coffee and eucalyptus.

Breathe in, breathe out.

"Well, I was kind of on a date and left without grabbing my phone and purse." I looked over my shoulder at the closed door and then up toward the large windows where Isaac's apartment was. "I really don't want to go back up there to get it."

"Are you okay? Did he... Are you hurt?" Chase asked, his brow furrowed as he stepped closer, his gaze following mine up to the window and back.

I shook my head. "Oh, no, no. He just... We just didn't see eye-to-eye with where the date was going—or where it was starting, I guess." I took a deep breath and looked up to meet Chase's dark, worried eyes. "I didn't want to just hook up, you know?"

Chase nodded, pressing his lips together as he eyed the metal door and reached for the handle. He twisted it a couple times before squeezing the tips of his free fingers between the door and the frame right above its ancient keyhole, his stance adjusting so his legs were at a lunge. As he gave the handle another tug, he lifted the knob upward while painfully pinching his fingers into the tight space of the doorframe.

Then the door opened, throwing Chase out of his lunge so he toppled backward, his heels ending up at my toes. Before I could appropriately freak out over what he'd just done, my hands were at his waistline, trying to steady him.

Well, my hands were definitely below his waistline. If Chase wasn't the giant he was, and I wasn't such a miniature human, I probably could have steadied him in a way that didn't look like I was posing for the world's most awkward prom picture.

"Um...what the fuck was that?" I asked, stepping aside so his surprisingly cute ass wasn't in my direct line of vision. I'd never called a man's ass *cute* before—nor had I ever really noticed how well Chase's jeans hugged him the way they did.

Actually, I'd never seen Chase in anything besides the typical khaki pants and gray trousers he wore to work paired with his signature, goofy—yet work-appropriate—button-ups.

And his yearly chicken costume.

"I lived in a loft like this a few years ago—the one right at the corner of the street, actually. I still live nearby...just a few streets over now. These doors look sturdy but are way too easy to break into. They updated most of these old apartments a decade ago but ignored the door issues," Chase said, walking toward the one he'd broken into with such ease. "It's why I moved out. I wish The Vintage Press wasn't in this part of town, but at least the area is on the up with Java Jude's under construction and that Wine Thyme place up the street. Visiting my old stomping grounds isn't so bad...especially when we have sour candy competitions to prepare for."

My mouth was agape in awe. I rarely had nothing to say, but words couldn't define the fuck-fest of thoughts flooding my brain. How could he shake this off as if he hadn't just broken into someone's home—even if it was just the staircase? Could he get arrested for burglary? Holy shit, Chase was about to become a felon all to rescue my phone and purse.

When I didn't say anything, Chase walked toward the open door in front of us. "Okay, well...give me a minute."

I watched him disappear up the staircase, and everything and everyone around me became harrowingly silent as I replayed the last ten or so minutes: the emotional battle stirring inside of my head and my heart, Isaac not taking no for an answer, the door locking behind me before Chase appeared out of nowhere to heroically—and illegally—save the day. I blinked away the warmth careening up my legs, arms, torso, until finally the heat flushed my cheeks. When I lifted my hands to rub away the unnecessary emotions attacking my system at full speed, I noticed flakes of white falling from the afternoon sky.

I'd also forgotten my jacket upstairs.

Fuck.

The door opened, and Chase ducked his way back through the doorframe with a peacoat slung over his arm, a leather purse dangling off his wrist, and a cell phone in his hand. His eyes were wide, and he was laughing quietly to himself as he handed me the forgotten items, not looking me in the eye.

"Thank you, Chase. Shit. Thank you," I said. His laughter grew louder as I pushed my arms into the peacoat and placed my phone safely in the pocket. It was sad how much safer I felt knowing my phone and purse weren't lost causes. "What...what is so funny?"

Chase shook his head and looked down at his sneakers, kicking some of the snowflakes out of the way between us. "Before I barged through his door, I was worried he may stab me or call the cops because some black guy he didn't know was breaking into his place."

"I hadn't thought about that." My eyes doubled in size, and my lips twisted into an O shape. With a throaty laugh, he stepped closer so the toes of our shoes were practically touching, and his hand fell atop my shoulder.

He finally looked me in the eye and my stomach dropped. "Some black guy breaking into his apartment apparently wasn't his number one focus. His door was open, and when I walked in, he was lying on the couch with his dick out. He didn't even stop jerking off when I grabbed your things and left."

I was speechless for the second time in ten minutes.

Chase's hand gently squeezed my shoulder, and another addicting laugh fell from his lips. "Let's go grab drinks. We both need some."

Chapter 24

EMMIE

I poured myself a hefty glass of chardonnay the moment I returned to my apartment. I wasn't a huge wine fiend, but I knew falling into a glass of something felt right after escaping the Lyra Center.

Plus, I couldn't get Cici's tits out of my head.

Which was why I topped off the glass before putting it back into the fridge.

I took a sip and scrunched my nose above the rim, falling onto the couch without unbuttoning my jacket or taking off my heels. The bottle I was finishing had been Marian's during her stay a few weeks back. I peered down into the glass, remembering how Fern always told me wine lost its mojo after a week of being open.

The bitter, month-old liquid felt perfect on my tongue.

Fuck that rule.

My coat pocket vibrated, and I sloshed the sip down as I fumbled for my phone, running a thumb over the screen to see Fern's name above a message:

Interesting attempt at a date with Isaac. Just come to Thirsty Theodore's.

The next blog desperately needed to be written. I knew if I waited much longer to bring my fingers to the keyboard, the emotions currently swallowing me whole wouldn't come out as effectively. I knew Al would probably send an email any minute, asking how the venture with Dr. Greene went—a not-so-subtle nudge to send the opening paragraph his way.

I also knew if I lay here, sipping this acid and sulking for the rest of the night, I'd never make it into the office the next morning with anything of substance written.

It took me a solid ten minutes to get my ass off the couch and an extra five minutes attempting to finish the wine before I stuck the half-empty glass in the fridge and texted Fern back to let her know I was on my way.

To my surprise, Chase sat next to Fern at the bar, holding a frosted glass between his two massive hands. Though I didn't directly work with the guy, I always poked fun at his towering size or his endearing dress shirts. He was one of five men who worked in the IT department at the Merlin Heights My Cup office and the only one who had a sense of humor—and a good one, at that. I would call him a name in passing, and he would joke about a point I made in my most recent blog, proving he was one of the few employees who actually read the damn things.

Though I now expected him to read the shit I wrote, I didn't expect to see him at Thirsty Theodore's.

"Look at this. It's the *BFG* and *FernGully* throwin' back some booze," I snickered, swinging myself onto the stool beside Fern.

"What does BFG stand for this time, Em? *Belligerent? Bodacious? Black* Friendly Giant?" Chase joked.

"Don't pull the race card, Chase. Two can play that game," I said, spinning back and forth on the stool. "It stands for *Bilingual* Friendly Giant this time. I hear you speak Spanish on the phone on a weekly basis."

Chase nodded, raising his eyebrows. "Those advanced classes in high school apparently were worth it."

Waving down the bartender and asking for whatever Chase was drinking, my peripheral vision caught Fern angrily finishing off her glass. When my beer was set in front of me, I paid for a second of whatever had been in Fern's glass.

She looked like a squished bug struggling to fly.

"So, what happened?" I asked, creating zig-zag shapes in the frost on my mug with my index finger.

Fern practically fell off her stool when the question was asked—as if she hadn't expected it. "With what? With, like, tonight?"

"What else would I be talking about?" My eyelids were low and voice monotone. She turned to look at Chase and then at the full cocktail being set in front of her.

"Oh, well... I guess it got a little too frisky too fast, and I wasn't there for that."

Chase snorted into his mug as his head fell back with a swig. "That's a good way to put it."

"Okay. Back up." I leaned my chest against the bar and squinted when Chase's smile widened under the dim lights. He was in on some secret before I was, and I did not like it. "How did *you* get involved in Fern's dilemma?"

"I was searching for our next sour candy competitor—and a comic book for myself—when I saw this little one beating up a door down the street." He tapped his fingers against the bar, shaking his head. "I went up to this Isaac guy's apartment to grab Fern's bag and saw him jerking off."

"Whoa. That escalated." A dark, caramel stout hit my palette, and I took a much longer sip than expected. Chase had great taste in beer. "I'm sure you didn't expect to see a dick tonight, but I didn't expect Fern to turn Isaac down either. That's the real shocker."

Fern finally turned toward me with her jaw dropped dramatically. "Excuse me, but I don't open my legs on every first date I go on."

I lowered my eyelids and stared at her. "Even if it's a re-date?"

"Yes...*and* even for someone who was once a sex god," Fern said, throwing her arms into the air. "Either way, he was pressuring me. It wasn't safe. So, he's off the list."

"I'm missing something," Chase added, flagging down the bartender for a necessary refill. At the rate the three of us were going, Chase would be joining us at Spellbound Beans in the morning to remotely work through a nasty hangover.

Leaning forward to peer around Fern as she anxiously hovered above her glass, I pushed a toothy grin toward Chase. "Yeah...this one is re-dating her exes. The guy's wiener you saw isn't a new piece of meat for Fern."

"After a decade, an old wiener is practically a new wiener!" Fern's squeaky voice caught the bartenders by surprise, their lips twisting into amused grins before going back to mixing drinks and overhearing other, much-less-interesting conversations.

"I feel like I heard something about this from someone in the office." Chase lifted his eyebrows and leaned away from Fern with a playful nod. "Well, well. Look at little Fern stepping out of her comfort zone. You're becoming a brand-new woman!"

Fern shook her head so fast that her burgundy hair practically slapped her in the face. "No, no. I'm still just me. My plan is to give people second chances and see if things work out this time around. That initial awkward phase isn't as—I don't know—awkward this time around when it comes to conversation, you know? Less nerves and more getting to the point."

"Your awkward phase hasn't disappeared, Fern." My voice came out hushed and monotone. "And from the story you guys are telling me, Isaac was getting right to the point. Or at least what he thought the point was."

Fern shrugged, sipping timidly from her glass. "I mean, I was just trying to keep tonight casual, you know? Go slow. I'm such a sucker for cute conversation and fluffy dates, but if I want something to work long-term, I can't really wait around for the fluff anymore. Right?"

"Isn't fluff what makes dating fun, though?" Chase added, sliding his glass from giant palm to giant palm as his eyes followed the movement. "All the flirting and unexpected handholding and all the little things that go into asking someone on a date. Isn't that supposed to be the fun part? That's what creates the spark everyone wants to feel. I mean, isn't that spark what makes something organic happen?"

Fern stared at Chase for a moment, and I could tell her brain was calculating every word he was saying and every expression painting his face. Fern usually took every word she heard either too close to heart or in a way that was far off the beaten path. This time, I wasn't sure how she was absorbing this.

In a way, I hoped she would let it crash around inside her skull a little bit.

His words were definitely crashing around in mine.

Chapter 25

FERN

Christmas came and went with the usual lineup of events. I forced myself through morning mass, watched my father preach to an enthusiastic crowd drunk on too much holiday spirit, and listened to Marian play with Thea and the Thunderclouds while my mother pressed back proud tears. After mingling with a few parishioners who asked way too many questions and begged me to join their weekly book club—something I half-considered—I snuck out and made it back to my apartment, where my body collapsed onto the sofa.

Slumping into the blankets with Loaf and Porridge warming my ankles, I looked at the lone bat and wheel I hadn't thrown clay on in weeks. It sat against the back wall beside the forest of pothos, spider, and monstera plants I'd somehow kept alive during the months I'd focused on men more than myself or my plants.

Even Legs, my beloved spider plant, looked a little limp.

Was that really what I was doing?

Making a relationship succeed meant I was working on myself in a way too. Right? I was bettering my social, emotional, and sexual well-being so I could stride into a lasting relationship that would actually mean something. I was trying to find something—someone—concrete. Someone who, by the My Cup Gala, would walk by my side with sparks in his eyes.

Sparks. Chase said I shouldn't skip the sparks but savor them instead. He made it seem like I needed to take a step back and rewire my approach.

Since listening to him at the bar, I actually was rethinking it all.

Well, overthinking was probably more like it.

I lived for those romantic scenes every holiday rom-com had and the cliché pickup lines that made Emmie gag. My chest grew warm just thinking of someone kissing my cheek after a first date, the feel of their soft lips lingering on my skin for an extra second longer than expected. Though I loved being pushed against brick walls, carried up the stairs, and thrown onto a bed, that first time holding hands gave me similar goosebumps like sex did.

Why was I pushing aside the sparks when those feelings brought me so much joy?

Ignoring emotions I dreamed about just to get right to the relationship didn't make sense anymore. I was starting to wonder if this plan had made sense in the first place or if my brain had been on autopilot during my emotional, drunken stupor at the reunion. If I wanted a relationship that would last, I needed to feel something real—not something forced. My heart needed to bruise the inside of my chest when someone's fingers laced mine. Genuine laughter needed to pull at my heartstrings, leaving my eyes damp as someone laughed just as hard beside me. I wanted the heat and the lust, yes, but I needed to feel the purity of those initial sparks and butterflies first.

Everyone deserved sparks.

I tapped my phone, and the screen lit up, my eyes squinting as I searched My Cup for the final name on my list.

The final person.

The grand finale.

My last hope at second chances.

3, 2, 1...and there she was.

Emmie's Monday morning knocks were right on time. She didn't knock on my door every single morning before work, but I knew this morning would be different. I knew the second she saw the reactions and shares and comments regarding *Expresso with Emmie—The Cheater Chase: Looking Good Naked*, her brain would shoot through the top of her head.

Instead, she shot into my apartment at lightning speed, slamming the door behind her as if a serial killer was chasing her. She twisted on her heel and ran gloved hands over her frizzy bedhead, breathing quick as her eyes hit mine like laser beams. From the looks of it, she was going into the office today wearing, what seemed to be, pajamas.

No. They definitely were.

"Holy shit. Just...fuck." Emmie walked in a circle around herself before rushing her hands back into her hair. No wonder her curls were fluffier than usual. She probably hadn't stopped touching them since waking up to all the notifications.

I jostled around her and smiled by the Keurig. "There are Espresso Strong and Bright and Bold pods."

"Both. Combine them. Rip open the pods and pour the grounds into my mouth."

"Oh, the drama." I popped an Espresso Strong into the machine and listened to it rumble to life as I slipped one of my many travel mugs beneath the machine. Though she wasn't a fan of my sticker addiction, this mug was covered in vinyl stickers of cats dressed as garden gnomes that she'd just have to deal with.

Or learn to love them.

Emmie whipped her phone to the front of her face, struggling to swipe across the screen with her gloved hand. "I quote: *'Emmie, you go, girl!'* First of all, do people really still say that? Didn't that phrase stop being cool when we graduated high school?"

"It definitely stopped before we graduated. But alas, we still say *cool*, so what do we know?" The Keurig began spitting out the few last drops, and I reached for the cover, twisting it on tight. "Keep reading."

"Okay, okay. *'I'm so glad you showed her who's boss. You're the boss of your body, and now, I'm going to be the boss of mine and pull a Naked WoMan on my ex too. He'll never see it coming.'*"

"That's a play on that *How I Met Your Mother* episode, right? The Naked Man?"

Emmie's eyes thinned and remained locked on mine, her thumb scrolling. "This one says: *'Yaaaaas, queen! Dr. Greene deserved this for the shit she put you through! Karma is a mighty fine bitch.'*"

I felt a lump form in my throat as I handed over the travel mug, knowing exactly why that quote was making her eyes double in size. "At least she didn't say *you go, girl.*"

"How the hell did this person know it was Cici? I purposely code the names in my blogs to keep identities safe. Well, besides Manny...his blog title made it a little obvious. I may be a bitch, but I'm only trying to save my job—not ruin all of theirs."

"How far down is that comment?"

Emmie scrolled a little further before bringing the phone closer to her glasses. "Two hundred and three."

"I think you're safe if that's the only one throwing her name around," I said.

"But how did that person find out?"

"Maybe she's another one of her exes, and she connected the dots. She connected the dots as she connected with your writing on a personal level! Isn't that kind of, well, the point? To make readers feel like they're not alone? Feel seen?" I walked back toward the apartment door, twisting the handle and pushing it open. With slumped shoulders inside an obviously unwashed sweatshirt, Emmie followed, and I locked the door behind us.

"Maybe my Grinch-sized heart is growing or something. I guess I care more about these assholes than I thought," Emmie said softly.

"But it feels so good too, right?" I asked, rapidly lifting and lowering my eyebrows—a movement I'd never truly perfected.

"Holy shit, it feels *so* good."

Pouting my bottom lip and leaning in toward Emmie, I rubbed her shoulder playfully. "You don't have a heart. I knew it really wasn't growing in size."

Emmie flailed both of her hands in my direction, leaning away and soaking sneakered feet into snow alongside the sidewalk. I shook my head, laughing at how ridiculous she looked carrying a stickered coffee mug while trekking through feet of snow in sweatpants and Reeboks circa 2001.

Reaching into my coat pocket, I slid a gloved finger across the screen and clicked onto the My Cup app. DJ's profile stared up at me. He was the final ex and my final chance. I didn't want to throw my own anxieties at her about our upcoming date when she was already drowning in her own. Helping her took priority—especially when her unkept emotions overpowered any hidden urge she had to shower.

Even as Emmie huffed and puffed beside me, I couldn't stop staring at DJ's profile now that I'd gotten beyond his initial coffee page. Nostalgia bit down on my heart. It was like a song you hadn't heard in years but still knew every word to. His expressions, his stance, his attire. It all threw me back into a whirlwind of fading memories I was ready to breathe new life into.

The red hair he'd shocked me with on our first date a couple years ago now leaned more toward a burnt auburn hue that matched a well-trimmed beard falling just below his chin. His frame was thinner, his shoulders maybe even a little broader, but his smile hadn't changed one bit.

That smile could steal hearts.

I planned for it to steal mine.

For the second, and final, time.

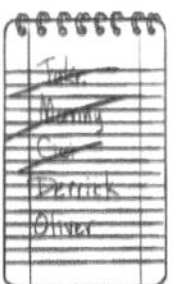

Chapter 26

Emmie

"**I** think a round of applause is in order for both Emmie and Izzy on their impressive rankings over the last few months." Al lifted his hands into the air, blocking his awkwardly shaped goatee with plump palms slamming together. I rolled my eyes at Izzy who stood next to Kyle, both returning the irritated gesture. "However, this doesn't mean we should lose this energy. Corporate is still *very* much pushing toward podcasts. The gala is in less than two months, and if we want to impress the shorts off those guys, we have to *all* spill the beans on a regular basis."

No one laughed.

Crickets made less noise.

"What if some of us caved and just started podcasting? Would they be okay with keeping, like, Emmie, Izzy, and Kyle for content since they always rank?" Melanie asked, adjusting her glasses before repeatedly wrapping a finger around her braided hair. "I'd be okay trying out the podcast trend."

Quiet little Melanie taking charge of a microphone? I couldn't see it.

Judging from Kyle's wide-eyed gaze, neither could he.

"That's something we could discuss come March." Al scratched his fuzzy chin before adjusting his weight onto the opposite foot. "Actually, raise a hand if you'd be okay trialing podcast content."

Four hesitant hands lifted into the air, each one making my throat grow tighter as their fingers stretched upward.

"Okay, okay. We can work with this," Al said, placing both of his hands flat on the desk. "Those who showed interest, stay. The rest of you, great work. Keep it up, and get out of here."

My feet raced to the door the second the last syllable was said. Though I tried to ignore the sweaty forefinger as it tapped my shoulder, I turned to face Al.

I never got out of these meetings without some form of unwanted one-on-one.

"I know, I know. You want me to keep spilling the beans and ranking until the gala. I'll keep up the mediocre work." Again, I tried to escape as he added his middle finger and thumb to the sweaty mix on my shoulder.

"You ranked first for clicks within the first hour, Emmie. That's phenomenal."

I turned to face the man who had just called me *phenomenal*. Well, he'd called my work phenomenal. I buried the compliment somewhere close enough to yank out when the content team was asked to switch to podcasting—a fear that never stopped lingering. "Thanks."

Another step toward the hallway. Another fail.

"Corporate asked me to choose someone to speak at the gala. You know, talk about why working for My Cup changes relationships, you know, for the better. They want someone from Merlin Heights to do it since we're the founding office," Al whispered, nodding over his shoulder at four co-workers willing to give up their passion just to keep their below-average hourly wage. I guess maybe they didn't have the same drive I did. Maybe they *only* cared about the paycheck, like most millennials did. I guess I was an exception—another badge I wasn't used to wearing. "Three people give speeches. They said if we want to keep some of the bloggers, then one of ours should speak. That's you."

"Are you asking me or telling me to speak at this thing?" I didn't need to get onto my tiptoes to look over Al's shoulder. I could easily see Howie struggling to stand behind Melanie, his eyes slowly shutting as the four of them impatiently waited. Stepping closer to Al and nodding my head toward the sluggish bloggers, I whispered, "Um...they're all waiting to hear about their next big break. You should probably tend to them."

"I need an answer, Emmie. Will you speak?"

I shuffled slightly toward the door, one foot comfortably in the hallway while the other stood in an inferno. "Yeah. I'll do it."

Finally, he let me free.

But I didn't feel free. I felt caged. Manipulated. Proud. Terrified. Anxious.

I was an emotional wreck.

I practically jogged down the hall and around the corner to where my desk was, my leather swivel chair looking more glorious than ever. I collapsed into it, already feeling the sweat seeping through my jeans sticking to the seat. Pinching the side of my glasses, I closed my eyes and set the frames on the desk before taking a deep breath. I rarely allowed myself to fall into some sort of meditative state, but now it was absolutely necessary.

Maybe I could sneak into Najma's office and hug her salt lamp for a little while.

I never thought I'd return to a microphone after Jeremy Boone started to chant, "Mixed M&M," during the ninth-grade spelling bee. If it weren't for his acne-ridden crew of soccer players joining him with his little ditty, I would have won.

Was I still bitter? Yes. Was I still annoyed with being called that stupid fucking name? No. I'd moved beyond that. My confidence was at a height I hoped would never fall. I'd worked too hard to get my physical and mental self to the place I was at, and I wasn't going to let a few silly memories tear me down.

Running my palm across my desk to find my glasses, I perched them back on my nose and widened my eyes. I twisted the chair to face the monitor with my body still slouched into the leather, clicking the mouse as the screen came to life. My *Cheater Chase* spreadsheet appeared, and my heart nudged my ribcage when the next name came into view.

Derrick.

He'd almost been the one to keep me monogamous. He'd almost been the one to convince me a diamond was what I wanted. He'd *almost* helped me see a mother figure in the mirror when I'd always seen some chubby, mixed woman who wanted nothing more than a life of freedom and independence.

He'd almost been the one.

Almost.

"Just give me the damn coffee, Oliver." I grabbed the mason jar in front of me that was filled with unnecessary tips and lifted it in front of his face. "I'll dump this. Pennies will fly."

Oliver snickered, his eyes barely lifting from his phone's screen. "Holy shit, what's got your panties in a bunch?"

I could have vomited. I did a little bit but sucked it back down along with the overused cliché. "Never talk about my underwear. Just give me my drink. I have shit to do."

"You used to like it when I talked about them," Oliver whispered before nodding toward the back corner of the coffee shop. "And I don't need to show you where you can go if you have *shit* to do."

I was going to kill him.

I would be locked away for murder before I started writing my damn gala speech.

I reached into the jar and threw a handful of pennies at Oliver's face before slamming the jar on the counter and turning on my heel. I strode by Joan—the middle-aged accountant who sat at the table next to us every Friday—who now clapped slowly with an approving nod. It wasn't surprising to see Fern also clapping when I sat down across from her.

"Whoa," she said, looking over my shoulder to see Oliver casually tossing pennies into the jar with a sadistic grin. "I haven't seen you get that mad at him since you guys broke up."

"And I wasn't even mean to him when we did. I wish I had been." I turned casually to watch Oliver as he picked up the remaining pennies before finally making his way to the drip coffee.

I just wanted my fucking coffee.

Taking a deep breath, I watched Fern's eyes return to her phone screen. "So, you have a date tonight, huh?"

"Yeah. We've been texting all week, and it's been...well, kind of great." Fern pushed the phone away and sat back against the booth, her arms crossing over her chest to hide a heavy sigh. "I'm trying not to get too excited. I'll just stick to being mildly hopeful."

"Mildly hopeful is appropriate. Do you think this guy will whip his dick out and start jerking off right after you leave too?"

Oliver practically threw my mug on the table, hot liquid pouncing through the air and onto my sweater. He leaned his elbow onto the table and set his chin on top of his fist, fluttering his eyelashes in the most obscene way. "So, your next blog is about porn, huh? Is the next ex a porn star?"

"You know nothing of her blogs, Oliver," Fern spat, pointing over my shoulder toward the counter. "She needs napkins. Go get her some. Rude."

"You don't think I've been following this little *Cheater Chase* Emmie's been on?" Oliver started walking back to the counter, slowly pulling napkins out one by one as my spine turned to ice. "Since that video went viral, I had no choice but to subscribe. Em, you sure got a knack for screwing people over. Or maybe you just have a knack for screwing all the right people."

I wrapped both of my palms around the mug and lifted it to my lips, the burn numbing my taste buds as a few customers looked in our direction. Oliver's voice was too vile to be ignored by anyone in his vicinity. I wanted to throw the boiling brew between my palms over Joan's head, nailing Oliver smack in the chest.

The act would excite that little dick of his too much.

It wasn't worth the entertainment.

I finally lifted my gaze to looked at Fern once Oliver decided to shut his mouth, and I decided I didn't have the energy to keep this petty conversation going. Fern's fingers were jackhammering away on the screen of her phone with such speed that she was growing out of breath.

"I've never seen your fingers move that fast," I said. "And your eyeballs are practically climbing into your skull."

Fern scrunched her little nose, rolling her eyes and setting the phone down. "I'm fine. My eyes are fine. My face is fine."

"Now you're looking at me like I'm on my period without espresso or Advil."

Fern's eyebrows lifted even higher. "Well, are you?"

"Advil plus espresso is the only cure for this uterus pain." I shifted my gaze to her leather work bag. "Give me the goods."

Without a second of hesitation, Fern reached into her bag with one hand to retrieve a travel-size bottle. Twisting off the top, I popped two tablets into my mouth followed by a long, hot sip.

"It's pretty messed up that I know your cycle," Fern said, slipping to bottle back into her bag before her fingertips returned to her phone.

She had yet to touch her tablet.

"It's pretty messed up that I still have a cycle after being on the damn shot for three years. My body is broken." I reached across the table and set my hand over Fern's bouncing fingers. She slowly looked up from her screen, but her fingers continued to type as her eyes hit mine. "Stop. The date will be fine."

"Oh, I know it will be. It'll be great." Fern shrugged as she began scanning the room, pupils shimmying over Joan's table and Oliver's pathetic tip jar. "Well, maybe not *great*. It'll be average at best."

"If you don't rekindle something, at least you'll make a memory." I lifted my hand from hers and threw both of mine into the air with an echoing snicker. "I mean, hell. Isn't that what we've been doing over all these stupid months? If anything, we're making memories we can look back at, laugh about, and maybe learn from. We're covering up some bad memories with a few...well, average ones."

Fern nodded, her gaze returning from its trek through an unusually quiet Spellbound. "We can make a few great memories while we're at it too, though. Why waste our time, you know?"

Lifting my mug into the air, Fern brought her lukewarm latte to meet mine with a dull clink. "There's that positive attitude I adore."

And if there was a God, he or she or they knew I'd need every ounce of positivity out there to get me through the night ahead.

MY CUP O' JOE
@JavaGinger_DJ
ESPRESSNO
STIR & COME BACK
LET'S BREW IT
DJ, 34
Teacher
Sips with WOMEN
Looking for RELATIONSHIP
Hot or Cold
I used to be a self-proclaimed hot coffee aficionado...
but then I discovered the hype around cold brew. Now
I drink three cold brews a day.
Sweetness
Some days, I like it black. Some days, I need every
ounce of sugar I can get. Either way, I'm drinking it.
With A Side Of
Video games, ceramics, and another cold brew...
because I officially have a problem.

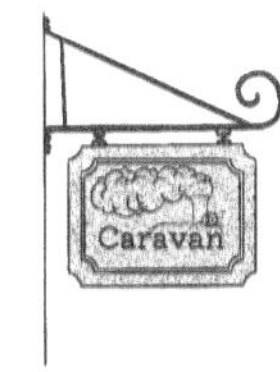

Chapter 27

FERN

This date would be the final attempt at this little experiment we'd concocted. If DJ and I didn't click, I'd be back to square one. I'd be back to disappointing my parents by being a single twenty-seven-year-old without a serious boyfriend in tow. I'd push aside the white picket fence paintings pinned to my eyelids since middle school for a little while longer. I'd force myself to stop searching for someone special and just hope someone special found me.

In all honesty, that didn't sound all too bad right about now.

Well, besides the disappointment part.

And the waiting.

"Stop. He's going to text you in, like, two minutes," Emmie spat, switching out her dragon slippers for heeled, suede boots. I hadn't asked her much about the cheater she was next to face, but from the looks of it, she was going to make the meeting short, sweet, and sexy as hell. Her lips were blood red and the upper edges of her eyes had tiny, false eyelashes glued to them. Her high-waisted skirt ended right below perfectly propped and perky boobs, where an inch of tan skin met her red, cropped sweater.

Wherever she was going, heads were going to turn.

"I know, I know. I'm nervous." My shoulders bounced up and down playfully as I leaned forward against the counter, the plastic edge biting into my chest. "Just a little."

"I can't tell." Emmie looked over her shoulder as she walked toward the peacoat hanging near the door, and a grin took over her ruby lips. "Stop pressuring yourself. I'm so done with all this pressure. After I do this thing, I'll meet you out for drinks. Where will you be?"

"He said we're going to the place he works at part-time because he can get us a good table. He's picking me up in a few minutes." My eyelids flew open, and my spine straightened. "Maybe it's a club. Holy shit, what if it's a club? I can't wear flats to a *club*."

Setting the peacoat over the side of the sofa, Emmie dramatically placed her palm over her chest. "You didn't stalk this place out or ask him more about the location in your texts? Fern, who are you?"

"I'm trying to take it slow, remember? I need to stop being so reactive and clingy." My phone vibrated, my hand pausing it before a second text could tremble the countertop. "Okay, okay. He's here. I'll text you where we are later if you want to meet us after your next attack."

Emmie saluted in my direction before slipping herself through the arms of her peacoat. "Good luck. And please, just take a deep breath. I hate telling people to relax, and people hate hearing it, but try to. Just a little."

"That's not in my genetic makeup," I shouted, the door shutting behind me and forcing my legs to shift forward. My feet fell over the staircase like concrete, and when I sunk onto the bottom step right before the front door to our building, I closed my eyes. I inhaled deeply and then released the anxieties pinching my throat shut.

Again, I breathed in and out.

One more time.

Opening my eyes, I pushed through the doors into the late-winter chill, where a light wall of snow was building between me and DJ, who stood only a few feet away, leaning against a scarlet Nissan. I couldn't help my lips from twisting into a grin as my feet left prints in the fresh dust behind me.

I was seeing red.

If this was a sign, my body was ignoring it.

My heart was, yet again, taking the lead on this one.

"I'm sensing a theme," I said, pulling the edges of the knit hat I was wearing that barely covered the tips of my ears, loose strands of burgundy falling out below. He stepped back, reaching up to adjust a similar style winter hat that also showcased the tiniest bit of auburn hair peeking out from beneath.

"I like this theme." His voice had a hint of gravel to it, roughening up the last syllable of each word. It was a voice I hadn't heard in over a year, but one that immediately caused memories to reappear with every blink.

In all honesty, we'd barely dated. Our fling lasted off and on for three months—four months at most. We'd gone out to dinner a few times and hooked up routinely after. He'd made me breakfast in bed when I had a sinus infection and had even gone as far as to stock my cabinets with nasal spray and Mucinex. When I visited my parents one weekend, he made sure Porridge and Loaf didn't go hungry and even cleaned their litter box.

Twice.

That was something even Emmie avoided at all costs.

A year and a half ago, he'd been traveling often for work as a tutor, visiting city schools who needed additional support. Though he'd been uncertain whether to jump into a concrete relationship or explore the world, DJ had left a concrete imprint on my world at the time.

It seemed worth revisiting how those imprints felt on my heart.

"Wait... are you still tutoring, or did you totally switch gears and become a chef?" I asked, his Rogue turning off as I squinted through the fast-falling snow to read Caravan sculpted into the sign dangling by the front door.

"I'm teaching science part-time at Merlin Middle School, actually. I stopped doing the traveling tutor program about six months ago." DJ closed the car door behind me, his hand quickly finding my waist as he led me to the sidewalk. "I barback here a few weekends a month. My dad's best friend owns the place."

"Your dad's best friend *owns* this bar?" The heavy door would have crushed my forehead if DJ hadn't gently pushed me through the entrance. "Like...they owned the train this bar was built inside of?"

DJ laughed with a shrug, warmth filling his freckled cheeks. "I'm not entirely sure. All I know is they bought the train car and were the ones who made it into a bar. Maybe they owned the train too. I really don't know."

"Let's just pretend you're friends with a family of famous train conductors," I giggled, DJ stepping in front of me to lead us to a large corner booth situated up on a small platform. I stepped up the three stairs and slid onto crimson velvet cushions, running my hand across the satisfying fabric and watching as DJ removed his jacket. "I'm sure they have to be careful sharing their fortune with you on weekends, being that they're world-renowned conductors and all."

My winking attempt made an eyelash jab my pupil, and I couldn't hide the mortifying expressions as I reached for the cocktail list.

Why had I put on that new mascara?

"You've never been here before? It's one of the oldest bars in Merlin," DJ said.

Leaning away as I angrily plucked my eyelashes, I tried to scan the menu. "I haven't...no. Is that weird since I've lived here pretty much my whole life?"

I felt DJ's knee brush mine below the table, and I looked away from the menu to meet his gaze. "Maybe you just don't get out enough."

"You think so, huh? Well, then I guess it was about time something like this happened. It's been, what, almost two years since we saw each other?" I wagged my index finger between us before pointing it toward the top of the menu. "I think I'm going with the pomegranate mojito. I like those cute little arils."

"Ariels?" DJ leaned forward to look over the edge of the menu. "I didn't know they put baby mermaids in mojitos."

"Um, aren't *you* the teacher, Mr. Jackson?" I asked, dramatically scoffing before handing over the menu. Thank goodness he was a barback and not a bartender. "Arils are pomegranate seeds. Although, baby mermaids would be cute swimming around in there."

"But then you'd have to drink them," DJ said, his face emotionless.

My eyes widened before I saw him snicker from behind the menu. For a moment, I really thought we were having a serious conversation about mermaid cannibalism. Thankfully, he still understood my odd sense of humor—something most people didn't. "I'd rather drink fairies."

DJ set the menu down and intertwined his fingers together, his knee brushing mine again. "Because then you'd gain their magic. Right?"

"Precisely," I said with a confident nod as the waitress appeared at our booth.

As strange as our conversation sounded, and as atrocious as my twenty-dollar mascara was behaving, I felt pressure free itself from my shoulders the moment our drinks were ordered. More pressure released when DJ brought more mythical creatures into the discussion.

The more we talked and the more we laughed, I felt vines of hope weaving around within my chest.

Maybe, just maybe, he would be the one to stay.

Chapter 28

Emmie

It was fucking cold.

I was pretty sure my nipples were cutting through the fabric of my sweater.

Mean Girls 2.0.

With falling snow causing my curls to instantly frizz before I even caught a glimpse of Derrick, the night was not off to a good start. With Merlin Heights being one of the coldest towns in the Finger Lakes region, we knew winter better than anyone else. We were used to extended winters, short summers, and falls we wished would never end.

My eyes shifted from my soaked boots up to the door of the quaint building set back slightly from the sidewalk. There was a little cobblestone path leading to the front doors, and when I read the sign dangling beside them, I hauled my frozen body toward it. With a gloved hand wrapped around the handle, I straightened my spine and inhaled deeply.

This was just like any other time.

Get in, get out, meet Fern for drinks.

So what if he's the only person I've ever been in love with?

Don't let that matter. Don't let those emotions in.

With thousands of thoughts numbing my brain, I took one last deep breath before yanking open the door.

Chapter 29

Fern

It only took another mojito for our discussion to go from giddy mentions of fairies to realizing we'd both attended the same ceramics convention in New York City not long after our breakup. We both raved about Blake Foltz, a vinyl sticker artist with an award-winning Dungeons & Dragons podcast. Clicking our glasses together, we promised to get together after the next episode released later that week.

My stomach was twisting into knots from the ease of it all.

The knots tightened every time his knee skimmed mine or he placed his hand over my own—something that had already happened three times.

If the knots grew any tighter, I feared the game my emotions would play.

A cool wind hit my cheek as the door to Caravan swung open, a flurry of white crawling onto the rug. Shifting my weight a little so I could see around DJ, I immediately recognized the peacoat and suede boots shuffling across the entrance mat. Lifting my hand to wave, I looked toward the clock above the main entrance.

DJ and I had barely been sitting there for an hour.

I hadn't expected Emmie to meet us for drinks just yet—maybe once our date had at least hit the halfway point, but not now. I hadn't even texted her the name of the restaurant we were at.

"Hey, Em!" I shouted, my voice catching in the back of my throat as my hand waved quicker, and DJ turned to look over his shoulder. "I'd told my friend I'd meet up with her later, but I didn't expect—"

"Emmaline?" DJ's voice was soft. It was a tone I'd only heard a few times during our relationship. I'd heard it when he'd spoken of his father's passing. I'd heard it before he told me his traveling tutor job was going cross-country instead of statewide as expected. I'd heard it when he'd kiss me below my ear, heating it up with hushed words that created a wildfire within me.

His tone took me by surprise, but what shook me even more was the look on Emmie's face when her eyes met his.

No, when her eyes met mine.

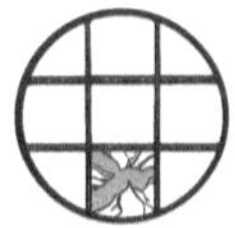

Chapter 30

Emmie

I'd planned to walk in, find Derrick talking to some bimbo, and dramatically break his cocktail glass on the floor. That glass would be the *break* we'd supposedly been on when I found out he was seeing someone else a week after the *supposed break* had started. That glass would symbolize how my heart had felt for weeks, months after the break transitioned into a break-up. Those little shards of fucking glass would be the pain I had felt as I numbly hooked up with strangers for months after, until realizing I was better than every shard of fucking glass turning my heart to shreds.

I'd finally put those pieces back together to create one hell of a woman standing in front of Derrick. Even though I knew, and believed, I was now one hell of a woman, I couldn't help but choke down the idea of Fern being Derrick's *other woman*.

"Emmaline?"

The sound of him saying my name—my whole name—gave me goosebumps I was sure Fern could see. I stood merely feet away from the booth they sat in, snow melting inside my boots. I wanted to hide inside my damp socks before I began sinking further into the puddle I was creating on the restaurant floor. Every second passing without my saying a word made me realize I actually was sinking.

Fast.

"Oh my gosh, you guys know each—" And just like that, Fern's eyes blinked open wider, doubling in size. Her mauve lips hung open slightly as she looked from Derrick, to me, and then back to meet the bearded, freckled face stunned before us.

Had she touched every one of his freckles too?

Had she run her fingers through his beard, joking about the tiny strands of silver coming out to play?

Had he told her how beautiful she looked when the morning sun created a radiant beam across her face?

The deep breath I took pained my chest. "When did you guys date?"

Derrick laughed and adjusted himself so he was facing away from Fern, squaring his shoulders in my direction. "Fern and I? It was a long time ago, Liney."

Pretend he didn't use the nickname.

Pretend you didn't hear a fucking thing.

"Not *you*, Derrick." I stepped closer to their table, placing my body so it stood directly in front of Fern's tiny, slumped frame. I hated how my fists immediately found my hips and how I pressed my chest out as if the fire burning inside could be seen. I didn't want to lean onto one leg and press my lips together, but my body and mind were nowhere near in sync. My eyes locked on Fern, and I watched as she swallowed down the boulder lodged in her throat. "When did you two date?"

"Um…not too long ago, I guess." She turned away from my intent stare, swallowing and forcing out a slight smile in Derrick's direction. "Right?"

"Fern, just fucking say it." I placed my gloved hands down on the top of their table, leaning in toward my best friend—my co-worker, my neighbor, my non-biological sister—as the ice in their glasses shook.

"We dated less than two years ago." She was staring at the mojito squeezed between her palms, eyes trembling as the pieces of the puzzle clicked together. Though her eyes switched back to meet mine, her frame didn't falter. She was trying so damn hard to stay strong. "But it was *so* casual. DJ was traveling, and we just hung out a few times before he left. We both know this all happened *years* ago, Em. We can't let this get in our way now."

We'd both purposely brought the past into our present.

We both purposely wanted it to get in the way of our lives now.

Why else would we have locked ourselves into this rollercoaster zigzagging around cheaters and exes and everyone in-between?

I leaned onto one arm so my angry, icy nipples practically pressed into Derrick's eyeballs. I still needed to play with that pretty little brain of his to some capacity…even if it pained every bone in my body to do so. "Really, *DJ?* You just needed something casual before leaving? Even less than a week after our initial chat about taking a break?" I stepped back, slapping my leg and letting my head fall back with echoing laughter. "And the irony of you going back to your college nickname brings forth a whole new set of questions, I must say."

Fern's spine straightened as she leaned across the table toward Derrick. "You said you and your ex broke up because of your job." Fern turned to face me, her hands flat on either side of her drink. "And what nickname?"

"You call this bastard DJ, and I call him Derrick. His name is Derrick Jackson, as I'm sure you know. This is probably why we never thought twice over the last few months when throwing names around," I said. "But I don't remember us mentioning him. Obviously, this date didn't top your list."

The slow dropping of Fern's jaw combined with her lifting eyebrows made my heart crumble within my chest. My mind continued to burn through every layer of my brain. There was no stopping the fire this night had created. My heart couldn't extinguish flames growing this fast in a brain burning to ash. Worst of all, these flames were circling the first person I'd ever loved and the one person I trusted more than anyone, forcing them both into the center of an inferno.

My fingers found the mojito sitting between Derrick and Fern, and I brought it to my lips. I knew it was Fern's before even lifting the glass, welcoming the heat as it flooded my system. Remainders of mint and pomegranate sloshed around the bottom, and I lifted the glass up, squinting at the mint leaves as if my eyes could magically refill the damn thing. Instead of reaching over for Derrick's beer, I held the empty mojito glass between my index finger and thumb and looked up at the wall ahead of me. It was made of some kind of teak lumber with a rounded window perfectly positioned so my reflection stared directly back at me.

The woman staring back at me was fierce, sure. But tonight, she was filled with a rage she wasn't quite familiar with. It was a rage fueled by anger and jealousy and love and betrayal. It was the most emotional game of tug-of-war her heart had ever played.

And the emotions were winning by a landslide.

I'd never been the fastest runner, and I'd never had the perfect pitch, but the second that glass crashed through the window, I knew this body was a hell of a lot stronger than I ever believed.

Chapter 31

FERN

My hands were turning to clay. Every time I shoved them into the bucket, every wrinkle on my palms filled. When I slapped the slab down onto the bat, every crease grew heavy. My wrists were stiff as stone and sore beyond measure, but nothing compared to the bag of bricks sitting on top of my chest. With every mug I sculpted, my lungs pushed harder against my ribs. With each spoon rest or soap dish placed into the kiln, I wanted to run upstairs to borrow Emmie's inhaler.

But I couldn't.

I couldn't just show up at her door or scream up the stairs from my apartment doorway. I'd texted her, called her, and even emailed her My Cup account the night before, staring at my dimly lit screen until deciding to take out some clay. I'd ended up warming the kiln at four o'clock in the morning while responding quickly to DJ's apologetic texts. He knew I had more important matters to deal with and, kindly, stopped texting.

For the first time in months, I didn't care about how I'd look walking into the gala alone or what my mom would say when I showed up to a wedding dateless.

All I cared about was the girl upstairs.

"I'm here…with coffee." A breathless Marian pushed through the apartment door. She quickly stopped—standing in her puffy coat and boots—and just stared. "Whoa. Fern."

"I felt creative."

"If shock and depression inspire you, that's great. There's just…a lot going on here," Marian said, stepping inside and sliding off her boots without setting down either coffee. She flipped her dark hair out of her eyes and walked toward me, setting my coffee on the floor by my slippered feet. "Do you even *use* spoon rests?"

I shrugged. "Someone might. Emmie cooks."

"Emmie doesn't need *seven* spoon rests," Marian said, leaning back against the couch, watching the wheel spin to a stop. Her eyes were heavy as she ran fingers through her perfectly combed—and conditioned—dark-chocolate mane. "You know she isn't home, right?"

"She isn't?" I looked up while reaching down for the coffee, heated drops burning the tops of my thumb and forefinger. Without a wince, I immediately brought the roast to my lips.

"She's over at Kyle and Rae's. She said she's staying there for a little bit."

"And *you're* okay with that?"

"Fern. Emmie and I aren't dating," Marian said with slow, lowering eyelids. "I feel like I repeat myself whenever I visit. We just fool around, and I'm absolutely fine with that."

Slumping over to rinse my hands in the water bucket, drops dampening the faded fluff of my slippers, I took a deep breath and forced myself to stand. I placed my palms at the small of my back and arched, the popcorn of my spine causing Loaf to hiss. Marian looked down at Porridge, who had practically wrapped himself around her calves, his little ears pointed and alert.

"Grab your coffee, and put on actual boots," Marian said. "We're leaving."

Oliver scoffed when we walked into Spellbound, but the scoff quickly tightened in his throat. My undereye circles and bloodshot eyes must have burned a hole right into that dark, dismal soul of his, forcing him to reach for his phone and begin scrolling.

Benji probably sensed the tension and made his typical exuberant entrance from the depths of the kitchen to the cash register in front of us. Oliver never shifted an eye from the phone in his hands. Requesting refills on the coffees Marian had just purchased—specifically asking for the hi-caf *Voodoo Brew*, we decided on taking over the Victorian chaise and wingback in Spellbound's far corner.

Bruises began covering my heart when we walked by the table Emmie and I usually sat at.

"So, let me make sure I got this right. You met up with the guy, DJ, that you used to see, who happens to be the Derrick who cheated on Emmie a couple of years ago?"

I nodded, my eyes struggling to blink. "I had no clue."

"Neither of you ever mentioned the same person at all?"

"We call him different things. It never seemed weird." Blinking long and hard, I took a deep breath and leaned back against the chaise. "I should have asked her more about her date. If she'd said she was going to Caravan to meet up with some guy named Derrick at the same time I was going, maybe I would have caught on."

"Honestly." Marian leaned forward, cupping the coffee in her hands. "Would you have believed it, though?"

I pressed my lips together and shook my head. "Probably not. No."

"I mean, who would have *really* caught on to this? The thing is, Fern, this isn't either of your issues right now. This is something from the past that's pissing off your present, and it's definitely not something your future needs."

"You're wise beyond your years," I whispered, the haze of heat making my eyes water as Marian snorted out a laugh.

Marian reached over the table and gently knocked her knuckles on top of my maroon locks. "No, I'm just a tad more practical than you."

The two of us jumped as Oliver's voice echoed off the walls. Cold air rushed through the front door as a man in an almost identical plaid button-up and dark jeans hugged Oliver, handing him a paper bag. Oliver peered inside, nodded, and hugged the shaggy-haired man again before our eyes unintentionally met.

My heavy squint must have terrified him, because he squirmed away and shoved the bag beneath the counter before waving his friend off.

I wasn't sure what impressed me more: this new ability to intimi-date Oliver or his inability to cover up what seemed to be a drug deal in plain sight.

Either way, as I turned back to face my sister, neither impressed me as much as they would have if Emmie had been there to make some inappropriate comment about it.

Chapter 32

The sound of footprints scuffing hardwood grew louder until the blinding screen of Kyle's phone floated mid-air into the living room. With his matching dragon slippers wiggling near the coffee table leg—the ones we'd purchased on a whim after a horrible My Cup meeting last year, he tossed his phone onto the couch. I watched it bounce twice before it hit the side of my thigh, plopping next to the laptop warming my legs.

"Dude, it's almost three in the morning," Kyle whispered.

"Are you stating the obvious or hinting at something else?" I asked, attempting to wiggle tired eyebrows as my hand patted the couch beside me.

It was a failed attempt.

Kyle shook his head, running his fingers through messy, dark hair before the dragon slippers carried his body to the couch where his weight fell against the back cushion. "You should probably pass the hell out. The whole office has the big gala meeting first thing tomorrow, and if Al catches you sleeping during it, he may just pass the speaking role to me."

"Perfect. I'll fall asleep as soon as my ass hits the chair tomorrow." Pinching my lips together, I pushed a sarcastic grin in Kyle's direction before facing the jumble of words on the screen in front of me.

Jumble was a kind description for what sat on my laptop screen. Sentences were short and quick. Descriptions were weak. Hidden messages were more than hidden—they were nonexistent. The only way I was going to create anything of substance was to completely call Fern out.

The angel on my shoulder was surprisingly overpowering the devil laughing in my ear.

Kyle leaned in closer. "Are you still working on Fern's blog?"

My dirty look punched Kyle in the face, my neck practically snapping with how fast it turned. "I hate that we call it that. Can we stop calling it that?" I took a deep breath and turned back toward the screen. "Breaking a window feels fucking exhilarating. That's the only message I can find to write about."

"That's it. Just spend the entire blog talking about how you're leaving marketing to become a world-renowned pitcher."

"Al would appreciate the athletic twist until he sees the blog getting way less engagement...and realizes I'm joking about leaving a job I genuinely love. I'll be podcasting in no time if I don't overflow the damn beans on this one." I rubbed my palms upward from my cheeks until the rough skin was scratching my closed eyelids. Al's flabby, crimson face and wide eyes had haunted the two hours of sleep I'd attempted. I couldn't imagine his response if I walked into the office without completed content. It was a nightmare I couldn't afford.

The real nightmare, however, consisted of me living in a world without Fern in it.

"Maybe just make the final blog—I don't know—*bigger*. This one can be mediocre and the next one can be the badass. Make it the grand finale of the series before the gala." Kyle's fingers pressed against my bare thigh. Goosebumps lifted against his palm as his hand crawled beneath the bottom of the warm laptop. With a gentle squeeze taking my mind away from the turmoil on the screen in front of me, he laughed. "Dude. You're sweaty as fuck."

"This laptop has been overheating on my lap for the last two hours. What do you expect?"

"I mean, you're always sweaty...but this is a whole new level." His fingers closed tight around my thigh, wandering up toward my practically nonexistent pajama shorts hiding below the laptop.

For the first time in a very long time, I wasn't sure I was in the mood to get feisty. Even a little. I was obviously a breathing ball of sweat and anxiety, and I definitely hadn't shaved anything—anywhere—in a week.

Even Kyle, who had seen me in absolutely every form—and position—wouldn't want to handle this stressed-out body tonight.

"Are you hoping I experience an even sweatier level of sweat, or can I finish *Fern's* blog?" I asked, lowering my eyelids as his fingers grazed the outside of my underwear. My heart trembled for a second—something I swore was cold as ice after these last few months. Somehow, my body still reacted to the touch of others. I tried to ignore the dampness I was unexpectedly adding to the sweaty mess Kyle's hand was smack in the middle of.

Kyle paused, sighed, and released his hand with a knowing expression. After over a year of living a polyamorous lifestyle—even though Rae hated putting a title to the partnership we had—Kyle remained very aware of my boundaries. Unlike many partners I'd had, he actually listened to the words coming out of my mouth and was cognizant of social cues. He often used the fact that we both had mothers of Asian descent who had forced respect upon us since birth. Though it was true my mother had thrown morals my way, my father had solidified them in our household.

I wondered what my father would have thought about this blog series, if he would have felt that same punch in the gut I'd felt leaving Caravan last week. If there really was some spiritual existence going on above us, I wondered how everyone up there enjoyed the shitshow going on down here.

More than that, I wondered how disappointed my dad would be knowing I was not only stabbing back at those who'd stabbed me first, but also pushing away my best friend.

Al looked like a drunken troll standing next to Najma at the front of the conference room. I couldn't tell if he was trying to waft her scent in his direction or hinting something to someone leaning against the far window as his chin subtly jerked up and then down. My eyes darting between Al, the far window, and the conference room door, I ignored the trembling of my hands as I lifted the coffee to my lips.

Since when did I shake from being nervous?

And why the hell was I nervous?

The answer to my question walked into the conference room practically on cue. Her faded burgundy hair was tied into a low, messy bun with a knit cap forcing bangs down to hide her eyes. My body immediately began walking in her direction—a conditioned reaction I couldn't escape. When I forced myself to stop, the coffee met my lips—and the front of my sweater—just as firmly as my feet hit the floor.

My chest burned of coffee and uncertainty, and I wasn't sure which was easier to see—the stains on my sweater or the expression painting my face.

"Do you need a bib?" Kyle's voice hummed by my ear, and his fingers gently squeezed my elbow, handing me over the familiar comfort I needed.

"Yeah, go get me one, please?" I asked, facing him and forcing out a smile. My eye twitched toward Chase, who ducked beneath the doorframe and nodded at Fern, who waved him in her direction. As he made his way toward her, his eyes scanned the room, and when they met mine, his brow furrowed, sending my stomach sinking to my toes. I couldn't stop watching their interactions: Chase's perplexed expressions and Fern's twitchy, lip-biting babble in response to whatever he'd asked.

I felt as if I were back in middle school, slammed into a locker, and forced to watch friends pass by through the metal slits. I couldn't do anything but painfully watch and wait.

"Okay, let's get this thing started." Al's booming voice silenced the space, and everyone in the conference room turned in his direction. It had been several months since every team from the Merlin Heights

My Cup office was in one room. Excitement and uncertainty dripped from all our pores.

"We need to start off by giving a round of applause to everyone in this room. Every team is doing magnificent work, and that work will be recognized at the gala," Najma said. Her voice had an impressive way of enticing everyone around her. It was hard to stray our eyes from her perfect poise and flawless skin.

Hell, I had to hold back an orgasm every time she spoke.

Somehow, amidst the applause and Najma's lustful essence, I twitched my gaze to Fern, who mimicked the actions of everyone else in the room. Najma continued, "The gala is one month from today, and we are *still* voting on a theme. Corporate in New York City wanted to choose it at first. After some discussion, the theme is fully in the hands of our staff members now. This shows how mighty our little office is."

"It's also probably because we're the founding office," Al said with a shrug before facing the group in front of him. "Okay. We need theme ideas!"

"Redneck rodeo!" a voice from the far side of the room shouted. The room erupted into laughter, and I turned to see a few marketing analysts slapping each other's backs.

I began making a comment before realizing it was Kyle standing beside me—not Fern. I stole a look at her from above Kyle's shoulder and gray, bloodshot eyes met mine like an arrow to the chest. The room quieted, and Al's nasal requests sounded like ones given by the teacher of Charlie Brown. Though our connection lasted maybe two seconds, at most, it sent a jolt of unease straight to my stomach.

Al coughed loudly to hush the crowd. "Uh, Emmie?"

I swear I cracked something in my neck when Al's voice sounded. "Oh, yeah. Sure. What those guys said."

"Do you have anything you want to add?" Al lowered his gaze, eyebrows raising toward his ridiculously shiny head. "... about your speech?"

"Oh," I stuttered, stepping forward as if that would help everyone hear me better. Really, did I want them to? "I'm speaking. At the gala."

I heard Kyle laugh a cough into his fist, and I looked over my shoulder to meet his eyes. "Just say something so we can all leave," he whispered.

Purposely avoiding eye contact with anyone on the right side of the room as I turned to face Al, Najma, and the three other supervisors, I took a deep breath. "Okay, you all know I was asked to talk about the company and what's been going on over these last few months with the content team. I'll probably talk about how My Cup has brought so many people together in just a year. Couples—okay, yeah, we've helped a few."

Gentle laughter helped bring my mind back to where we were and why we were there. Another deep breath grounded my feet further, but I could still feel the edge of my sight wanting to wander. I forced my voice to speak as redirection. "We've helped people meet their partners through our content and coffee, but we've done more than that. We've brought people together. We've brought communities together. We've brought *friendships* together."

Breath stung the back of my throat, and when I pinched my eyes shut, they opened toward the right side of the room. Instead of Fern standing uneasily beside Chase with an anxious foot tapping the floor, Chase hovered above the emptiest damn spot I'd ever seen.

Chapter 33

FERN

I will not cry. I will not cry.

I repeated this out loud all the way back to my desk the moment I felt Emmie's gaze make me want to vomit. I couldn't stand in that room with my watery eyes and agitated stance, feeling an aching blaze climb farther and farther up my throat. When her eyes had strayed, my feet seemed to float toward the small opening of the door my body could barely sneak through without anyone noticing. When I collapsed into my chair, breathing as if I'd run a mile—something I hadn't done since the hell that was seventh-grade P.E.—laughter floated from the conference room, making the skin beneath my sweater itch.

The thing I hated most about all of this was that neither of us knew how to feel. Even though I wasn't physically inside her mind, I knew her well enough that she, too, couldn't get a grasp on these emotions. It wasn't middle or high school. We couldn't slip a note through the slits of a locker, circle *YES* when asked *Can we still be friends?* and agree to move on. Instead, we were forced to navigate these damn feelings as adults, even though our actions at Caravan mimicked something only reality stars could pull off.

We had to awkwardly coexist, feeling too many things instead.

"Did you check Spike?" Chase's hushed voice practically sent me across the top of my desk, my hip bone crashing into the ledge of the laminate as I looked up to see him a few feet away.

I set my hand over my hip and pushed out a painfully forced smile. "Hey, hi. Spike?"

"You haven't checked yet today, huh?" He laughed and took a step closer, lifting his chin in the direction of the barrel cactus balancing on the top of our cubicles. "Check it."

Twisting to face the line of plants, I noticed a small, colorful bag laid at the bottom of Spike's ceramic planter. Reaching for the yellow bag, I looked down to see familiar green and orange and red colors, but the illustrations looked like they'd hopped out of a time machine.

"I'm slightly disappointed you went for such a popular candy…but this bag is *definitely* not from the last decade."

"Try the last few decades," Chase said, leaning against the cubicle separator with a modest grin. "My aunt found these."

I looked up from the bag with squinted eyes, my brows narrowing below the scratchy edge of the knit cap. "Were they locked in a safe from her childhood?"

"In the pocket of a jacket she used to wear when she was around our age, actually. She did a major closet dump this weekend since they're moving to Greyport soon," Chase explained.

"I hope she kept that jacket or else I may search through every Merlin thrift store to find it. An original Sour Patch Kids bag from the 1980s? This is gold." I ran my finger over the faded plastic and felt my smile fading as the laughter in the conference room grew silent.

"Let's go," Chase whispered, looking over his shoulder toward the shuffling sound coming from behind him. The clock ticking on the wall told us the meeting would probably be over soon, and my fingers started crinkling the wrapper against my palm.

"Let's go, meaning...let's eat these things?" I looked down at the Sour Patch Kids and lifted one brow toward Chase who was slipping his arms into his coat. "Because we may end up at St. Merlin Hospital if we do."

"You know what I mean. I can tell something is going on." Chase was not someone to pry into the business of others, but I could see the gold casing of his heart shining through his chest. "Let's finish the day at Spellbound."

A rumble of applause sounded again, and I lifted up onto my tiptoes to see if the conference room was emptying out. Luckily, the doors were still shut. "She may go there, though."

Chase reached for the oversized sweatshirt hanging over my chair and gently pushed it in my direction. "She has a content team meeting after this. I can tell you need some strong coffee to go with some stale Sour Patch Kids."

*

Word-vomit was inevitable once coffee hit my lips.

It was so easy talking to Chase. He listened with such intent and asked questions in such a soft, genuine way. Those dark eyes never strayed once they hooked onto mine, and it made my heart pour out truths even faster. After his heroic performance at Isaac's apartment, the shell of his introverted persona seemed to crack a bit. I felt as if he were now this therapeutic bodyguard thrown in front of my cubicle, who also blessed me with sour candies and succulents.

Or in this case, the therapeutic bodyguard turned coffeehouse therapist.

"So, that's why you *really* needed those passwords in the fall?" Chase said, nodding while wrapping his fingers around the cup. The cup looked like a dollhouse miniature sitting between his palms.

"I mean, kind of. We have access to most of the profiles in the database as is." I lifted my gaze from my fingers that hadn't stopped intertwining with one another since I sat down in the booth. "I just thought it could help us find who we needed without having to go through every file, you know?"

"Was it worth it?" Chase asked, his eyes pinned to mine in a way that forced mine open wider. "I mean, I'm guessing that's a dumb question since you and Emmie are where you are now."

"I don't know," I said, my voice growing even more quiet. "I'm always willing to give people the benefit of the doubt. Hell, that's exactly what I've been doing over these last few months! Obviously, second chances don't always work out for everyone, but I was willing to try, and I guess I'm glad I did." I peered over Chase's shoulder, which was much easier to do with him sitting down, to see Oliver snickering at his phone as his thumb slid across the screen.

If Emmie were here, she would have called him out on how annoying his laugh was.

"You're just too kind," Chase said, breaking me away from my gaze and the distracting thoughts that went along with it. "I mean, I don't think Isaac deserved a second chance. I could be wrong, though."

"Yeah, he wouldn't have been a good date to the gala. He would have just wanted to hookup in the bathroom all night."

Shocked, Chase's lips fell open. "The *My Cup* gala? Is that really why you're re-dating?"

I guess I'd forgotten to mention that part of the plan.

"Here's your raspberry latte." Oliver placed Chase's drink on the table alongside his empty cup of coffee. "Sorry it took so long."

"You forgot he even ordered it," I spat, rolling my eyes so they disappeared below messy bangs. Crossing my eyes to look up at the dark scarlet strands, I blew a few out of my vision so I wouldn't miss any of Oliver's sickening expressions.

Oliver shrugged and began walking backward toward the counter. "Have you replaced your partner-in-crime with this dude now?"

My stomach leapt into my throat. "Stop being a dick."

"It's just a question." Oliver reached into his pocket and clicked on his phone, an arrogant smile going right back to its usual place. "I'm putting pieces of the puzzle together. More pieces than you'd expect."

Chase leaned forward and cocked his head to the side. "He's smart enough to use a metaphor?"

"No. Actually he's not." I reached into my pocket and scrolled through my own phone, tapping the little coffee cup logo so the screen went to the app's main menu. Clicking onto the *Coffee Bean Banter* tab, three new blogs were bold at the top of the page.

Emmie's was first on the list.

"Shit. It's Monday." Obviously, I hadn't whispered quietly enough because Oliver snorted from behind the counter.

"Shouldn't you be the first one to read your best friend's blogs when they go live? I'm sorry, *ex*-best friend." Oliver shook his head, his eyebrows lowering and his lips curling into a disgusting pout. "Maybe you shouldn't steal people's boyfriends. Hmm? Then you'd pay more attention."

I skimmed the article enough to hit the main points and messages before skimming it again and looking up at Oliver. "There's nothing in this article that says I did anything. What are you talking about?" I felt Chase's hand wrap around my phone, and I let him snag it to read the piece. I could tell from the slight rise of his eyebrows and the pinching of his lips that he, too, was surprised.

Nothing related to my name, personality, or appearance was in the blog.

I was nowhere to be found.

Oliver leaned over the counter, where he set his hands flat in front of him, tapping his fingers to the rhythm of the music overhead. "I may come off as an idiot, Fern, but you'd be surprised." The bells over the door jingled, and he didn't blink away as three middle-aged women shuffled in. "I know shit, and I'm ready."

Oliver's body disappeared behind women who requested half the sugar and extra oat milk in their overly complicated orders. I was grateful for the distraction because I liked Oliver being forced to do the job he barely ever did anyway. However, the complaints of the women and the quick, jarred movements of Oliver behind the counter didn't distract me from the words I'd just heard him say.

Chase slid the phone back in front of me, his hand gently covering mine for the quickest second before it returned to his latte. "She may have brought up the incident, but she didn't even hint at you being involved. If anything, that's a start." He nodded his head in Oliver's direction, Chase's lips twisting into a grimace. "What's that dude's problem?"

Once Oliver handed the three women their drinks and leaned back with his phone in hand, my heart rammed against my ribs. He looked from his screen to my eyes and back down. It was that quick, twitchy look that set my nerves on fire. A spark flickered inside my brain, and like Oliver's puzzle metaphor, I was putting the pieces together too.

I scooted closer to the table so when Chase leaned forward, I could practically taste the raspberry flavor floating from his lips. "Emmie dated Oliver a year or so ago. Right around when My Cup went live."

Chase looked over his shoulder in his direction before returning to my glance. "Why the hell would she do that?"

"She thought he was hot," I said, the words turning my stomach. "And Oliver thinks strictly with his dick, so he obliged."

Chase blinked quickly, his eyes wide. "*He's* who women are attracted to?"

"We're getting off track." I was practically on the table at this point, the palms of my hands flat over the tops of Chase's. The velvety smoothness of his skin took me by surprise, but Oliver's obnoxious chuckle snapped me back to reality. "Oliver reads her blogs. He's been following her series this whole time, and he overhears us whenever we're here. He knows exactly what's going on."

It took about thirty seconds of unblinking thought before I saw the same spark I'd felt minutes before flicker behind Chase's dark eyes. Blinking slowly, he bit the inside of his cheek and shook his head. "Shit. He's next, isn't he?"

I looked up over Chase's shoulder, forcing everything within me to remain calm, even though I knew I couldn't hide the crazy-eyes I was wearing. "Yeah, he's next. He knows it, and he's ready."

301

MY CUP  ’ JOE

Rae, 24

Massage Therapist
Sips with WOMEN, MEN, NON-BINARY
Looking for CASUAL

Hot or Cold

I'm a sucker for iced lattes. A seasonal flavor with a
little oat milk...and I come undone—like, immediately.

Sweetness

i'm a secret sweetheart

With A Side Of

Espresso. Please give me a latte with an extra espresso
shot on the side. I'm pretty much the Energizer Bunny
in disguise. Tail and all. 🐰

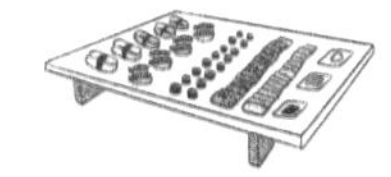

Chapter 34

Emmie

In two weeks, I'd walk into Three-Ring wearing a gorgeous gown—one I had yet to purchase—prepared to make a speech I had yet to even think about. I would giggle when Al introduced me to some corporate big shot and solidly shake hands with everyone Najma shook hands with simply because I wanted to touch whomever she touched. I'd walk around, sipping my third tequila on the rocks—because beer is too casual for these upscale things—smiling when Kyle and Rae winked in passing. If I'd asked Marian a month or so ago, maybe she would have been by my side wearing a skintight number my eyes wouldn't rip away from.

Instead, I'd be walking around with Patron in my glass and a plastic smile painting my lips.

Without Fern.

The thought made a giant sigh escape my lungs, my body flopping over Rae beside me, who lifted her arms so I could place my head in her lap. Her hands, busy holding a controller, contently landed on my shoulder, and Kyle let out an angry grunt from my opposite side. Rae pressed the controller down into my shoulder before I felt the sharp ping of teeth press into my upper thigh.

"What the fuck, Kyle?" Leaning so my elbow jabbed into Rae's tiny waist, I twisted to watch Kyle toss the controller onto the floor after releasing himself from my flesh. "You haven't bitten me like that in—I don't know—four months!"

Rae adjusted herself, and as she scooted her tiny body upward on the couch, her oversized sweatpants lowered to reveal sheer fabric that barely hid her landing strip from peeking through.

Fuck.

That adorable landing strip of hers made me quiver every time I laid eyes—or my mouth—on it. I reached toward the elastic band of her sweatpants and dramatically pulled it up so it sat right below the sports bra she was wearing, and I tied the drawstring tight so it wouldn't slip.

My pulling her clothes farther on rather than off caused a puzzled line to grow between her brows. However, Rae rarely questioned my quirks. "Didn't he bite you a few weeks ago?" Rae looked over my shoulder toward Kyle, who remained slumped into the couch, reaching to loosen the knot I'd made without his eyes leaving the screen. "When we all tried that edible massage oil stuff? The one that tasted weirdly like Almond Joys?"

Sitting up straight, Kyle cocked his head over his shoulder and paused the game. "Oh yeah. I did."

"It tasted like sunscreen and took forever to scrub off," I said, watching as Rae contently slid her sweatpants—well, Kyle's sweatpants—back to her hipbones.

"But he *did* bite your leg that night, right?" Rae asked, reaching forward and sliding her hand from my chest, to my belly button, to the inside of my right thigh, where her index finger pointed at a small, faded green bruise. "Right there! I knew it."

I rolled my eyes and pinched her fingers between my soft, warm legs. "Okay, okay. You're right. Moving on."

"What's got your panties in a bunch?" Kyle asked.

I tried not to gag at the word everyone knew I hated as Rae's hands traveled lower between my thighs, a finger adding pressure on the sensitive nerves she knew I'd give in to. She knew I despised that word. Undies. Drawers. Freaking skivvies was better than...*panties*. Forcing the word from my thoughts, I reached down and squeezed my hand over hers. "Same shit. I'm not in the mood."

That was partially a lie. The sight of her body and her hand gently caressing my skin was usually all it took for me to turn savage.

Maybe I didn't feel as savage as usual, but Rae usually found a way to pull some of my feisty side out when I'd pushed it far down.

"Is it still Fern? Because you guys should be beyond this by now." Kyle reached for the controller before sitting at the edge of the couch, gesturing for Rae to grab her own. She shimmied her hand out from my grasp, but not without an overly dramatic eyeroll. "And isn't your last blog due, like, in a week?"

"Oooh! And the draft of your speech? I can't wait to hear it." Rae pointed her controller at the screen and turned away. "You better practice it for us. I love having an in."

"You love *getting* it in," Kyle whispered.

Rae winked and licked her lips. "Shut up and push play."

My head was spinning, the screen in front of me a mess of fuzzy graphics blurring at the edges. I shifted myself to a seated position and felt the walls of my brain pulse heavily against my skull as if it had its own heartbeat.

How had I gotten myself here? Was saving my career worth losing my best friend? What about ruining the lives of those who'd ruined mine? Was feeling sexy and confident worth losing the person I felt closest to?

I really wasn't sure what was worth my energy at this point.

My knees and palms hit the floor, and I crawled across the rug until I was sure I wouldn't block the screen Rae and Kyle were very intently staring at. Getting myself to a standing position was a hellish feat, and I wondered why I felt so hungover when I hadn't consumed a drop of alcohol in days. My feet were bricks dragging across the kitchen tile toward the spare bedroom where I'd been staying, my hands heavy at my sides as I hauled myself through the doorway. Once the bed was in front of me, I faceplanted atop the crumpled comforter coughing up the scent of black coffee, half-assed foreplay, and guilt.

I wasn't sure how long I lay there suffocating in my own filth. Long enough to hear Rae and Kyle turn off the television and click off the living room lights. Long enough for my feet to lose feeling and my hands to go numb from dangling off the end of the bed. Long enough for my own brain to sit in silence for the first time in a week.

My brain going quiet forced my eyes open and my aching body to shimmy up so it was fully on the bed. I felt like an inchworm, shifting myself across the bed until my head hit the pillow. My eyelids had never closed so quickly, and I pressed my thumbs fiercely over them until I swore I could feel my brain.

Was this how it felt to be broken? Once the madness stirring inside your brain fell quiet and there were no more feelings left to feel, could you title yourself as insane? Did you just become a shell of a human filled with stale air, sour blood, and guilt?

Guilt.

My eyes shot open.

I still felt something. I couldn't be broken if I felt some whisper of emotion. I would focus on that feeling. I'd stare deep into the depths of it. I'd rip it apart and dissect it until I knew what to do with it.

I would do all of that and more once I finished this series.

I had to fuck Oliver over first.

"In front of people?" My mom never spoke with her mouth full, but from her uncomfortably direct gaze, I could tell she needed details. "*Real* people?"

"Yes. I will speak in front of hundreds of human beings, Mom." I handed her a napkin so she could wipe the soy sauce dripping from her lips. Though I knew she wanted specifics, redirection was in order. "Are you glad I brought food from Hen Hao Chi this time?"

My mom's eyes pinched when her cheeks lifted into a grin. I loved watching her face shift into a smile. "Oh yes, yes. Much better." Once she swallowed the bite and lifted her finger, I knew my attempt at redirecting had failed. "Will you talk about work or what? What will you speak of?"

Lian, 1. Emmie, 0.

"They want me to talk about how my job brings more people to My Cup. Well, they *really* want me to talk about how our blogs make more relationships happen. I don't really know how I'll twist that into the speech. It'll be a stretch."

"No, no, no." My mom wagged her hand in front of her face before reaching down for chopsticks so she could fiddle with another dragon roll. "You do help. You bring people together."

I watched my mom slop her roll in soy sauce before shoving it into her mouth, her cheeks mimicking those of a chipmunk. For a tiny, conservative woman who was quite the opposite of her daughter, when she was hungry, she ate. Though I'd eaten in the same abrupt way she had for decades, it took me too long to realize our metabolisms were much different.

However, our destructive IBS was not.

"We bring some people together, yes. I'm sure we also mess things up too, you know? We probably mess up some dates...maybe friendships too." I immediately stuffed two avocado rolls into my mouth. I looked like a hibernating chipmunk instead of a daughter with a secret.

"Ah, that's life. That's real. You write real things." She took a moment to finish chewing this time before finishing her thought. The soft line of her smile and calm eyes told me she was coming down from the *hangry* podium she had been sitting on when I arrived at the office. "But you make people see real things. Wants. Needs. Cares. Those are real."

I placed my chin on my knuckles and listened to my mother's words. She'd never spoken much about my job since I'd started working on the My Cup research team three years ago. In truth, I wasn't really sure she knew what a dating app was or how different my position was now from the one I'd started with. From the few short phrases she'd stated in the last fifteen minutes, however, I realized she followed my career more than I knew. She obviously read my blogs. She felt the genuine messages I forced into them.

Hell, she officially knew I'd shown up naked to a fake dermatologist appointment.

"You don't think what I've been doing over the last few months is—I don't know—selfish? I see it all as selfish, karma-fueled chaos that will probably bite me in the ass before it teaches anyone legitimate lessons on love."

I was still sore from karma's recent ass-biting.

My mother chuckled as she reached for a napkin. "That too. Yes. A little selfish."

"Thanks for the honesty."

"Genetics," she said, smiling before looking at the clock above my head. "You're honest, and that's good. Stay honest in your blogs and your speech. That's why people like the blogs—and you."

Except, all the cheaters I'd hunted down didn't like me very much. And Fern.

"That's the only reason why people like me, huh? My deadpan honesty?" I asked.

My mom leaned forward and playfully patted my cheek with a shake of the head. "No, no, no. You're so much more than that, Em."

She wasn't wrong. She wasn't wrong about honesty being one of my most appreciated traits, and she wasn't wrong about my job. The goal of My Cup was to connect people through coffee and good conversation. The content team focused on writing pieces that were relatable, realistic, and empowering. Wasn't that really the reason behind everything I'd been doing with *The Cheater Chase*? I was trying to help others feel empowered about their future relationships, right? What I was doing wasn't the kindest, but the reactions my blogs received and the increase in My Cup profiles being created were proof some good was coming of this.

I'd never been someone to dig deep into my emotional well. Hell, usually that well was desert dry. However, my heartstrings tugged a little tighter every time I celebrated a successful publishing day. Whenever I watched Fern's beloved bean graphics overflow below my post, my lips curled robotically into a grin I couldn't ignore.

Maybe this venture wasn't just proving how mentally strong I'd become, but it was also forcing me to look at the strength already sitting behind my ribs. Maybe these stupid emotions were steppingstones leading me right to where I needed to be—even if where I stood felt unstable as hell. The stones would smooth out in time. I just had to listen to the damn heart in my chest. That would be the hardest part.

I adored my job and needed to save it.

But I adored my friendship that much more.

Chapter 35

FERN

Could the damn coffee machine be any slower?

For a business that focused on coffee culture, you would think they'd splurge on some technologically savvy appliances and maybe an espresso machine. Instead, staff searched daily for coffee pods that weren't outdated and stared anxiously as our mugs were filled at a snail's pace. There was never a day the machine didn't cough, stop, start back up again, and then cough a little more. The entire process was worse than watching bad acting during a series finale, and I didn't have time for it.

This was why Spellbound was my go-to.

Our go-to.

Today, though, I was forcing myself to step outside of my comfort zone. Well, most days I was stepping outside of my comfort zone in some way. However, this time it felt like a much larger step. This step was slippery and caused my hands to tremble beneath the hot mug I slowly carried around the cubicles. Facing confrontation was something I avoided and, to be frank, was never discussed with me growing up. I was always told to *listen to Jesus* or *God's word will guide you.*

Well, I hadn't shaken hands with Jesus over the last couple of weeks, and Marian's visit was the closest I'd gotten to anything Godly in decades. Therefore, I was listening to the one piece of advice stitched into the crevices of my brain since childhood: *Always give second chances a try.*

Even though that's what got me here in the first place.

Scalding liquid dripped over my index fingers, and I hoped my choppy bangs hid the beads of sweat bursting from my brow. The mug in my hands was a gift from Emmie, given around the time we'd both started at My Cup. She'd enthusiastically run over to my desk that day, sliding the mug in front of me so I could see my name sculpted across it. Emmie had been adorably proud of the find since we always joked about how our names rarely were found on anything.

And now the memory was trying to push through the dam in my tear ducts.

Fucking emotions.

I stood with booted feet together and coffee burning my palms when I arrived at the content team's corner of the office. I directed my gaze at Emmie's empty desk and took a step closer, thinking maybe she would magically appear in her chair. The weird thing was, her chair didn't even have a coat or sweatshirt slung over the back of it. Her laptop wasn't even open on her desk. There wasn't even an empty mug or thrown-out Spellbound cup anywhere to be seen.

It was Monday. She was *always* in the office on Mondays.

"She's not coming in." I turned to see Kyle spinning in his swivel chair to face me from his desk across the room. "She said she's off finishing her series today."

"Finishing her—" My eyes widened as an imaginary lightbulb flickered above my head, and the mug in my hands practically hit the floor. I fumbled for the ceramic cup as russet drops flung onto my sweater and more dripped down my hands. Kyle got to his feet and jogged over to me, reaching for tissues from someone's desk. Izzy turned toward us, and Ahmed took his earbuds out just as Kyle gently placed his hand atop my shoulder and gestured us away from the corner.

"Look. Since the *incident*, she's pretty much been comatose in our spare bedroom," Kyle whispered as he released his gentle grip on my shoulder. We rounded the corner toward cubicle country, Katie from finance cursing at the coffee machine in passing. "Like...she's seriously a mess."

My face was shocked when a smile pushed through.

Who in their right mind felt even an ounce of happiness when their best friend was miserable? I hated that I had to force away the curl of my lips as they inched upward. Looking down at the coffee I was supposed to give to Emmie, I took a sip as we neared my desk. "I've been a hot mess too."

"Well, then...do something. You're both acting like middle schoolers fighting over the same *dreamy* guy to take to prom...when you both don't actually want to go with him at all," Kyle said, shaking his head. "It's really not worth it. Your friendship is."

Chase peeked above the cubicle wall when he heard Kyle's voice and asked, "Do they even have prom in middle school?"

"No one says *dreamy* either," I whispered, the mug pressing against my chin.

"Your mom might." Chase laughing quietly at his own joke was the redirection I needed. I held myself back from telling Chase that *Your Mama* jokes hadn't been trendy in twenty years, but the look of pride painted across his face was too cute to disrupt. However, it took only a second of realization before I set the mug down and placed my hands on Chase's shoulders.

My eyes widened when his met mine. "Emmie's going to get Oliver. Now."

"*Get* him?" Chase asked.

My foot stomped the tile, and I flung my head back, doing everything in my power not to cross my arms over my chest and pout like a pissed-off toddler. "He's the last cheater on her list. Remember?"

Chase eyed the clock above my head before shifting back to meet my gaze. I could tell the figurative lightbulb had shifted from my head to his. These lightbulbs had been on fire recently. "She's meeting him, like...now?"

"She's going this morning. That's what she told me." Kyle slowly reached toward the mug on my desk, keeping his eyes locked with mine. "Since she's not here, can I—"

"Yes, yeah. Take it. Thank you, Kyle." Skittering around Kyle as he walked back to his desk with a lukewarm mug of crappy coffee, I grabbed my jacket and slipped my arms through the sleeves. "Put your coat on. Come on."

Chase stood up and leaned over the separation between our desks. "Are you going to Spellbound to tell her Oliver is up to something?"

"*We* are going, yes. We both heard him last week. He might, like, drug her coffee or something." The thought made my stomach climb into my throat, shocking my eyes open wider. "Holy shit. He's going to drug Emmie."

"Do you really think he'd do that?" Chase asked, reaching down for his hooded sweatshirt and sliding it over his head.

"I saw him whispering to some creepy friends of his and taking a bag from them a few weeks ago," I said, the memory flickering through my mind like a black-and-white film. "Fuck, Chase. He's definitely going to do something. Let's go."

Chase laughed gently as he rounded the corner of his cubicle, the chuckle turning into a cough when he saw my intensely serious expression. "Okay, okay. I just hope this guy isn't jerking off into an espresso machine when I get there."

Chapter 36

Emmie

I was ready to end this.

At the beginning of all this, I'd felt that adrenaline rush. I'd whispered to the strangers at Jake's open house, their grimaces and disgusted expressions causing bubbles of excitement to pop in my chest. I embraced the look of shock on Manny's face when he recognized this *new* version of me, not feeling the guilt I should have when our video went viral. Even when I walked into the Lyra Center, prepared to nervously drop my coat for Cici, I'd left with more confidence flowing than I expected.

Then I saw Derrick...with Fern.

It was then that I questioned everything I'd done over the last few months. I questioned the emotions I'd felt, wondering if they were true rumbles of joy or just my own expectations forcing feelings upon me. I questioned the feelings I still had for him, those emotions I had tucked away in the darkest corners of my mind—and heart. I questioned whether I'd thrown the glass out of genuine anger or just because it would make the blog beans overflow. I questioned how much I did care about my job and whether my naivete toward Fern was valid.

I knew two things for sure: I loved my job—like, I *really* loved my job—but I loved my friend more.

I was ready to end this blog series, but I needed to do it the right way.

When I climbed into my own bed well after midnight and for the first time in over a week, I felt calm. My familiar comforter definitely needed a wash, and clothes were still strewn across my bedroom floor from when I'd quickly packed for my stay with Kyle. My quick departure had been a little immature now that I'd had time to think about it. Fern lived downstairs, but that didn't mean I needed to completely ghost both her and my place of comfort.

We were grown, dammit. I needed to act the part.

I stepped through a few sodden piles of snow still lurking curbside on my walk from the apartment to Spellbound. It was finally warm enough—at a whopping forty-five degrees Fahrenheit—to stomp through slush instead of start up my cold car. When the shop door stood directly in front of me, I watched my reflection take a deep breath before pushing into a haze of espresso. My eyes immediately darted to my usual spot—*our* usual spot—that sat lonely opposite the cash register. I quickly set my bag down on the chair and slipped my tablet onto the table before turning on my heel to face the counter.

Oliver leaned back against the brick wall with arms crossed over his chest. Tattoos snuck out below his short sleeves, and a few swirls of dark ink peeked above the V-neck of his shirt. His thin, closed lips turned upward ever so slightly as they pinched his pale cheeks, causing small wrinkles to claw at the edges of his eyes. His ringed fingers weren't sliding across the screen of his phone like they did most mornings, and he had yet to make some snide remark about my job or my choice of oversized sweatshirt. Instead, he stood like a statue straight out of a grungy 80s film, waiting for the right time to crack.

I threw him the typical scowl, hoping my expressions wouldn't hint that anything was different about this morning. "What's with your face?"

He chuckled low, releasing his arms and stepping away from the wall. "What, this?" His hand circled around his head, taking another step closer. "This face you used to love?"

"Don't make me vomit, Oliver." There was definitely vomit already in my throat, and I pushed down the sour taste as my fingers met the cold counter. "I never loved you. Lust, maybe. Just give me my coffee, please."

So far, so good.

Well, all was good except for him. Everything about Oliver's poise and demeanor seemed—I don't know—off. Almost forced.

It gave me a headache.

"You're just going to ask for your drink and go back to working back there, huh?" He nodded toward my table behind me. "Just like it's a normal day? I mean, a normal day *without* your best friend, that is."

I bit the inside of my cheek when my stomach dropped to my feet. "Don't bring her into this. I'll gladly find somewhere else to work from." Going somewhere else was definitely not part of the plan. I genuinely wanted my Spellbound Beans brew and, preferably, now.

Oliver snickered and reached below the counter, his hand returning with a mug where newly decorated froth sat atop steaming liquid. It looked to be the exact latte Fern usually ordered most days we visited Spellbound. However, this was not one of our usual days to visit Spellbound, and if we did, we always asked for a to-go cup.

Why had he assumed I—or we—would show up this morning?

"What the fuck is that? You're some magician now?" I said monotonously. "You know what I ask for. Coffee. Black. Now."

"You could say I'm a wizard of sorts." Oliver set the ceramic mug on a saucer and placed it directly in front of me. "I'm a barista—knowing things just comes with the job description. I see things; I hear things; I *read* things. I'm pretty much a psychic."

"Your scrawny ass doesn't know shit," I snorted.

"You liked my scrawny ass once." He nodded toward the mug with a grin I wanted to scratch right off his face. "On the house. My treat."

I looked around the room to find two other customers quietly minding their own business, not even throwing a second glance our way. As I reached for the mug, realization froze inside the icy walls of my brain. "Excuse me, what?"

"You heard me. It's yours. You lost your best friend. The most I can do is give you a free drink in memory of her," Oliver said.

Skeptical was an understatement. "I'm not hooking up with you in the bathroom, Oliver."

"I wouldn't expect you to." He eyed the bathroom door in the corner before his eyes daggered into mine. "You haven't gone near that bathroom since our breakup. I'm still surprised you come in here every week after that. Takes some real guts...and I know your guts can be a little irritable most of the time."

My hands reached for the mug the second he mentioned that embarrassing scenario—one I continuously tried to push from my memory. "I'm a strong-ass woman. I've moved beyond that shit."

"Literally." His eyebrows hit the top of his knit cap, and another raspy laugh left his lips. "It's on the house. Just take it."

I wrapped my hands around the warm mug, taking a deep breath as the shop door opened, and a gust of crisp air smacked my face.

Chapter 37

FERN

"I ... don't... run. Ever," I panted, my run turning into a pathetic jog at Chase's hip. Shifting my gaze toward him, I realized he wasn't jogging. He wasn't even power walking. "Is this *seriously* your casual walking speed?"

"I wouldn't say this is my *casual* speed." Chase looked down at me with a close-lipped grin as I slowed my pace to a grisly speed just below power-walk mode. "My legs are just double the size of yours."

"True. Yeah." I had to stop. As pitiful as it looked—and felt—I needed to catch my breath. My Cup was barely half a mile from Spellbound, and being that I didn't own sneakers and had been sprinting for the last two minutes, this was the hardest workout I'd probably ever done. My gloved hands fell to my knees, and my spine rounded, my breath creating clouds.

"You okay?" Chase set his hand on my hunched back, and I bolted up, his touch sending a surge of unexpected electricity back into my limbs. The hood of my jacket flew back as I flung my body upright and the top of my head crashed into Chase's chin, causing him to step back and cup his jaw.

"Holy shit, holy shit! Are you okay? Oh my gosh, Chase!" I stepped closer to him, and I gently pressed both of my hands to either side of his face, my right hand falling over his. When the wool of my gloves touched his bare, sienna skin, the twinkle of pain once in his eyes subsided.

"I'll probably need a jaw replacement." His voice was low and monotone, every muscle in his face morphing into a serious façade. "I don't think I'm going to make it, Fern."

I stepped a little closer, my thumb gently outlining his jawline until it hit a spot, causing him to writhe just the tiniest bit. Seeing him in pain, even if it was being dramatically overdone, was a ping to the heart I didn't feel coming. My body lifted onto my toes—way, way onto the tips of my toes—and my left hand climbed its way to the back of his neck.

Before I could stop myself, my lips fell over his.

His warmth immediately flooded every blood vessel in my being, and his familiar scent felt therapeutic, my palm loosening against his jaw. His hand wrapping around the small of my back, pulling me in closer, awakened emotions I hadn't felt in months, maybe years.

I wanted these unexpected emotions to keep terrifying me.

They felt so fucking good.

However, I couldn't focus on how perfect his plump lips were or how his woody scent forced me to forget our time and place.

I had somewhere to be.

I released my hand from the back of his neck and fell onto my heels, making my stumble backward look as planned as possible. "We can call you an ambulance in five minutes. Okay? Will you survive five more minutes?"

Chase lifted his brows and removed his hand from the side of his chin. "I'm not sure. If I don't make it, promise me you'll do whatever all of that just was again to help me regain my strength."

"Okay. Yes. I can heal you again if need be." My mind began painting flowery scenarios I wanted to experience in real-time, but I forced away the daydream. I blinked three times and began walking down the sidewalk, shaking myself back to reality. "Let's go, let's go."

It took about a minute and a half before Spellbound's cauldron-shaped sign was within view, and my awkward jog went back to the sprint I had started with, Chase walking briskly at my side. I wanted to stop and ask him what the hell had just happened back there. I wanted to ask him how that painful accident had somehow turned into an unexpectedly beautiful one.

"She's right there," Chase whispered, keeping his lean frame a few steps away from the door. "She's talking to him. Go do your thing."

I reached for the door handle, stopping mid-twist to turn toward him. "Wait. What is the *thing* I'm supposed to do, exactly?"

Chase shrugged and reached for his chin, massaging his jaw with an oversized palm. "Follow your instincts. If that doesn't work, follow your heart." His lips creeped toward the hand returning to cup his face. "You seem to work magic when you just follow your heart."

Fuck. The butterflies I felt soaring through my system were getting in the way of the mission at hand.

I took a deep breath of bitter air—a hint of Chase's subtle, earthy cologne handing me some needed tenacity—before twisting the door handle and throwing myself at the counter.

Chapter 38

Emmie

Wind bit my face, forcing my eyes shut. Just as I squinted them open, a small, redheaded creature pounced onto the counter, sliding toward the cash register. She knocked over three ceramic mugs on her way across, mimicking a flailing penguin trying out a Slip 'n' Slide for the first time. When my mug I'd been holding met the tip of her tiny nose, her gloved hands clutched the ceramic at such speed that the steaming liquid flew into Oliver's face. Coughing and spitting drops of latte into the sink next to him, he hunched over and continuously wiped away the liquid from his lips and tongue.

"You're not drugging my best friend today, asshole!" Fern shouted at Oliver as she remained belly-down on the counter. Her hat had flown off during her attack, causing her hair to become a disheveled mess over her face. When she slowly turned to look up at me, I couldn't help but smile.

"What the fuck was that?" I asked, shaking my head and watching Oliver fill a glass of water with trembling hands before chugging it all in one gulp.

"I saw Oliver being a sketchier sketch-ball than usual a few weeks ago. He was whispering with some guy, and then the guy brought him a paper bag." Fern finally slipped her feet off the counter, standing up and running a hand through her hair. "There was probably coke or Molly or Flakka in your latte."

My eyebrows shifted in shock. "Since when is Flakka in your vocabulary?"

Fern shrugged, reaching behind herself for her hat before stuffing it in her jacket pocket with a shrug. "I Googled. A lot."

I turned toward Oliver who was still chugging water by the sink. "All because you thought Oliver was going to *drug* me?"

"He's been following your blogs, and he knew he was next." The door opened behind Fern, and Chase walked in, lifting his hand for a quick wave by his hip as some college-aged students entered at his heels. "I didn't want my best friend to die."

Her fixed, bright eyes met mine, setting ablaze a warmth within my chest I'd so desperately missed. Hearing her say *best friend* meant more to me than the possibility of losing my job or, hell, losing the freedom to come back to Spellbound ever again. Even with emotions burdening our minds over the last month, we could still see each other as friends—not shells of our past selves. That meant everything.

She wasn't the girl who had once dated my ex.

I wasn't the girl who had misunderstood what *taking a break* meant.

We didn't need to give our pasts second chances when we knew our present was already kicking ass.

No, *we* were kicking ass. We were the reasons the present looked so damn good.

"You've got to be shitting me." Chase's voice took us all by surprise as he stood with half of his body behind the counter. "Like...literally. Fern. These are the drugs you were sniffing out."

Chase slid an empty box down the counter, and Fern snagged it, reading the font scrawled across the front. "*Speedy Lax Supreme. The ultimate colon cle—*"

"For fucking real?" I grabbed the box out of her hand and chucked it at Oliver's forehead, watching it bounce off skin still damp from the espresso. "You really stooped *that* low?"

The grin Oliver attempted made my fingers mold into fists on top of the counter. "I mean, I only stooped to your level, right? Karma, is it?"

"*You're* the jackass I found making out with that blonde slut-bucket in the bathroom." I gestured toward the doorway before slowly twisting to smile at the girls behind Chase, their arms crossing over their chests impatiently. "No offense."

"So, you don't deserve to be screwed over for messing up the lives of the guys who messed up yours? Karma, right?" Oliver turned the faucet on and filled up his glass before chugging the entire thing in a few, jittery gulps. As he swallowed, he held a finger up to the girls standing behind Chase. "I'll be right with you."

"We can wait," the taller blonde said, wagging her hand in our direction. "This is good."

The shorter, younger blonde—but still old enough for tattoos and lip fillers, apparently—stepped closer to her friend with a nod. "I want to see where this is going. Class can wait."

Though the crowd surrounding us wasn't terrifying, I knew the longer I stood there, the more people would arrive for their mid-morning coffee and, instead, walk into this. I didn't need cameras recording this interaction. I was not in the mood to go viral again—even for My Cup's sake. I just needed to end this conversation, grab Fern, and move the hell on.

"Karma was already played, Oliver, and not at your hands." I looked at Fern, who now stood next to Chase, who was rubbing the side of his chin—and not in the pensive way I'd expect.

Her pale skin, her naive yet knowing eyes, the lipstick she never forgot to apply that looked a little out of sorts, to be honest. Fern was the person I raced to when I needed to do nothing but snuggle quietly on her couch with Porridge and Loaf clawing at my hair. She was the person who ate bad Chinese food with me after a feisty night with Kyle and Rae, listening to details going beyond her interest level. Hell, Fern was the person who'd seen me at my lowest and helped lift me up to my highest potential.

"Karma played us before you could. We got there first," Fern said as her eyes met mine. "Unfortunately."

I lifted my eyebrows and tried to push aside any emotion carrying me in Fern's direction, trying to convince me to smother her in an embrace. I was not a hugger, and though all of this was softening me up a little, I wasn't going to break.

Well, maybe I'd let myself crack at the seams just the tiniest bit.

"Why is there such a long line?" Benji shouted from the doorway, shuffling his feet quickly behind the counter before noticing the broken mugs on the ground. "How did those mugs break, and...did you spill coffee on yourself, Ollie?"

"Shit." Oliver's voice was so fleetingly soft it was surprising anyone heard it as he raced to the opposite side of the counter, around two tables, and into the bathroom. The second I heard a low groan escape below the bathroom door, I threw my hands into the air and turned to face Benji.

"Can I just get a black drip coffee?" I asked. "I trust you won't put laxatives in it."

Benji grabbed a to-go mug with his brows curling beneath his glasses. "Excuse me?"

A painful growl shot from the bathroom, causing the group of us by the counter to crunch our noses in disgust. The older couple, who had been attempting to quietly drink their coffees in peace, grumbled under their breath and threw their arms into their jackets.

"The guy shitting his brains out in the bathroom put laxatives into Emmie's drink." Fern stood up straighter, adjusting the collar of her peacoat as her chin seemed to lift upward. "But I threw it into his face. Obviously, some got into his system."

"And that, my friends, is karma," Chase said, clapping his hands slowly a couple times before stepping back to let the two girls go before him in line.

"I'm going to deal with this once all this shit dies down," Benji said.

Fern giggled, and I elbowed her waist. "What? There are so many good poop jokes going on."

I could, thankfully, laugh at them now too. A year or so ago, when I'd found Oliver in the bathroom with that girl, this situation wouldn't have been so funny. I'd had such an unexpected anxiety attack, from seeing him fucking that girl against the sink, that my bowels began screaming. I'd practically pulled down my pants and sat on the toilet before they'd pulled their pants back up.

It was that horrific day that I'd decided to change things.

It was also when I decided I wouldn't avoid Spellbound and Oliver.

I knew I was a bigger person than he could ever be.

I grabbed the coffee and my belongings and stood by the front door as Chase and Fern ordered their drinks, still waiting for Oliver to sneak out of his clubhouse in the corner. When I pushed the door open and the three of us walked out into the cool morning, Fern stopped and lifted her shoulders to her ears.

"Wait. What were you supposed to do to Oliver?" she asked. "For the last blog?"

I smiled, lifting the cup to my lips for a quick, satisfying sip. "Nothing. I wasn't going to do anything because I knew he would try something. I just didn't know what. It wasn't worth my time to try to figure it out. He isn't worth my time." I gestured one hand back and forth between Fern's little body and my own. My other hand lifted the coffee to my lips, bringing all my icy organs back to life. "*We* are."

Chapter 39

FERN

"**I**'m in love with Thea."

My father leaned forward over his plate, almost vomiting mimosa onto the French toast in front of him. "Excuse me?"

"I love her, Dad. We're dating. Thea is my partner." Marian's voice was the most confident I'd heard in months—and that said a lot because she was confident as hell. However, if there was ever a time when that energy dwindled, it was when she was around our parents.

And for good reason.

"Friendship is such a nice thing," my mom stated, delicately cutting a piece of bacon with her fork. *Bacon.* She was cutting her bacon with a fucking fork. Reaching across the table, I broke the floppy, repulsive piece of meat with my fingers, and my annoyance was met by her smile. That only made my frustration build. "'*A sweet friendship refreshes the soul.*' Prover –"

"'*Better is open rebuke than hidden love.*' Proverbs 27: 5-6," Marian shouted, cutting her off and slamming her hands on the table. "Guys. I'm a lesbian. That's just that."

My dad sat still, staring at their perfect child. "It's fine. It's probably a—"

"Don't you dare say it," I said, eyeing my father. I thinned my gaze as he finished off the mimosa in his glass, washing it around in his mouth. "Just believe her, congratulate her, and move on."

My mom turned so she was fully facing her youngest daughter. "Honey, give it time. The Lord knows your heart and purpose. Trust in Him to lead you toward marriage."

"He has, and it's Thea. Thanks, God," Marian said.

"Marian!" My mother's jaw dropped, color draining her cheeks as she turned to face me. "Has she been visiting you more often? That Emmie is not a good influence on our Marian."

I closed my eyes and took a deep breath as I counted out loud, "1, 2, 3..."

My trance was broken by the snapping of my mother's fingers. "What are you doing? Where did you go? Stop always being in such a fog, Francis."

I cupped my hand over my mother's snapping fingers and whipped my eyes open. "I am breathing, Mom. I am trying to relax my body and mind because of how furious you're making me."

"Fern, let's not speak this way at brunch," my dad said, gesturing over to the waitress for a mimosa refill.

"When will speaking like this *ever* be okay?" I asked, gazing over my mother's shoulder to meet my father's eyes. Behind his thin, dark frames, I could see his eyebrows slowly loosen from their furrowed position as his body slumped back into his chair. "Marian and I have held our tongues for far too long. We've been ourselves, but the versions of ourselves we knew you'd be most proud of. We've added way too much frosting on top of these versions of ourselves when, really, the lives we're most proud of lay hidden beneath the sugar."

Marian leaned in my direction. "That was good."

I nodded my head toward the waitress walking in our direction, waving my hand awkwardly above my shoulder. "It's really just because I want one of the cinnamon buns going around on those trays." I pointed at the tray the woman was holding, and she leaned down, letting me pluck a bun from it. I bit into the warm, gooey goodness and couldn't stop the smile forming. "Damn, these are perfect. You guys should get one."

"Your minds are clouded. What's going on?" My mom's head hadn't stopped shaking back and forth in confusion since Marian threw her truth in front of them. My dad, on the other hand, was sitting quietly in his chair. He held a newly filled mimosa between his forefinger and thumb, his graying eyebrows lifting the slightest bit so they crawled above his frames.

"They're being honest with us, Bernie. That's what's going on." His voice was hushed, almost hoarse. Leaning forward, he set down the glass and met my eyes. "You've always been the more opinionated one, Frannie. That's for sure. But knowing you've been hiding yourself from us out of fear that we won't accept you? That's not Godly on either side of the coin."

My mother faced my father and then reached for his mimosa, taking a long gulp.

"I haven't hidden too much from you guys. There's nothing really about my life I haven't made into somewhat of an open book," I said, lifting the cinnamon bun to my lips and feeling the hot glaze dot my chin. "If anything, I feel forced into being this person I just don't want to be whenever I'm around you."

"Do you feel this way too, Marian?" My mom set her hand on Marian's shoulder, cocking her head. "Do you feel that we've forced you to feel or be a certain way in the eyes of our Savior?"

To my surprise, Marian snorted out a laugh. "Absolutely. The thing is, Mom, I love serving God. I just want to do it *my* way. God wants me happy, and He knows I'm happy with Thea." Marian turned to face me, reaching over to pick off a piece of the frosted dough. "Also, Fern wasn't finished. I think you need to really listen to her and ignore me. I'm fine. I feel great now after getting that off my chest."

My heart palpitated when all eyes clicked into place with my own. "I mean, I wasn't saying anything much different than what I've always said."

"No, you were definitely saying something they should hear," Marian whispered, leaning closer. "*Feeling forced to be someone you can't be. Ring a bell?*"

"Oh, yeah, right." I wasn't used to giving monologues—especially unexpected ones during family brunch. If I had something important or confrontational to say, I'd casually bring it up over time or ignore it completely. This, though, felt different. Since my home-run slide onto Spellbound's counter, my words were hot, and my thoughts were ablaze. Maybe it was Emmie's energy slowly seeping its way back into my life after a month without it. She was setting all the molecules back into their necessary places.

Hell, maybe kissing Chase clicked my confidence into the spot it needed to be in.

"I know I've never lived the life you guys hoped I would." I lifted my arm into the air and gestured toward the swirls and shapes of black and gray ink. "I mean, the day I started getting tattoos, you mentally disowned me. I felt that."

My mom shook her head. "No, no. *We* didn't. God—"

"Don't." My dad set his hand on my mom's shoulder, nodding in my direction. "Let's just listen to her."

I could feel Marian smiling without even meeting her gaze, and I took a deep breath. "I'm not married yet. Hell, I haven't had a serious relationship since Davis—and I even gave him a second chance. I actually gave a bunch of my exes second chances, hoping, by now, that maybe I'd have a specific ring on a very specific finger." I paused, looking down at my ringed hands. Almost every finger was dressed in silver except for that beloved one on the left. "The thing is, I don't think I ever let myself be okay with not being married or in a serious relationship at this age. I'm almost twenty-eight-years-old, and I've always cared more about how you guys would react to my life choices rather than how I feel about them. And dammit, that's not fair."

I wiggled in my seat a little bit, straightening my spine as I reached for the mimosa. "Sure, I want a boyfriend. Hell, I'd take an engagement right about now. But I'm also okay being single—even if it's not exactly what you saw as being ideal for my life. I'm not going to force anything. These last several months taught me that forcing emotions in the wrong direction can lead to more than heartbreak. I'm not going to lose who I am, or my closest friends, just to please a plan you both think works for me. I'll do what works for me...like eating another one of these." Practically tripping the waitress as my free arm flew out from my chair, I snatched up another cinnamon bun and took a messy, satisfying bite.

With sugar dripping off my lips, a mimosa in one hand, and my parents staring at me with half-puzzled, half-proud grins on their faces, I almost missed my phone as it vibrated from my lap, Chase's name lighting up the screen.

Chapter 40

Emmie

"Well, fuck." My words hung in the air as Al's chubby fingers wagged forward to gesture away the attitude clinging to my voice. He heaved himself onto his desk to sit where we found ourselves eye level with his knees, and I swore if he opened his legs any wider, the crotch of his pants would rip. I'd been called to his office alongside Melanie, Ahmed, and Izzy—the four of us now seated in front of his desk in tiny wooden chairs as if in some coffee-fueled Saturday detention.

Except, I hadn't yet had my coffee.

"So, what are the others going to do?" Melanie asked quietly. "I didn't expect to stay on writing *and* have this happen."

"Shut up. You're a good writer," Izzy said, her abrasive tone slapping Melanie with both confusion and pride. "Melanie is the only one here who started podcast training. What does that mean for us?"

"Are you sure corporate wants someone with this strong of an ac-cent on a podcast?" It was embarrassingly obvious Ahmed was trying to exaggerate his accent as he shrugged his shoulders. "You don't want bad reviews because people can't understand me. That could happen."

"Don't pull the race card, dude. I've tried before and failed," I said, expressionless, without turning to look at him. Instead, my eyes stayed focused on avoiding the ripping seams of my boss's pants. "So, you want us to keep our four blogs going *and* do a combined monthly podcast? While the other four stop writing and do strictly podcast work?"

Snickering, Al closed his knees the slightest bit. Thank fucking God. "I did just say that, yes. In fact, I'm hoping it can go from monthly to maybe—"

Both of my hands flew into the air, and I sat back farther in my tiny, children's chair. "Monthly is fine. Let's keep it once a month."

Seriously, where the hell had these chairs come from?

"Have you talked to the other four? How are they taking it?" Melanie asked quietly.

"They're doing well. Kyle has been promoted to podcast manager, and I'm confident he will do a solid job keeping the four of them on task every week, since they're doing weekly and bi-weekly casts."

I could barely get through the day hearing my own voice without needing a nap. If anything, I was thankful I'd only have to suffer at the microphone a few times a month to record and, probably, re-record.

Al scooted in my direction, and I swore I was going to have to catch him from falling off the desk. "Oh, Kyle did want Emmie to guest on his show a couple times a month. Melanie, Howie was interested in your take on a few things for his cast too."

Well, the fuck with my luck.

"Wasn't Kyle talking the other day about something called Polly Pocket he wanted to start?" Izzy asked, turning to look at me from the end of the line of chairs.

"PolyPod, yeah," I laughed, sitting back and crossing my arms over my chest. "I'm guessing he's starting a podcast highlighting the poly life, right?"

"Something along those lines, yes." My heart finally relaxed when Al's feet hit the floor, and he walked over to the opposite side of his desk. "Since My Cup has been so in-tune with inclusive matters of the heart over the last year, we think it's a good idea."

"It is a good idea," Melanie said in her usual quiet tone. She looked up, adjusting her glasses with a subtle smile angled in my direction. "My partners, Neil and Lamar, would gladly guest on his podcast as well."

The second I walked through the door at Thirsty Theodore's, Marian's eyes met mine, and she reached for the full beer at Fern's elbow, immediately handing it over. Nodding appreciatively as I flung my coat over the back of the chair, I felt her own beer glass clink against mine and saw the edge of a smile before the glass hid her perfect lips.

"I heard. You did it," I said.

"I did it, Em!" Marian's free arm flew around my shoulder and a few drips from her lager scattered the left side of my shirt. Luckily, I hadn't washed this one in about a month—only spritzed it with some perfume on my way out—so this was proof it was time. "I don't think they believed me, but I don't care. I feel like I freed the weight of the world off my shoulders."

"Don't be so dramatic," Fern added, twisting in her seat and failing at the dramatic hair flip she attempted on her way around. From the looks of it, her roots were newly crimson, and her bangs were freshly chopped back to right above her eyebrows. "They'll throw some weight back at you soon enough."

"Debbie Downer for the win," Chase's voice cut in as he handed Fern a pomegranate mojito, setting aside his own bourbon concoction by her elbow. I wasn't sure why anyone trusted Fern's elbows as the ideal places to set down extremely full beverages.

I knew better.

Fern lifted a pomegranate aril out of her drink and popped it between her darkly stained lips. "I'm waiting for my mom to send me some passive-aggressive text. It'll happen soon, and I'm okay with it."

"Are you, though?" I asked, squishing myself between Fern and Marian before lifting my elbows up onto the bar. Simply absorbing Marian's fresh, familiar scent made my entire being feel at ease as I brought the beer up for a swig. Even standing this close to Fern made my heart falter a bit. I was grateful to be back to watching her stumble through thoughts and words instead of stumble through the office avoiding our eye contact.

I felt at home in her awkwardness.

"I am," she said with a smile, clicking her mojito against my beer so the glass pinged my front teeth. "I've always been fine doing whatever I want to do without their approval. It just felt damn good getting it all out there and not feeling like I have to impress them anymore. I only have to impress myself."

"That's the only person who really counts." Chase's voice always came in as an edgy purr, and as I watched their eyes meet, I wanted to hear him talk more. I wanted to watch their interactions blossom. I wanted to know what the hell was going on with my best friend and her candy-sharing cubicle neighbor.

My best friend.

Damn, it felt good to have those three words back in my life.

Chapter 41

Fern

“**W**hy the hell did I choose this color?”

Emmie set her purse and phone on the table the content team was assigned to before rolling her eyes in my direction. “You said you wanted to change it up. *This* is definitely a change.”

“Cotton-candy pink, though?” I looked down at the gown and ran my hands over the soft silk clinging to my hips. “I look like a fucking unicorn.”

“It’s not as bright as you think it is. It works well with your hair.” Emmie picked her phone back up, scrolling quickly over the screen. “They’re, like, on the same color board or something.”

“Color *palette*,” I responded. Watching her thumb attack the screen of her phone, her lips moving as she read whatever words she was skimming, made me see some raw emotions this brave, beastly human rarely showed. I stepped forward and set my hand on her wrist, my fingers clicking together with a metallic chime. “Em, you got this.”

"I hate speaking!" Emmie twisted toward me, throwing her hands into the air. "Well, that's a lie. I love to talk. I just hate my voice and hate speaking to more than the few people I like, and I just don't—"

My hand softly grabbed her raised wrist again, the long-sleeve sheer fabric of her dress itching my palm. "Girl, breathe. You always do fine with this shit."

As Emmie's arms lowered, I watched the rise and fall of her chest, realizing she had listened to my meditating demand. Below the curls falling in front of her dark frames sat even darker eyes heated with an anxiety I was all too familiar with. I'd known Emmie for a while and never had I seen her emotions with such clarity. Instead of holding them tight behind her ribs, she now put no effort into hiding a single tremble of her fingers or twitch of an eyelid.

It was obvious that she, too, had learned to let down her guard during our month apart.

Maybe it wasn't our time apart allowing us to rip at the seams a little bit. Maybe that alone time let us look deeper within ourselves, giving ourselves permission to fall apart and stitch ourselves back up how we pleased.

We didn't need to sew ourselves up for anyone else except for ourselves.

And we all knew my sewing skills were nowhere near perfect. They'd come undone sooner or later, and I'd be ready when they did.

"The last time I spoke to a crowd this big was in high school during a stupid debate club event." Emmie's voice shook my focus back to the table, away from whatever part of my brain I'd gotten lost in.

When I lifted my gaze to meet Emmie's, I caught Chase's instead as he walked into the gala, clad in the sharpest cobalt suit I'd ever laid eyes on.

We exchanged quick grins before turning back to the frazzled Emmie in front of me. "Well, did you win the debate?"

"Of course I won," she said, her tone razor-sharp. She noticed I had edged toward the opposite side of my seat, and when she saw the direction my body was floating in, she let out a throaty snort. "Go. Go get him."

"Get who? What?" I twisted up onto the narrow heel of my shoe so I faced her, my hands both on the back of her chair. My back was now in the direction of wherever Chase was, because, obviously, I didn't care.

However, the thought of not caring lodged a lump of guilt into my throat, causing me to gently look back over my shoulder at him as he walked in our direction. He strode toward us, looking so tall and so handsome—and so utterly kind that it hurt in all the best ways.

"Shut up, Fern," Emmie whispered, leaning closer so the spearmint of her chewing gum wafted toward me. "After all we've done over these months, all the second chances we've given to people—including our friendship—Chase *must* feel different. There's no way he doesn't, and honestly, I bet it feels fucking good."

When I felt a finger tap gently on my shoulder—a flurry of heat and uncertainty climbing beneath my skin—I couldn't help but agree with her.

Emmie nodded toward him, and I stepped away from her chair, practically tripping over his Oxfords. I turned around to stand as solidly as I could in my silver heels, my face looking up into his. "Hey. Hi."

Shaking his head and stepping closer, he smiled the most genuinely handsome smile I'd ever seen. "Hi." Fumbling back, he reached into his jacket pocket. "I found something."

From the corner of my eye, I watched Emmie walk away toward the front stage where Al stood with Najma and a couple other tall, white men who looked way more important than they probably were. I followed Chase toward the back wall that was only a few feet from the bar we needed to get to before the line grew longer as his balled hand appeared from his pocket. He slowly uncurled his fingers to reveal two little yellow-and-black packages sitting in his ginormous palm.

I opened my eyes wide, looking from the candy to his eyes and back. "Toxic Waste? No way! I haven't had one of these since, like, elementary school."

"These are as sour as they get." Chase reached for my hand, twisting it over and slowly opening my palm. It opened flat in the space between us, my fingertips almost touching the pale shirt beneath his suit. Setting one of the tiny packages in my hand, I folded my fingers around it but never looked away from his gaze.

I couldn't. I physically couldn't stop staring into the eyes of someone who did something so beautifully weird to my heart in a way I never, ever saw coming.

"Yeah? Are we doing this now?" I broke the gaze I never wanted to break to look down at my hand between us. Stepping forward, he curled my hand into a fist and lifted my bent fingers to his lips, placing the softest, gentlest kiss atop my knuckles.

"Would you like to?" His voice was hushed, kind, and so damn sexy. How had I never melted into the chocolate of his voice the way I did now? How had I only seen our exchange of Warheads and Sour Punch Straws as friendly banter when, really, it was more?

I'd missed a chance at something in the present because I'd been too busy chasing the past.

My closed hand was a pumping heart beneath both of his, and as I lowered my fist, his hands continuing to peacefully hug mine, I stepped closer. "I would, Chase. I really want to."

The corner of his lips inched upward into his cheek, a snicker whispering between his lips. "I want you to kiss me, but I'm afraid you'll hurt me again."

My head fell back, letting out a grunted laugh before I pushed myself up onto my toes. "I'll do my best to avoid pain."

This time, it was he who pressed his lips against mine, pulling me in so my chest pressed against his hard stomach and forced my toes higher inside my heels.

"It's been painful overhearing your dating ventures these last few months," Chase whispered, our lips still touching, but barely. Man, those lips. I wanted to suck on them harder than the candy heating up my palm. "I didn't like you hurting."

"I brought it upon myself, Chase," I said. "I'm at fault. I didn't stay in the present like I should have. I...I didn't look right in front of me."

His lips twisted into a smile against my own. "Well, then why don't you try living in the now a little bit. I can help with that." Instead of shifting forward for another kiss—an inappropriately timed kiss as employees now filed in toward the bar—he released his grip on my fist and gripped his own candy. "Ready for this?"

Another throaty laugh escaped me, and I stepped back, lifting the candy into the air and ripping the edge. "Hell yeah, I'm ready."

"Are you sure?" He eyed the naked candy between my fingers as I tossed the wrapper into the trashcan near the bar, missing it completely. "Because these are the real deal. You can't get rid of this once you start."

"No second chances," I said, smiling and stepping forward. "One...two...three."

With that, we both tossed the candies into the air, catching them perfectly in our mouths.

Chapter 42

Emmie

I hated technology.

I realized now how much I despised the digital era. Instead of typing up my speech and printing it out like most of us did in high school—and still did today—I'd emailed it to my phone. I mean, that was what every maid-of-honor and important corporate person did these days, right? However, instead of being able to read it smoothly, whenever I needed a hint from the script, the screen would go dark, and I'd have to click my password back in.

Since walking over to the stage, I'd re-clicked my damn password seventeen times. I swore the numbers 6666 were now burned into my fingertips.

I smelled Kyle's citrusy cologne before seeing him walk up to me. "What's up, Quasimodo?"

No expression was written across my face. "What?"

"You're hunched over your phone like Golem hoarding the ring." Kyle reached for my shoulder, giving me a gentle shake. "It's a two-minute speech. You've done harder."

Snickering beside him, Rae hugged his arm closer against her thin frame. "It's true. You have."

"Are you guys just coming over here to throw dick jokes my way? I'm sure that'll *really* help my nerves." I dramatically looked from Kyle to Rae and then repeated the head bobbing charade. "Because you should have brought me a—"

"An old fashioned, perhaps?" Kyle stretched his hand in my direction where the most beautiful, sweating glass stared at me with metaphorical eyes no man or woman could ever match. "You like hard liquor when you're nervous. Beer is for after."

After my hand wrapped around the cold, gorgeous glass, I collapsed into Kyle's and Rae's arms. Their inability to confidently hold me up was proof they either weren't prepared for my hug, or they'd already had a few too many drinks.

Or both.

"Thanks. I'm fine. It'll seriously be fine." My blabbering was shut off when the drink hit my lips, and the devilish heat started drowning my body. I set the glass on the side of the stage, half of the ice cubes already poking out. "It'll be great."

Kyle and Rae just stood in front of me with uncertain smiles painted across their faces until Al and Najma walked over to discuss the opening. The two of them backed away, thumbs-up gestures pressed against their chest, and I was forced to focus on the two supervisors in front of me.

Hell, now with Najma standing this close, focus would be impossible.

I believed this until Al set a hand on my shoulder, and it was extremely obvious he'd forgotten to put on deodorant.

Or brush his teeth.

"You're going to hit the stage in ten minutes. Everyone is getting seated," Al said, his hand going from an uncomfortable shoulder grab to an even more awkward back slap. "Go crush it. The draft was great."

Najma leaned forward, and I could practically taste the cherry blossom clinging to her skin. "You'll do great."

I couldn't stop my body as I reached for Najma and brought her in for an embrace, her arms solidly hugging me back before stepping away. Her expression wasn't of shock, like most people's would be after being unexpectedly hugged by a non-hugger. Instead, her face wore a warm, prideful hue to it.

It was just the glow I needed to see before being called backstage.

The CEO talked about how proud he was of the business, and he threw out some numbers in regard to how many couples had been connected in our one year since going live. A few office supervisors from across the country praised select employees for excellent leadership skills or quality design work. Our little Merlin Heights office even got recognition for having the smallest yet mightiest number of staff on board.

Then, my name was called.

The steps I took from behind the curtain into the incandescent spotlight seemed to take half a step rather than three. With my phone in hand, the screen was lit to full capacity, and my right thumb kept actively grazing the top. I raised the microphone slightly before clearing my throat and giving the bobbing heads before me a white-toothed smile.

Here the fuck went nothing.

"I began working as a content writer for My Cup O'Joe right before the app went live. I started off writing press releases for upcoming announcements and prepared copy for the website, app pages, and social media platforms. Again, this was all before the app even started making couples fall in love through the magic of coffee culture. Even before that, I helped out behind the scenes with research and data collection.

"It wasn't until I had a few backlogged blogs posted and the app was out there for the world to see that I realized the work I did was actually important. It wasn't that I didn't enjoy writing press releases—well, that's a lie. I definitely didn't *love* writing those."

Luckily, I got a few laughs as my thumb brightened the screen in front of me. "It was that I loved writing content that could connect on the most personal level possible. I loved that the words I wrote about experiences I was going through meant something to the people reading them. My experiences opened our clients' eyes to what could actually happen in their own lives if they took the first step."

I took a deep breath, and even though my thumb lit the screen up and I knew what segment was next, I didn't peek down. "Being a bisexual, polyamorous, mixed-race woman isn't easy. Hell, even though I'm completely confident with my lifestyle, it doesn't mean I haven't hit road bumps or gotten speeding tickets." The laugh I snorted out was not part of the script whatsoever. Why did I find my speeding ticket metaphor to be so damn funny? "But it's those bends in the road that led me to where I am now. Those stories made me the top content writer for this company—a company unlike any other.

"Now, I know I wasn't asked to talk about how amazing My Cup is." I lifted my arms up and gestured around the filled room before me.

"We're all here, so we already know this. I was asked to talk about how our content writing builds connections within the app's community. The *writing*. At first, I wasn't sure how to respond. Being someone who always has something to say about everything, you can imagine how shocked I was being as close to speechless as I can get."

Out of the handful of laughs echoing throughout the room, one high-pitched, throaty grunt stood out, and my eyes directed immediately to Fern. Unsure if she knew I could see her or not, I watched as she brought fisted hands to either side of her face, forcing out a cheesy smile with both thumbs pointing upward.

I looked at the darkened screen of my phone before placing it on the podium in front of me, the screen facing down. "Relationships are what most people aim for in life and, sometimes, those relationships start with a simple cup of coffee. You don't realize how sharing conversation over a latte or cup of tea can turn into something more: a relationship, a sexual partner, a forever friendship. Whatever it turns into, the writing I've done has helped build some amazing new connections and even strengthen existing ones.

"Over the last several months, I chased down those who had done me wrong in my past, in hopes of feeling some kind of karmic release. And you know what? I did get that satisfaction, but I also almost lost one of the best connections I've ever build within the My Cup community."

Pinching her dark lips together, Fern nodded, and I watched as Chase leaned in closer to her, a smile widening on Fern's face as his fingers laced with hers. "You can chase down your past all you want in hopes of learning some big, bad lesson from it. However, you can't change it. You can only move forward with what you've learned now.

"The content we write teaches lessons. It builds trust. It proves that you don't need to be perfect to find love or happiness or whatever it is you're looking for in a relationship. Our words get the engagement they do because readers believe that a single cup of coffee can lead to something bigger, something better. They believe they can find something so genuinely perfect for their lifestyle that no one will think twice. Why? Because the members of our content community have lived it and written about it. Because My Cup has incorporated every kind of lifestyle and pronoun into the profiles being created behind the coffee cup symbol that pops up on your screen. No one is ignored or pushed away. Everyone is accepted."

Fern's gaze hit mine, and I held back whatever emotions were trying to escape the corners of my eyes. "And acceptance tastes even better than the best cup of coffee."

About the Author

JENNIFER ALINE writes stories that combine the steamy elements of romance with the raw realities of friendship and family-focused themes of women's fiction. She loves creating quirky characters with big personalities who are forced to challenge themselves and step outside their comfort zone...while also finding love — or something like it — along the way.

Jennifer lives in Western New York with her twin daughters and grumpy miniature schnauzer. She has an unhealthy obsession with vintage typewriters, owns way too many plants, and is a self-titled coffee snob. When she isn't writing, reading, or chasing her daughters around, she can be found singing karaoke, taking dance classes, or searching for the newest local coffee shop to obsess over.

If you loved hanging out in
Merlin Heights, you'll love
visiting Greyport!